SAVE HER

ABIGAIL OSBORNE

BLOODHOUND
— BOOKS —

ALSO BY ABIGAIL OSBORNE

The Puppet Master

For Elle – my reset button, my best friend

1

Had her mother-in-law not been a cold, manipulative bitch from the first day she met her, Flora was sure she would have been distraught to be responsible for putting her in the hospital. As it was, she could not deny that the only reason she felt guilty was because of the anguish it was causing her husband.

The waiting room was crammed full of people perched on clinical plastic blue chairs. The collective fear of the anxious relatives was palpable and it engulfed her like a thick fog. Her eyes followed her husband as he paced up and down like a metronome. The squeak of his shoes on the linoleum echoed around the room each time he turned, but he was oblivious to it. Lines had appeared on his face that had not been there before tonight. Flora's heart ached for him. At least when her parents had died it had been quick. There was no agonising wait in a room full of posters warning about the risks of smoking and spotting the signs of cancer.

Flora was ashamed to admit that it had crossed her mind that if Cecelia died her life would change for the better. She banished this thought to the dark recesses of her mind. Usually mild-mannered and warm-hearted, Flora was devastated that she was now capable of such thoughts. That she had developed such a capacity for hate was as a direct result of the war that Cecelia had waged upon her since their first encounter.

It was laughable that Flora had ever thought that Cecelia Cavendish, the matriarch of the million-pound ancestral legacy Cavendish & Sons, was going to willingly welcome an orphan with no social standing into the family. But having lost her parents in a car accident at fourteen, the thought of belonging to a family had been seductive. Hearing Sam wax lyrical about his family had caused the embers of hope to burn. She had even harboured the possibility that she may find a surrogate mother and father figure. Visions of shopping trips, afternoon tea and family dinners had played like a cinema reel in her mind. It hadn't helped that Sam had shared in her naïveté. His certainty that his family would accept her and welcome her with open arms prevented her from considering the alternative. The reality.

'Sam, honey, come and sit down.' It was a request she regretted immediately as soon as he sat down and his knee began to bounce up and down, shaking not only her seat but the whole row of connected seats. Sending an apologetic glance to the couple sat next to her she wrapped both her hands around his, attempting to calm him. Her two small pale hands were not even close to covering his one large hand. Her gentle giant. To the world, Sam looked like a force to be reckoned with. Intimidatingly tall with perfect blond hair, he looked like he'd stepped off *Dragon's Den*. His ocean-blue eyes were never seen without a twinkle. He exuded the easy confidence that came from being born into money and status. But Flora knew that he was so much more than that. He was a man who loved to play Pokémon Go, cried at *Love Actually* and who loved to walk around in her fluffy pink dressing gown.

'She's going to be okay.'

But he ignored her empty words. He stared at the door to the room with such intensity she was surprised it did not burst into flames. She willed the doctor to come through, give them the news they needed so she could get out of this place.

The worst day of her life had ended in a hospital. She tried to ignore the memories, but the sickly smell of disinfectant seeped into her skin like a poison. She dared not breathe through her nose because she knew the memories would overwhelm her if she did.

Sam placed his head in his hands, sighing loudly. She reached out and rubbed his back consumed by guilt and a sense of helplessness. Her husband was a good man. Which was why he had yet to acknowledge the elephant in the room. The fact that it was her fault that his mother was in the hospital. If Cecelia died, could Sam forgive her for killing his mother?

2

It was spite that made her do it.

Friday Night Dinner was a requirement in the Cavendish family. Each week they were obligated to convene at Cavendish Manor, the stately home that housed Sam's parents Cecelia and Alistair, where Flora was treated to four courses of rich, decadent food along with generous helpings of thinly veiled criticisms and disparaging remarks. Over time she had learnt to deflect or ignore Cecelia's subtle but persistent attacks. But still reeling from her day at work, she had returned fire with the only arrow she had in her quiver. One she knew would not miss its mark. If only she could explain to Sam about Linda, to explain why she had lashed out.

Linda's face filled her mind once more and tears pricked her eyes.

From the first day since she had opened Harper's Art Centre for Autism, Flora had had to force herself to leave each day. She would find art supplies that just had to be organised. As she held each brush and pencil, she would relive the tiny steps of progress in each child who had used it. She had opened the centre to give children with autism a place to thrive, to grow and meet others like themselves. It didn't suit every child: some with severe social anxiety couldn't cope with the sensory overload of being around other people. But for many of the children she worked with she was able to help them to use art to communicate. It was fulfilling, emotional and she loved every minute of it. That was until today, when she met Linda.

On the first Friday of every month Flora ran an introductory session where parents could bring their children to see what facilities were on offer and how their children interacted in the sessions. Generally, the fathers came to see what their money was being spent on, whilst the mothers were normally brimming with hope that they might finally find a way to connect with their child.

Flora made her way around the room, stopping to interact with each child. Some were hesitant at first, picking up their paint brush as if it was a bomb, whilst others confidently flicked paint onto their canvas. There was always mess, which horrified the mothers, but Flora quickly assured them that they could make as much mess as they want. It was important to her that the children had the freedom to express themselves in whichever way they chose.

Whilst the rain lashed at the windows, Flora had been with a bespectacled and skinny young boy named Oliver. Oliver had decided to paint with his elbows much to his mother's disgust. She kept trying to wipe the paint off his elbows and shove a paintbrush into his hand. A red tinge coloured his cheeks and Flora could see a 'meltdown' building.

'Oliver! Cut it out,' Oliver's mother whispered sternly, looking around red-faced to check no one else was watching. Flora hastened to intervene when she saw the boy's hands reach for the scissors to begin cutting, believing his was following the instructions to 'cut it out'. Gently, she encouraged Alison, Oliver's mother to let him paint with his elbows and suggested that they both joined in. Flora hid a smile at the horror on Alison's face as her son began to smear dollops of red paint on her elbows. It was just as Flora was applying yellow paint to her own elbow to reassure Alison, that the door to the centre had flown open.

A woman hurtled through the door, windswept and soaked through. She looked like she had tried to fight the elements and lost. Behind her stood a small boy with black hair plastered to his face and terrified brown eyes. Cleaning herself up, Flora had approached them with a warm smile. The woman was using her sleeve to wipe furiously at the rain trickling down her face, smoothing down her black bob that framed an angular face. Her son stood resolutely behind her, hiding from the room. Skin darker than his mother's, he was striking, with his piercing and intelligent brown eyes and caramel skin. He couldn't have been more than nine years old, but it was already possible to see he had the makings of a handsome man.

'Can I help you?' asked Flora.

'We're here for the introductory session. The bloody bus didn't turn up, so we had to leg it.' The woman's jaw was tensed, and she squared her shoulders. She had the posture of a someone used to fighting for their right to exist. Some of the other parents were looking over at the bedraggled woman with obvious distaste, already making snap judgements. Flora bristled and shot them a pointed look that had them return their focus to their own children. Turning to the pair, she tried to smile as widely as possible.

'Not a problem. Let's get you dried off and then I can show you around.' She gestured to them to follow her. 'Sorry I didn't catch your name?'

'I'm Linda. This is Ethan.' She pointed over her shoulder to her hidden son. Flora's heart went out to him when she saw the unadulterated terror in his eyes. His little body was quaking where he stood, his knuckles white from gripping his mother's coat so tightly.

'Right, Ethan and Linda. My name is Flora. We are going to go to the room over there to take off your coat and hang it up to dry. Then I will show you the different rooms in the centre. Then, if you would like to, Ethan, you can try painting or drawing.'

Flora was always careful of her words when she was at work. It was so important to be clear and unambiguous. She'd learnt the hard way on her placement at university when she had told a girl she had been working with to 'go and wash your hands in the toilet.' She had found the girl washing her hands in the actual toilet.

After taking them into the back room and introducing them to her assistant, Charlotte, she had hung up their coats, trying to ignore the tell-tale smell of the charity shop that wafted from them along with the scratches and stains. She settled Ethan and Linda at the chalk station and the rest of the afternoon had gone as planned. At the end of the session the room had begun to empty.

Flora felt elated as each family who left seemed excited to return. Squeezed budgets and over-worked teachers meant that the mainstream education system was failing children with autism. Consequently, many autistic children found it hard to integrate and have a normal life. Flora had been determined to do her part and had fought tooth and nail against the odds to open her centre, a place with the tools that could help autistic children to express themselves in a world that seemed unable to accept them because they did not conform or act 'normal'. Flora had seen so many parents gaze in wonder when previously hidden depths in their children were revealed as they began to communicate and develop by being given an alternative way to express themselves.

Flora went to lock the door, when movement in the corner of her eye stopped her. Linda and Evan were still where she had sat them earlier, at a table allocated for chalk painting. Ethan's head was down, his tongue pointed out at the corner of his mouth, his now dry black hair tucked out of his way behind his ear. He was utterly absorbed in his task. Linda had her back to the table, looking down at her lap, seemingly lost in thought. Her short black hair was covering her eyes as she looked down, picking at a hole in her faded black shirt.

'I am sorry, Linda. I didn't see you both there. Time's up I'm afraid, the session is finished now.'

Linda looked up and Flora had been shocked to see tears were tracking down her face. The pain and desperation in her eyes pinned Flora to the spot. In the light, Flora could see how gaunt she was, her cheekbones jutting out. Her eyes were sunken into her face with large dark circles underneath that only the severely fatigued and malnourished could achieve.

'Linda, is everything okay?'

Linda didn't answer straight away, she just stared at Flora. The silence became deafening and Flora was about to insist that they leave when Linda spoke in a quiet voice. 'I just want the best for my boy.'

'I can understand that.' Not sure where this was going, Flora pulled a chair over from another table until she was sat opposite Linda.

'You don't understand, though. Look at me, I can't afford a place like this for Ethan. I can't even afford new clothes.'

Flora's face burned hot. Linda's shirt had most likely been as black as night at some point but was now a faded dirty grey and stretched from being washed too often. It hung off her too skinny frame denoting the size she used to be. All of a sudden it hit Flora like a ton of bricks. She knew where this was going. Aware of what was coming next, she panicked trying to work out what she could say. Her brain was firing random words that she tried to piece together into a placatory answer. She wished she could help but if she gave one person a free place, then how could she justify charging everyone else?

'Listen, Linda, I'm sorry but...'

Linda cut her off. 'Don't. Just don't. I know it was stupid of me to come when I can't afford to send Ethan here. But I just thought.' Tears choked her off. She cleared her throat and continued. 'I just thought if you could see Ethan, meet him... you'd wanna help. I saw your advert on the internet and watched videos on your website. Read the reviews from parents whose children have "thrived" here.' She looked around at the room with longing in her eyes. 'I couldn't help myself. I brought him here knowing I couldn't afford it. But I had to come just in case there was the slightest chance you might help us. I had to do that for my boy. The school he's in, they don't know how to help him. They talk about getting him in-class support or moving him to a special school, but they pass his case from pillar to post. They don't care about him.'

She looked imploringly at Flora again. 'I work three jobs just to put food on the table,' Linda added with an it-is-what-it-is shrug which told Flora she did not say this to garner sympathy. 'I can't afford a special needs school for him. I can't do anything apart from watch my talented, clever boy be let down by ignorant people. Each day he comes back from school, he loses a bit more of his sparkle. You know what I mean? I am spending so many days holding him on the floor as he screams because his senses are just overwhelmed. He can't communicate with me. With anyone. He needs your help. Please, is there any way that you can help us?'

Again, Linda carried on before Flora could respond. 'Mind, I don't want to be a charity case. I can't afford the price of each session, but I can afford to pay something towards it. I could work for you as well? I can clean. Do you need a cleaner? Anything you need I can do it. Just please don't say no.'

The hope that shone in Linda's eyes broke Flora's heart. She opened her mouth to speak but no words came out. She looked at Ethan. He was smudging the white chalk to make smoke from a chimney. It stopped her from saying what the sensible side of her brain was screaming at her to say. Her heart was already picturing welcoming Ethan to the group for free. So, Flora had taken the coward's way out and given herself more time.

'Let me discuss it with my business partner and I'll get back to you, okay?' Flora did not have a business partner. But Linda wasn't to know that.

With a heavy heart she had locked up the centre, said a glum goodbye to Charlotte, her heart and head in turmoil and Linda's contact details burning a hole in her pocket. Guilt made bile rise to her throat as she thought about the four-course dinner she was about to consume whilst Linda was probably going without to ensure Ethan got enough food.

3

Linda and Ethan's plight had consumed Flora's mind as she drove her battered red Vauxhall Corsa out of Manchester's city centre. Orange brick terraces almost mounting each other gave way to stone semis with expensive cars until these were replaced with gates leading to large, towering mansions bordered by great swathes of countryside. Usually she spent the journey fascinated by this visual representation of the class system. It was the type of day she would normally have loved. The sun was apologising for the earlier rain, its rays reflecting off the residual droplets, making everything around her sparkle. The green grass enhanced by the sunlight would dazzle her, each vibrant shade of green vying for her attention. On any other day, the beauty around her would be making her feel lucky to be alive. But she noticed nothing, driving purely on autopilot. Unable to think of anything else but Linda and Ethan.

It was with a bad taste in her mouth that she went up the tree-lined driveway leading to Cavendish Manor. As she handed her key to the valet, she wondered if Linda had ever been able to afford a car. It was the hole in Linda's shirt that she thought of as she gave her coat to the butler, a frumpish elderly man called

Reginald who probably earned more in a week than Linda did in a year. It was Ethan's grey raincoat with the rip in one sleeve that she pictured as she listened to Cecelia agonise over whether they should have Christmas at their French mansion or in their holiday home in Spain.

And it was just as the lemon soufflé was served and Cecelia was informing them that she'd had the chef throw out the first batch because they didn't all match – that Flora's misery and frustration erupted like a volcano. She didn't mean to do it. Her impotence at being unable to help Linda combined with her dislike of Cecelia had silenced her sensibilities. Before she knew it, in a voice that she hoped mirrored Cecelia's when she was delivering one of her backhanded compliments, Flora interrupted her mother-in-law.

'Oh, Cecelia, before I forget, we won't be around for Christmas this year as we are planning to have it in our new house on our own.'

The room went as silent as a crypt. Sam's spoon had hovered in the air as he looked at her, incredulously. They had agreed to wait until they signed the paperwork and Sam had wanted to talk to his parents on his own. As soon as she had spoken, she knew she'd made a mistake. She wanted to chase after the words and gobble them back up. She closed her eyes praying that it was all just a dream, like the many occasions at night where she would picture what she should have said to Cecelia but was never brave enough to actually say it.

But when she opened her eyes and looked across the table to her sister-in-law Sophie, she saw her face had lost all its colour. She had done the unspeakable. Greg, Sam's brother looked dumbfounded, his mouth wide open in shock. Alistair, Sam's father was looking at her intently, but she could not read his expression.

She wanted to explain to them that Cecelia had made her do

it. After years of abusive snide comments, she had finally had enough. That being with Linda and Ethan, two people in genuine need, had meant she could not stand the shallowness of Cecelia's conversation anymore. Cecelia used none of her wealth to help people. Did she even realise that people like Linda existed? That they had real-life problems that were more important than which house to spend Christmas at and whether they should get there by bloody plane or helicopter. Accustomed to the power that came with the family wealth, Cecelia was only concerned with the chess game that was her own life. She put her pawns where she wanted them and expected them to do as they were told. Sam and Flora lived in the house that Cecelia had bought for Sam when he turned eighteen, a house that was next door to the one she had bought Greg, his brother. These houses were, coincidentally, five minutes around the corner from Cavendish Manor.

Flora had known that she would be apoplectic when she found out that Flora and Sam would be moving away. Cecelia did not allow her pawns to move of their own accord. However, she did not foresee her mother-in-law collapsing to the floor like a statue, clutching at her right arm.

4

Cecelia clutched her right arm and fell to the floor. If Sophie's brain had not been distracted by trying to process what Flora had said she would have found the entire thing comical. Before Flora had opened her mouth, nothing would have pleased Sophie more than seeing Cecelia falling to the floor, apparently having a heart attack. But as it was, Sophie was so stunned that she felt she could quite easily have joined Cecelia on the floor.

Her heart thumped in her chest as she tried to take in Flora's words. Flora was moving. And worse still: she had not said a word to Sophie. It made the blood boil in her veins.

Since they were four years old, Flora and Sophie had been best friends. A friendship that started with them both liking the green crayon the best, it had transformed into something unshakeable, twenty-four years later. Although they loved the same colour, in looks and personalities they were polar opposites. Flora was shapely and brown-haired and still obsessed with the colour green, her wardrobe reflected nearly every shade of green available. Sophie was stick thin and blonde and favoured suits and dresses in muted creams and blacks. She was sophisticated and spent a lot of time making sure not a hair was out of place. People were drawn to Flora as she was kind, chatty and trusting whereas they found Sophie was reserved and ruthless. But they had been inseparable since that day and their friendship grew with them, leaning on each other throughout the journey to adulthood through the good times and the bad. They'd even married brothers, which made it all the more devastating that Flora would not have discussed with her something so momentous as moving away.

Sophie felt like the world had shifted around her. Nothing looked quite the same. Flora was her entire world: their friendship was all that got her through the day. People envied the close bond between them, it was a profound connection. Or so she had thought.

Flora would not meet her eye, even after Alistair had leapt from the table and yelled at Reginald to call an ambulance. Greg and Sam hovered uncertainly around their mother as Alistair cradled her head in his lap. Cecelia looked serene, like she was sleeping. But Sophie could not focus on them. She kept looking at Flora, willing her to meet her eye. But Flora's head stayed resolutely down, as tears spilled onto her pale green dress, leaving blotchy stains. Sophie was about to give voice to her stormy thoughts, to force Flora to look up and meet her eye when Reginald burst in, followed closely by two paramedics.

The next few minutes were a blur. Greg's hand on her back pushed Sophie roughly out of the house and into a car. The chauffeur pulled away and they were following the pulsating lights of the ambulance to the hospital. Greg was holding her hand so tightly it hurt, but Sophie could not really feel the pain. For Flora did not understand the damage she had just done. But she was going to.

5

The doors to the waiting room burst open. Each door slammed against the wall making everyone jump, such was the force of Greg's push. Greg was two years older than Sam and although they both had a similar giant build, Greg exhibited none of the gentleness that Sam possessed. Brash, loud and ruthless he was the polar opposite of Sam. When Sophie first introduced her to Greg, Flora thought she was joking. But apparently their shared ambition and passion made them a formidable couple. They both worked in the family firm and despite Cecelia's protests, Sophie had risen up the ranks and played a vital role in securing new business for the company. Flora would have thought it would have garnered Sophie some respect from Cecelia, even grudgingly. But if anything, it made Cecelia hate her more.

Sophie headed straight to Flora and took the seat next to her. Greg walked over and sat at the other side of Sam.

'Bad news, she's going to be fine. Just a panic attack. Drama queen,' whispered Sophie. Sneaking a look at the men to check they weren't listening, Sophie continued, 'Shame, though, I was really hopeful for a while. Can you believe she tried to make it look like a heart attack? Bloody actress.'

Flora looked at Sophie for the first time since she had revealed their plans. In lashing out at Cecelia she knew she had badly hurt Sophie. There had never been a time in her life when she had not told Sophie something. Every time something happened to her, no matter how trivial, Sophie was the person she wanted to tell. Sophie was the one she cried to when the parent-shaped hole in her life became too much to bear. Sophie was the one she turned to when she had her first period and thought she was dying. They had grown together, two damaged little girls grappling with their traumatic childhoods and who only had each other to rely on. But that was exactly why she could not tell Sophie she was moving. How could she admit to her best friend that she was no longer that broken little girl who needed Sophie as much as oxygen? That she was now a married woman ready to embark on the beginning of her 'happily ever after'? Sam was so patient and kind when it came to her relationship with Sophie. But a few little hints here and there had told her he was ready to start coming first in Flora's world. Flora gave Sophie a weak smile but said nothing.

A flicker of emotion passed over Sophie's face, but Flora could not decipher it before her face became expressionless once more.

Flora opened her mouth to speak but Sophie took her hands. 'Let's talk about it later.'

Flora opened her mouth again, but Greg stood up. 'Sophie, let's go.' His tone brooked no argument. Sophie stood obediently and walked to his side. As soon as she got close, he grabbed her arm and led her out of the room. Flora could have sworn she saw Sophie wince in pain. But the thought was driven from her mind at the feel of Sam's arms wrapping around her. This always happened: whenever he touched her the world disappeared around her and she was consumed by the feel of his skin and his smell. She had been resistant to him at first, put off by his money and status.

She had thought everyone that had a life of privilege, who had things handed to them on a plate, could not possibly share her values. But she soon came to see that although Cecelia embodied everything that she hated about those with wealth, Sam was the one apple who had fallen far away from the tree. He was her entire world and she was glad she had not killed his mother. She loved this man with all her heart and resolved to never let Cecelia get under her skin again. He was worth taking any nasty remark that Cecelia threw at her.

After all, Cecelia's weaponry consisted of empty words. She would never actually hurt Flora. Would she?

6

The next time that Sophie and Flora saw Cecelia was at Alistair's birthday party. Like the Queen of England, Alistair had two birthdays. A family one and a public one. This was the public one, where anyone who was anyone was invited. Michelin star chefs cooked up tiny portions of pretentious food and the gardens of Cavendish Manor rang with fake laughter only rich people can produce. Impeccably dressed waiters appeared before the guests could even register that they were thirsty. Classical music played from speakers sequestered among the shrubs. Not slowed down by her 'funny turn', Cecelia had gone all out.

Sophie walked on the outskirts of the gardens trying to avoid everyone. Normally, she and Flora would have teamed up and spent the entire time together, giggling, dodging Cecelia and making fun of the guests. But Flora had been spending less and less time with her since that fateful dinner. Every day she seemed to be 'working late at the centre'. When they did see each other Flora would talk endlessly about Linda and Ethan and what she was going to do. Every time Sophie went to broach the subject of moving, Flora appeared to sense it and change the conversation or come up with an excuse to leave.

Sophie was becoming increasingly frustrated, as she knew that danger was coming for Flora. And she was the only person in the world that could protect her from it.

When they had married into the Cavendish family, Sophie genuinely believed they were both getting their fairy-tale ending. In Greg, she had found a like-minded, intelligent and ambitious businessman and Flora had found the gentle giant she always wanted in Sam. But to enter into the Cavendish family was to be swept up in their web of toxicity. Flora had kept herself on the outskirts of family life. She never accepted or used their money unless she had no choice; whereas Sophie had thrown herself in headfirst and fully embraced the Cavendish life, seduced by a wealth and power beyond her wildest dreams. But now she was inside she had been exposed to the secrets of how the Cavendish family retained their wealth and power. She had seen that Flora was in more danger than she could ever realise since her revelation on Friday.

Sophie had always protected Flora and she was not about to stop now. But she could not protect Flora if they were not talking. Sophie knew that Flora was a coward when it came to uncomfortable conversations. Her friend was beautiful inside and out, but her need to please people stopped her from standing up and saying what she truly felt. It saddened Sophie that Flora had felt unable to talk to her. Honesty had never been a problem between them before they married into the Cavendish family.

Did Sam have something to do with it? She always thought that he had begrudgingly accepted their close bond but now she wondered if Sam was just biding his time, waiting for an opportunity to get rid of her.

She knew she could be irritating, always turning up and

taking up so much of Flora's time. But he didn't – couldn't – understand what bound Flora and Sophie together. He was born with a silver spoon in his mouth and had not known hardship, neglect or cruelty in the way that Sophie and Flora had. Sophie had had to fight to get them to where they were today. She was not going to let Sam or any of the Cavendishes ruin it. She would protect Flora at all costs, whether she wanted to be or not.

The four of them – Greg, Sam, Sophie and Flora – had travelled to the party together. Greg had driven whilst Sam and Flora cuddled in the back. Sophie enjoyed watching the glow on Flora's face when Sam embraced her. After everything that she had been through, Flora deserved happiness. Sophie looked at Greg, his face compassionless and focused. She wondered what he was thinking. Did he even think about holding her hand? When was the last time he had cuddled her? She went cold inside and returned to surreptitiously staring at Flora and Sam through the wing mirror of the car.

Cecelia and Alistair had been waiting for them at the entrance to the house. Sam and Greg were held by their mother and the girls were pushed to the side like the spare parts Cecelia thought they were. Alistair bowed his head to Sophie and gave her a knowing smile. She went cold again. His smile was designed to remind her of the power he had over her. Everyone who met Alistair Cavendish instantly warmed to him. After all, he was charming, handsome, generous with laughter and an extremely shrewd businessman. It was only if you looked closely, behind the façade that you could see the psychopath in the bespoke tailored suit.

7

Escaping another dull conversation – no, she had not gone to Oxford University like Sam and yes, Manchester College of Art was 'coming up in the world' – Flora went around the side of the building towards the back door, intending to seek a bottle of wine from the bar inside. Since marrying into the Cavendish family, she had begun to drink more heavily. It seemed the only anaesthetic to the shallowness that came with this pretentious world of money she had married into.

Raised voices from around the corner of the house stopped her in her tracks. Was that Sophie? She almost did not recognise her friend's voice as it trembled with a fear she'd never heard before.

Greg's voice rang out, echoing off the stone walls. 'Dammit, Sophie. I don't even know who you are anymore.'

Flora tried to peer around the corner but whipped her head back, worried they would see her.

'Greg, please!' cried Sophie.

Unable to help herself, Flora peeked her head around the corner of the house again just in time to see Sophie lay what seemed like a placatory hand on Greg's arm. Greg ripped her hand off him, throwing it from him like her touch had burned him. Anger rippled from him and he appeared to grow even larger. He grabbed Sophie by her shoulders pushed her until her back hit the wall behind her. Flora heard the breath leave Sophie's lungs and the thud of her head meeting stone. He towered menacingly over Sophie and brought his head down, his face inches from hers. Flora's terror matched the fear on Sophie's face. She saw spittle leave his mouth as he spat words she could not distinguish into Sophie's face. She saw Sophie's lips move but could not hear a sound. The next moment, Greg let out a cry of anger and he pulled back his hand clenched into a fist. Flora saw the colour drain from Sophie's face, and cringe away. She was about to rush to Sophie's side when Greg's fist hit the wall right next to Sophie's head. He lowered his hand to his side, a trickle of blood on his knuckles. His whole body vibrated with anger. Flora turned away, her breath coming in rasps, and indecision flickering through her. What should she do? Her instinct was to intervene, but something stopped her. She cursed her cowardice.

Taking a deep breath, strengthening her resolve, Flora moved around the corner, determined to give Greg a piece of her mind. But Greg had gone. Sophie was slumped on the floor, picking at the skin around her fingers, eyes unfocused. Desperate to comfort her friend, Flora did not see the ornamental plant pot in front of her. She heard the crash before she registered what she had done. Soil and white hydrangeas spilt across the floor interspersed with shards of the gold-leaf plant pot. Sophie's head snapped to attention.

'Oh no. What am I going to do?' A wave of nausea swept through her, Sophie and Greg's fight momentarily forgotten. Flora leant against the wall, legs weak. She had once seen Cecelia scream for a whole hour when a waiter had spilt a drink on the floor. Once again, Flora had just handed Cecelia more ammunition.

As if summoned by thoughts alone, Cecelia came gliding around the corner. 'My hydrangeas!' she cried, hands on her face, tears springing to her eyes as she took in the sea of dirt, flowers and broken vase in front of her. Flora felt the gaze of curious guests, saw them inching closer to get a good view. Drawn like vultures by Cecelia's shriek, by the possibility of drama that could feed the gossip mill for weeks.

'I am so sorry, Cecelia,' said Sophie, stepping in front of Flora, blocking her from view. 'I was rushing to get myself one of those wonderful crème brûlées you told me about, and I didn't look where I was going. Oh, please say you'll forgive me. I couldn't bear it if we were to fall out.' Sophie reached forward and clutched Cecelia's hands in hers. She had raised her voice, ensuring everyone in the immediate vicinity could hear her desperate plea for forgiveness. The crowd and Flora watched with bated breath.

Cecelia looked behind her to see the hungry crowd waiting in anticipation. Her desire to yell at Sophie warring with her need to avoid becoming the latest gossip. Had they been alone there is no doubt she would have been scathing and tried to take advantage of the opportunity to belittle Sophie. But with Sophie apparently distraught with guilt in front of her guests, to be seen to be anything but forgiving would have ruined her precious image.

Taking advantage of Cecelia's indecision, Sophie grabbed Flora's arm and dragged her away from the danger zone. Shouting behind her that she would send someone to pick up the pieces and have the vase replaced. They wound their way through the corridors until they sought refuge in one of the guest bathrooms upstairs. The room was more like a spa than a bathroom, with a waterbed to rest on when you couldn't decide whether you wanted to use the walk-in rainfall shower or the opulent roll-top bath.

Flora opened her mouth to thank Sophie for taking the blame when her eyes processed the violent red marks on Sophie's arms. 'What the hell?'

Sophie looked confused. 'Er, I just saved you from a roasting from the Dragon Lady. You're welcome, by the way.'

'Sophie, your arms.' Flora stroked the fiery red marks that looked so vivid against her friend's pale white skin.

At first, Sophie closed her eyes, seeming to take comfort from the physical contact. But then she knocked Flora's hand away and moved to sit on the lip of the bath. 'Stop worrying. It was just a little argument that got a bit heated. We will be fine tomorrow.' Sophie wouldn't look at her.

'But your arms.'

'I bruise easily. Stop overreacting.' Sophie took a deep breath in and then looked at her. 'It was nothing. Honest. Just a silly fight. I did something that annoyed him, that's all. It was completely my fault.'

Flora was not mollified. She walked over and got into the bath and pulled Sophie in with her. Sophie let out a surprised laugh as she fell backwards. The sound echoed around the room and made Flora feel a little better. The bath was so big that they could sit at opposite ends of the bath facing each other and their legs only just met in the middle. Sophie pulled Flora closer so that their legs interlocked. She fiddled with the bow on Flora's shoe – her Primark shoes that she had once told Cecelia had been handmade by a designer.

'I remember when you got these shoes,' mused Sophie. 'Are you ever going to get rid of them?'

Flora looked at her in mock horror. 'I love these shoes. How dare you!' They smiled at each other and Flora's heart warmed. It was at times like this that she felt the bond between them like a physical tether. But her eyes fell once more on Sophie's shoulders. The imprint of Greg's hands branded on her skin.

'I've never seen him that angry, Soph. I was really scared. And he shouldn't have hurt you like that.'

'I told you, he didn't hurt me. It looks worse than it is.' She tickled Flora's feet in her shoe, trying to lighten the mood. 'You are making a mountain out of a molehill, my dear Flo.'

Her tone was jovial, she was trying to close down further discussion but Flora ignored her. 'But what did you do that annoyed him?'

Sophie looked down, ashamed. 'I made an important business decision without approving it through him. I thought it would be okay but then it ended up losing us a lot of money.'

For reasons Flora would never understand, Sophie had joined the Cavendish empire willingly. She happily took their money and seemed to enjoy the status and power that came with being a Cavendish. Cecelia didn't approve of Sophie any more than she did of Flora, but she was less vocal with her distaste because she knew Sophie was an equal match for her as a verbal sparring partner. Instead of the vicious barbs Flora was bequeathed, Cecelia would try to take advantage of Alistair being Sophie's boss.

Sophie had confided in Flora in those early days that Cecelia and Alistair had been relentless in trying to get her fired. Cecelia had even gone as far as hiring people to try and trick her into making dodgy deals or sell company secrets. And Alistair spent his time setting her impossible tasks. But Sophie was every bit the shrewd businesswoman that Cecelia was. Every ploy Cecelia attempted Sophie had already anticipated.

'But that doesn't give him the right to hurt you. No matter what you had done.'

Sophie sat up, her hands on Flora's legs and looking her straight in the eye. There was a flicker of annoyance in her crystal blue eyes. 'Flora, I will say it one last time. It looked worse than it was. Greg would never hurt me.'

But though Flora let it go, she still wondered who Sophie was trying to convince. They had spent so many of their formative years protecting each other that perhaps she was being oversensitive.

Sophie sat back in the bath and resumed playing with Flora's shoe. 'Have you spoken to Linda yet?'

Flora sighed. She could feel tears rising in her throat. Why was she so emotional lately? It was a knee-jerk reaction now every time she thought of Ethan and Linda. It was a catch-22 situation that had her moral compass spinning in useless circles. Her heart was desperate to help Ethan. She wanted nothing more than to say yes. But she couldn't do that because it wouldn't stop there. It would be impossible for her to say no to the next child who couldn't afford to attend. It would open the floodgates and ultimately result in the closure of the centre. 'No. I keep putting it off. You know what I'm like. But I'll do it tomorrow.'

Sophie raised her eyebrows. 'You know it is the right thing to do. Unless you take up Sam's offer to invest? Expand the centre?'

Flora narrowed her eyes at Sophie. Her hackles raised the way they always did when this topic came up.

Sophie raised her hands up in defence. 'Hey, I'm just playing devil's advocate. I know how you feel about the money situation.'

Flora immediately backed down, placated. The well-worn tirade she was about to launch at Sophie dying on her lips. Sam could never understand why Flora wouldn't embrace the family money. As much as reasonably possible she resisted taking a single penny. In the early days, Sam hadn't taken her seriously. But when Sam bought her a new car, she took it back. When he bought her fancy clothes, she donated them to charity.

Eventually, he realised that extravagance and Flora were like chalk and cheese. She liked to think she got this moral stubborn streak from her parents. They had lived frugally and given what they could to charity. They never wanted more than what they needed to get by and that was how Flora wanted to live. An evil voice in her head reminded her that her principles regarding the Cavendish money were also preventing her helping Linda.

Sophie must have noticed the internal strife within Flora as she changed the subject once more. 'So, when do I get to visit the new house? I need to pick out my room.'

Flora looked up at Sophie in surprise. So far, they had avoided talking about the move. But it seemed Sophie was fed up with treading on eggshells and it was a relief to talk about it. By bringing it up this way, Flora hoped Sophie was saying she was okay with her moving away. She knew that Sophie loved living next door to her. But this house they were moving to wasn't just any house. It was the house her parents had lived in. She took a deep breath and began to fill Sophie in on everything she should have told her months ago.

8

Flora had been with Cecelia when she got the news that her aunt had passed away and that she was the sole beneficiary in her will.

Cecelia was sitting at the breakfast bar in Sam's house. She had never called it her house and still thought of it as Sam's house though she had lived there nearly five years. Cecelia had helped herself to a satsuma from the fruit bowl. 'I much prefer the ones with the seeds. But then, I suppose not everyone has a distinguished palate. Honestly, the rubbish people eat these days.' She placed the orange back in the bowl like it was rotten.

It had now gotten to the stage that almost every word that Cecelia said poured fuel onto the already volcano-like rage that boiled within Flora. When she looked in the mirror, she was surprised she couldn't see the flashes of orange lava glowing as it flowed through her veins. Her hatred for this woman was becoming part of her DNA. But she ignored the anger and kept it buried deep within, for Sam's sake.

Cecelia was dressed impeccably in a black skirt and matching suit jacket with pearls gleaming at her neck, and her hair styled in her trademark chignon.

Flora imagined picking up the oranges in front of her and throwing them at Cecelia's head. She could see in her mind's eye Cecelia running from the house whilst she hurled oranges at her, some of them meeting their mark so that bursts of sticky citrus juice coated Cecelia's clothes, strands of her perfect white hair falling chaotically around her face.

Flora's fingers inched towards the fruit bowl, intoxicated by the tantalising daydream of a dishevelled Cecelia. The sound of the post falling onto the mat caused her to jump guiltily, and she quickly left the room to grab the letters, ignoring Cecelia's complaints that 'a Cavendish lady should not be getting the post. The help should be getting the post.' Cecelia still hadn't come to terms with the fact Flora had insisted that Sam get rid of his housekeeper if he wanted her to move in.

Cecelia – presumably fed up of not getting a reaction from Flora – left without saying goodbye. But Flora hadn't even noticed. Her hands trembled as she had opened the letter stamped with the 'Lucas & Jones Solicitors'. It was printed on thick, expensive paper. Official letters always made her nervous. Like when she drove past a police car, her heart would quicken even though she knew she hadn't done anything wrong.

Dear Mrs. Cavendish,

It is with regret, that I am writing to inform you of the passing of your aunt, Pauline Sanderson. As the executor of your aunt's will and as you are the only living relative of Ms. Sanderson I am writing to you to request an appointment at your earliest convenience to discuss some important matters in more depth. Please respond to this letter or call the number provided as soon as possible.

Our deepest condolences for your loss.

Yours sincerely

James Lucas

Senior Partner, Lucas & Jones Solicitors, LLB

A momentary sadness consumed Flora. Her last and only blood relative was now gone. She wasn't surprised that no one had told her. She was sixteen the last time she had seen or spoken to Pauline. But then memories of her childhood rose up and poured cold water on any sparks of sadness she might have felt.

The day of her parents' death, she had been taken to the hospital by a police car and introduced to a stranger who said she was her mother's sister Pauline. She informed Flora that they were going to live together in her parents' home, which had been left to Pauline in the will. 'It'll be such fun'. But the smile she gave Flora had made her shiver.

It did not take long for Flora to realise that all the malice and evil missing from her mother's character had been given to Pauline. Pauline's rancour towards her sister was evident from the first day she moved in. Everything that belonged to her mother was either sent to the tip or shoved away in the attic. The house was altered beyond recognition.

It was as though Pauline was on a personal mission to remove every trace of her sister. That included Flora. As soon as Flora was sixteen, she was unceremoniously evicted. A note was Sellotaped onto a pile of bin bags filled with her belongings. 'Time to stand on your own two feet.'

The day after she received the solicitor's letter, Flora found herself sitting in a respectable office, with a glass table and a friendly, professional man staring at her with concern. James Lucas had had to call in his receptionist to bring Flora a glass of water because she looked like she may faint or be sick.

Flora had stood up and looked out of the window, shocked that her aunt hated her that much that she wished to leave her entire estate to the 'British Arachnological Society'. *A charity for spiders for heaven's sake*. But Mr Lucas wasn't done.

'It was only when finalising the details of your aunt's estate that I discovered that 5 Trelawney Close was actually part of a trust and could not be considered part of your aunt's estate. This is why I have called you here today. According to your parents' will, the house was to be held in a trust, with your aunt and her late husband named as trustees, until you turned eighteen.'

At this, Flora had staggered backwards, her legs also in shock lost their primary function of holding her up and she felt herself collapse. As the ground rushed towards her, Mr Lucas jumped to his feet and pushed her into a seat before she could fall to the floor. The receptionist thrust the glass of water into Flora's shaking hands and stalked back out the room, oblivious to the bomb that had just gone off in Flora's mind. That her entire childhood had been shaped by the lie of one woman. She didn't seem to care what Flora had suffered since her parents' death and that she was just uncovering the extent of her aunt's deception.

In stilted sentences, Flora informed Mr Lucas that her aunt had neglected her duties as trustee and instead told Flora that she was the sole beneficiary of her parents' will. Flora was tempted to ask where her aunt was buried so she could dig her up and kill her again.

9

'She did what!' Sophie's head jerked back as if she'd been slapped. She couldn't process what she was hearing. Rage was building within her and she wanted to lash out at something.

'I know. I couldn't believe it either.'

'Why didn't you tell me straight away?'

Flora looked down again, her face colouring. 'I'm sorry. I know I should have said. I just knew you would be upset that we were moving, and I didn't know how to tell you.'

Sophie's heart winced. It made her desperately sad that Flora had kept this from her. After everything they had been through, after everything Sophie had done, it was like a knife in the back to find out Flora had been keeping secrets from her. She looked away, it was hard to cleanse her face of frustration and emotion.

'Flora?' Sam's head poked around the door. He was dressed in a blue suit that complemented his eyes. But there was no doubt that Greg was the more handsome out of the two. Sam was too gentle, and it oozed from every pore. Whereas Greg was authoritative and intelligent, you instantly respected him as soon as you saw him.

'Why are you both sat in the bath?' He looked bewildered. Sophie and Flora giggled.

'Hiding.' Flora chuckled.

'From who?' questioned Sam.

'Why from your delightful mother of course,' replied Sophie.

The skin around Sam's eyes tightened. Flora always beat around the bush when complaining about Cecelia to Sam, but Sophie had no qualms with voicing what she thought of his mother, a tendency Sam hated. She couldn't understand it. Unlike Sam, Greg knew exactly what his mother was like and how she treated Sophie. The difference was he did not actually care. After their first meeting, when Sophie had informed him that his mother was downright rude and disrespectful towards her and she was not having it, Greg had just laughed and told her it was character building. 'If she's rude to you, be rude back.' Although, not exactly supportive, at least he wasn't an ostrich like Sam.

'Flora, come on. Get out of the bath. Let's go and get a drink.'

Flora clambered out of the bath with all the grace of a three-legged donkey. Sophie laughed. Before she had time to get up, Sam had whisked Flora from the room leaving Sophie alone.

With no desire to re-join the party, she wandered around the house. It still marvelled her that it had so many corridors and rooms. It had been named Cavendish Manor because when built it was fancier than a normal house with its Romanesque pillars. But over time, wings had been added until it resembled more of a castle.

Sophie had only been in a handful of the rooms on offer and had a vague idea of where she was going but she had never looked in all of the rooms. One by one, she opened each door as she passed by and glanced in. Most were uniform guest bedrooms, containing a four-poster bed, solid oak wardrobes and the dusty smell of abandonment.

At last she found a room that was different to the rest, it looked like someone's study. With a thrill of curiosity Sophie wandered in. A framed photograph sat upon a magnificent mahogany desk that gleamed majestically in the sunlight. Sophie picked up the frame to see a picture of a young Cecelia with a baby in her arms and a young boy perched next to her. Cecelia was almost unrecognisable because she was beaming with happiness. It transformed her face, lit her up features and made her look almost motherly. Sophie had never seen her give a genuine smile in over five years. This version of Cecelia looked down at the baby in her arms and radiated love and warmth. What had happened to this Cecelia, the one capable of such beautiful emotion? She was looking at baby Sam with pure adoration, an expression Sophie would have given anything to have seen on her own mother's face.

Sophie placed the photograph back where she found it, feeling the sting of tears, readjusting it until she thought it was exactly where it had been. She could only imagine the grief she would get if Cecelia realised that she had been snooping.

She moved around to the black leather chair behind the desk. She sat down and let out a groan of satisfaction. Where on earth had Cecelia got this chair from? It was the most comfortable thing she had ever sat on. It caressed her back and gave support in all the right places. Sophie was no stranger to back pain from hunching over her laptop all day, thanks to Alistair dumping unsustainable amounts of work on her desk. She needed this chair.

Sophie looked around the room. It was almost as if it had been engineered to instil a sense of power and importance on the person who sat in it. Is this what a modern-day throne room looked like? What must it be like to sit in a room like this, in a mansion like this, knowing you had the money to do whatever you wanted in the world? She would certainly not be spending her life like Cecelia. She would take Flora and travel the world. To be fair, they had the money to do that now, but it wasn't hers. As much as she spent it like it was, there was always a boundary. It was always there between her and Greg, never spoken aloud but both of them knowing that it would never be her money. He was the keeper of keys and had the power to take everything away. She did not have the resources to completely change her and Flora's lifestyle, to never work again and spend her life seeing the world. Poor Cecelia. All she did was throw parties, terrorise her daughters-in-law and worship her sons. What a waste.

Sophie was distracted from her musing by the bookcase. The entire room was meticulously organised and uncluttered, which is why her eyes were drawn to a hardback book that was sticking out in its row. Sophie was about to push it in when she noticed that the book did not fit its dustjacket. She had just pulled the book out of its place, when a cough sounded behind her. She whirled around.

Alistair.

'Is there a reason you are in Cecelia's study?'

His tone was conversational but she was not deceived. Sophie's brain went momentarily blank as she stared into his compassionless eyes. He was thin and tall and his winter-white hair accentuated his bright blue eyes. Although he had crow's feet around his eyes, his skin was yet to become papery and translucent like others his age. She knew he was in his late sixties, but he did not look it. A rich diet of malice, cruelty and money appeared to have kept him young and vibrant.

'Er, yes. I'm borrowing a book of Cecelia's. Greg asked her for me, and she told me where it was.' She brandished the book. It was the first time she'd even looked at the cover. *What to Expect When You're Expecting.*

Alistair's eyes X-rayed her, his eyebrows raised slightly. 'I did not have you pegged as the procreating type. I thought you were much more sensible than that.' He sounded uninterested, but his eyes pinned her to the spot, searching for an ulterior motive.

'There are many things you don't know about me, Alistair. I'm full of surprises.'

'If only that were true, dear Sophie. I think you'll find I know everything there is to know about you. I think there are a few people downstairs that would be *crushed* if they knew what I knew.'

Her heart thudded in her chest. *Does he know?* she wondered. *No. It's not possible.* There were only two people in the world who knew Sophie's darkest secret. The secret she had locked in a trunk in the shadowy recesses of her mind where she pretended it didn't exist. No, he didn't know. He was trying to psyche her out. Hadn't she spent over five years watching him toy with people until they no longer had faith in who they were.

She straightened up and gripped the book in her hands, her knuckles turning white. She forced her body to saunter towards him and then stopped in front of him. 'My dearest father-in-law, I have absolutely no idea what you are talking about.' Clutching the book hard to prevent her shaking hands from betraying her, she walked out of the room, not realising that she had taken part in the first battle of a war she could not hope to win.

10

'Of course I bought this house for you, Sam,' Cecelia would always say, but in reality she viewed the three-storey, four-bedroomed terraced houses as an extension of her own home. She had her own set of keys and would come and go as she pleased.

Early on in her marriage, Flora had asked Sam to have a word with Cecelia. She was fed up with being on edge all the time, waiting for the next unannounced visit. It was only when she informed him that she was too nervous to have sex with him that he somehow managed to find the time to talk to his mother. He had informed her that same evening that it was taken care of and his mother would no longer visit without an invite and proceeded to carry her over his shoulder, up to the bedroom.

The next morning, she found Cecelia sat in the kitchen with a cup of tea, reading the *Financial Times*. Nothing had changed. In fact, it got worse. Cecelia began to have things sent to the house she thought would 'smarten the place up a bit'.

Sam could tell Flora it was a conciliatory gesture until he was blue in the face. But it was obvious to Flora that Cecelia was marking her territory. Why else would she think it appropriate for them to display a piece of art called 'Harpy'? Honestly, how Sam was successful in the business world when he was so bloody naïve was beyond her.

The fact that, today, Cecelia had knocked on the front door, should have warned Flora that something was terribly wrong. The steps up to the house meant that when she opened the door she was stood over Cecelia and from this vantage point, Cecelia looked shrunken and antiquated. That was until she pushed her way into the house without waiting to be invited in. The knock at the door obviously just for effect.

She walked through the hallway to the kitchen and made herself a cup of tea, tutting that there was no staff available to make her a drink. She didn't even acknowledge Flora, who just followed mutely like a sheep.

After sipping her drink, Cecelia set it down on the counter and pinned Flora with a steely gaze. 'We need to talk about this frankly ridiculous notion you've got of moving out of this house.'

Flora had expected Cecelia to go to Sam, not her. Surely, Cecelia realised that she would have more power over Sam than she would over Flora? Unless she had already tried, and Sam had stood his ground. That notion warmed Flora's heart and gave her strength. Her spine straightened and she stood taller, readying for a fight. This time she would face Cecelia and not rely on Sophie or Sam to fight her battles.

'If you feel you need a bigger space then we can help you look for something...' Cecelia paused apparently looking for the right word. '...suitable.'

'It's not about space, Cecelia. The house we are moving to belonged to my parents.'

Cecelia waved a hand dismissing her words. 'Yes, yes, I'm well aware of that. But surely, if your parents were alive today, they would want you to live somewhere like this.' Cecelia spread her arms wide, gesturing to the kitchen around them. 'I mean, really, Moss Side. Perhaps if they had lived in a better neighbourhood, they might still be with us.' Cecelia's words may have been spoken softly but they were designed to wound.

Flora swallowed the lump in her throat and blinked away unshed tears. Her body felt encased in ice, she was unable to move or speak. Not for the first time she wished Sam was here to see the vicious snake inside his mother that she kept hidden just beneath the surface, waiting for moments like this where she could sink her venomous teeth into Flora. He had never truly believed his mother was capable of saying anything cutting or despicable.

Cecelia pulled out a stool at the kitchen island. The metal screeched against the floor, making Flora wince. She took a seat and carried on, changing tack. 'What about Sam? What about what he needs? You may not be who I would have chosen for him...' She coughed and wrinkled her nose. It looked like it was physically costing her to say that. 'But I always thought you wanted him to be happy.'

'Of course I want him to be happy,' Flora said angrily.

Cecelia jumped on that. 'Well then, why are you forcing him to move away from his family, from his support network? He needs his family around him. You know what a tight-knit family we are. You don't have a family of your own so maybe you don't realise how important family is.'

The second callous reminder of her parents' death whipped at Flora like the strike of a rope on her bare back. 'But we are only moving to the other side of Manchester, not the other end of the country.' The meekness of her voice irked her. If only she could channel Sophie and be confident and strong. Her head was full of the things she really wanted to say. *We are moving to get away from you. Sam wants to move away. He wants to be with me.* But she knew as soon as she opened her mouth the words would fail her. She was the cowardly lion from *The*

Wizard of Oz. Only there was no yellow brick road leading to her courage.

'Exactly my point. Why do you need to move at all if you are only moving such a short distance? It makes no sense to me.'

They were going around in circles and Flora wasn't sure how to end the loop.

'Is it about money? If you had more money would you stay? I could make an investment in your little centre. Would that make you happy?' Cecelia asked.

Flora wondered if Cecelia's cup of tea was still scalding enough to do some real damage, were Flora to throw it in her face. The implication that she was a gold digger was not new, but the belittlement of her centre was a hard cross to bear.

'Cecelia, we are never going to agree on this. Sam and I are moving, that's that.' Flora placed her hands behind her back because they were shaking, betraying her emotions; but the tremor in her voice could not be hidden. Turning her back on Cecelia, Flora walked through to the front door and opened it. 'I think you should leave.'

Flora was astounded at herself. *Did I really just say that?* She did not dare to look at Cecelia. Choosing to study the floor whilst she waited for Cecelia to go.

'Flora, wait. Please.' Cecelia's voice came out strangled. Her eyes looked watery and she seemed diminished somehow. Flora shut the door and came back into the room. 'Please don't take my boy away,' she asked in a small voice. She stared down into her tea, avoiding Flora's eyes, a slight pink tinge to her cheeks.

Flora wished she knew if this was genuine or whether it was part of a ploy to get her way. She felt uncomfortable, not used to a Cecelia that could express any emotions other than hate and distaste.

'He is all I have, Flora; my reason to get up in the morning; my reason for living. Please don't take my boy away. I know it might not make sense to you, but I need my boy around me.' A tear slipped from Cecelia's eye, tracking down her face, peeling away Cecelia's mask to reveal a mother who loved her child. She quickly wiped it and drew her shoulders back, taking a shaky breath. Flora could almost see the barriers going back up like a computer rebooting.

'Anyway, I trust you'll consider what I've said. I wait to hear from you.' As she passed Flora, she whispered in her ear. 'Think very carefully, Flora. Decisions have consequences.' The threat hung in the air long after Cecelia strode from the house.

Flora slumped down on the breakfast bar, her brain and body weak from the onslaught of emotions. Part of her wanted to tell Sam that they were staying put. She was keenly aware of the importance of family, having had hers stripped from her so cruelly at the hands of a hit-and-run driver. But could she really give up her hopes and dreams for Cecelia? Surely Sam would have told her if he didn't want to move. Frustrated with herself she texted Sophie.

Just had the Dragon Lady at the house. She is trying to persuade me not to move.

Sophie's reply was instantaneous.

Not surprised, G said she's talked about nothing else since you told her. Don't let her get to you.

Unnerved by Cecelia's threat and needing some space from all things Cavendish, Flora had taken up residence in her favourite coffee shop. It had the most beautiful green fabric chairs she wanted to steal every time she visited. She ordered a double espresso, followed by a hot chocolate with all the trimmings. Inhaling the delicious scent of freshly brewed coffee she tried to let the buzz of conversation all around her replace the mass of thoughts in her mind. It did not work: she could not clear her mind.

She was so close to getting everything she ever wanted but she was worried about the lengths that Cecelia would go to stop her. Unused to her subjects disobeying, what would she do to restore order? Her words reverberated in Flora's mind: *Decisions have consequences.* She wanted to throw her drink across the room and watch it smash into pieces.

She was disturbed from her dark thoughts by the waitress putting down the plastic tray with her bill on it, a silent instruction that it was time to leave. Flora pulled her purse from her bag, unzipping the change compartment.

It was completely empty, her fingers roved around in disbelief, trying to locate the pound coins she had put in there yesterday whilst in Waitrose. It was then her eyes registered the empty slots where her bank cards should be. She felt sick and shaky all at once. With sweaty palms, she opened her bag wide, desperate to find that everything had fallen out of her purse into the depths of her rainbow-coloured handbag. Cursing herself for having such a stupidly large handbag, her hands frantically sought her missing cards and money.

It didn't make sense. The only thing still in her purse was her driving licence. Everything else had vanished. Coming up empty, she blushed when she realised that the young waitress who had dropped off the bill was watching her with a curious smile. Typical Alderley Edge, even their teenagers were obnoxious, she really only came here for the chairs and the great coffee. Flora checked the pockets of her coat, which was hung on the back of her chair. This had never happened to her before, she felt hot and sweaty. An irrational fear that the police might be called crossed her mind.

Her heart was racing as the slim waitress, who couldn't have been more than eighteen sauntered over. She had the stony teenage fed-up-with-life expression. 'Everything okay?'

'I'm really sorry but I've left my cards at home. I'm so sorry.' Flora's face burned hot with embarrassment. She felt paranoid that the eyes of everyone in the shop on her. Her legs twitched as she resisted the urge to run away. Flora could read no compassion in her eyes, only amusement.

The girl picked up the bill and looked at it. 'We have a budget to spend on hot drinks for the homeless, we can use some of that to cover this.' Her voice was purposefully loud so that everyone in the café could hear. Flora was mortified. She could see the customers taking in her nice clothes, hear the silent judgement. *Look at her, taking money from the homeless.* Thanking the girl profusely, Flora promised to bring the money in. She put on her coat with difficulty. Her hands were trembling so much it took several attempts to find the arm hole. She almost ran to the door such was her desire to escape. As she turned to close the door behind her, she caught sight of the waitress standing with her colleagues behind the counter, all of them were looking at her. As she pulled the door closed the sound of the girl's laughter entwined with the tinkle of the door's bell, cementing her humiliation.

Outside she pulled out her phone and called Sam. The words spilled out of her as she rushed to explain what happened to her.

'See this is why I told you to get contactless on your phone.'

'Well that doesn't help me right now, does it!' her voice was so loud that people on the street turned to look at her in surprise. 'Anyway, I think you are missing the bigger picture. My cards have disappeared. How could they have been stolen without me knowing?'

'Maybe they haven't been stolen. Did you change purses and forget?'

Flora shook her head emphatically. Realising at the last minute he couldn't see her, she answered. 'No, Sam, I'm not an idiot.' Tears lumped in her throat, stopping her from speaking.

'Hey, don't get upset. Just cancel your cards and order new ones. These things happen all the time. It's okay, sweetie. It's not a big deal.'

Flora tried to get Sophie to come over that evening, but Greg was home and that meant Sophie wasn't free. She only seemed to visit when Greg was away these days. Flora berated herself for being jealous of Sophie spending time with her husband. She had promised to come over the next morning and Flora heard her yelling her arrival at 8.30am, whilst she was still in bed, playing Candy Crush on her phone. Getting up, she wrapped her pink fluffy dressing gown around her, rescuing it from the floor where Sam had left it.

She chose to ignore the irony that she did not mind Sophie walking in unannounced but hated it when it was Cecelia. But then, Sophie wouldn't spend her time taking down pictures Flora had hung because 'it made the house look like a brothel'. Flora came down the stairs, the story of her missing cards on her lips.

Sophie was facing away from her, sitting at the breakfast bar, Flora wrapped her arms around her in greeting but was quickly flung off as Sophie let out a screech. 'Flora, you bloody scared me.'

Flora was about to laugh when she saw Sophie's face. It looked creased in pain. 'What's wrong. Are you okay?'

Within seconds, Sophie's face was smiling, and Flora wondered if she'd imagined the look of pain. 'Fine, fine. Like I said, you just scared me. Anyway, what did you want to tell me that you couldn't tell me yesterday?'

'Oh yeah. Wait here.' Flora dashed over to the sofa where she had left her handbag after emptying it across the floor last night. She grabbed her purse and turned to leave the room when she realised something felt off. Stopping mid-step, she looked down at the purse. It was heavier than it had been last night. She had handled it so much yesterday that she was more than familiar with its weight. With a slight tremble in her hand, she pulled back the zip and was greeted with the sight of all her cards in the slots. The seven pound coins she had got from Waitrose were back in the change compartment, like they'd never been moved in the first place.

'What's taking so long?' Sophie asked.

Flora felt her enter the room but could not tear her eyes away from her purse. 'They weren't there,' breathed Flora weakly. Her body was limp, her hands clammy.

'What wasn't there?' asked Sophie.

She slumped onto the sofa. 'This is going to sound ridiculous, but yesterday I was in a café and my purse was empty. All my cards, everything gone. It was so embarrassing. I just went to get my purse to show you it was all gone. But now...' She stopped, staring at the purse again. 'Now, it's all there.'

'That's weird.' Sophie joined Flora on the sofa and wrapped her arms around her. 'What do you think happened?'

'Thank you,' said Flora. Looking at Sophie with tears of gratitude.

'What for?'

'For not asking me if I checked properly. Or for thinking I imagined it.'

Sophie chuckled. 'I think after twenty years of being your friend, I'd know if you were a nutter by now.'

Flora's body warmed and she snuggled closer to Sophie, resting her head on her shoulder. It was a testament to the strength of their friendship that Sophie believed Flora automatically. That's what love was, knowing someone so completely that you always took their side. She wished she could say the same about Sam. All of last night he had refused to believe that someone had taken her cards, convinced she had just misplaced them. She didn't want to look too closely at what that meant for their relationship. That he wouldn't believe her automatically. But then, she reasoned, he hadn't known her as long as Sophie had.

'But it is really weird. You don't think...' said Sophie. Then she shook her head. 'No, actually, forget it.'

'What? Tell me!'

Sophie looked sheepishly at Flora. 'Well... the only explanation is that someone took your cards and then put them back.'

'Well, yeah,' said Flora, realising Sophie was voicing what her brain had yet to process. 'But who?'

Sophie couldn't look at Flora in the eye. Instead she addressed her knees. 'Flo, there are only two people it could be. Cecelia and...'

'...Sam,' finished Flora.

Sam and Cecelia. Cecelia or Sam. For the rest of the day, Sophie and Flora were trapped in the same cycle of debate. In the end, they had decided that Cecelia was the only candidate. It was a reach because stealing Flora's cards and putting them back just didn't resonate with the Cecelia they knew. It was beneath her, a menial task that they could not picture her doing. When Cecelia wanted to offend or upset Flora, she would do so in person to soak up the damage of her words or actions. Sophie had theorised that it could be part of a scheme to try and stop Flora from moving. But Cecelia was cleverer than that, surely? It would take a lot more than that to scare Flora into staying put.

Flora refused to believe that Sam had taken her cards. She would not admit that Sophie had a point that he was the one with the easiest access to them and that it would be harder for Cecelia to get to her purse than it would be for Sam.

Sophie had wondered aloud if they were working together until a scathing look from Flora caused her to change the subject. Flora desperately wanted to talk to Sam about it. But even if it wasn't him, she had never convinced Sam that his mother did not like her and was regularly rude and disparaging towards her. How was she going to convince him of something as incredible as this?

That night, as Flora coated the vegetables in pomegranate molasses, she couldn't resist furtive glances at Sam. He was sat at the breakfast bar, typing intently on his laptop. She wished more than anything she could peer into his mind. She thought she knew everything about him. But a tiny seed of doubt had firmly planted itself into her mind. *Damn Sophie and her theories.*

Sam's arms came around her, startling her from her reverie. 'Hey jumpy, is dinner almost ready?' he asked, nuzzling his nose into her neck, running his hands up and down her waist. Her body, seemingly ignorant of her worries, responded to his touch. She turned from the kitchen island and surrendered to him, letting his arms surround her.

His began to kiss her deeply, she tried to return his passion, but she couldn't relax into the kiss.

Sensing her reluctance, Sam pulled away, rubbing his nose against hers. 'What's wrong, sweetie? You aren't still worrying about your cards?'

She pushed him away. 'Of course I am. One minute my cards were gone and the next minute they were back in my purse.'

'Flo, listen to yourself. How would that even happen? Perhaps you took the wrong purse to the coffee shop. Maybe they fell out into your bag. There will be an explanation, we just don't know it yet.'

'Sophie doesn't think I've lost my mind. She thinks someone took my cards,' she retorted defiantly.

Sam shook his head and sighed. 'Why would they do that, Flo?'

'It's obvious. To freak me out. Scare me.'

'But who would want to do that to you?'

'I can think of one person who hates me enough.'

Sam's shoulders slumped. He groaned in frustration, the noise of someone desperate to stop listening to a broken record. 'Not this again.'

'When are you going to wake up and see your mother for who she is? Do you know what she said to me? She said that if my parents hadn't lived in such a rough area, they'd still be alive.' She began pacing up and down the kitchen, circling the island. 'Like hit-and-run accidents don't happen in posh areas. Only the poor people are stupid enough to be killed in a car accident. The rich are too safe in their limos and chauffeured cars!'

Her body was shaking in anger. She normally held back when talking to him about his mother, knowing it was the one thing they would never agree on. But the incident with her bank cards and Cecelia's callous comments had displaced her usual reserve. 'Oh, and she said that because my parents are dead, I don't have a clue what it means to be part of a family.'

'Flo, calm down.' He pulled her to a stop, gently placing his hands on her shoulders. 'I'm not justifying what she said but she was just lashing out. We both know she is taking our move badly. I'll talk to her again.'

It was Flora's turn to groan. 'Uggh. Why can't you see the way she treats me? She is always criticising me, throwing subtle insults at me. She hates me, Sam. Not once has she ever said something nice or kind to me. She belittles me at the slightest chance. You have to see that.'

'I know that you and my mother aren't close, but she does not hate you, I promise. She just isn't good at showing her emotions. It probably feels like she is cold towards you but that is just the way she is. She shows she cares through actions not through words. She invites you to every Friday Night Dinner. If she hated you, she wouldn't do that, would she?'

Flora's frustration gave way to sadness as once again she acknowledged the futility of trying to get Sam to open his eyes and see his mother for who she was. She stepped away and Sam's arms fell to his side. Flora took a seat at the breakfast bar, leaning over she rested her head in her hands.

Sam continued in a softer voice. 'My mother would never hide your bank cards and replace them. That is a childish prank, I don't know anyone that would do that. It doesn't even make sense to do that. What would someone accomplish? It's much more likely you just had the wrong purse, or the cards fell out.'

'That is not what happened, Sam,' she said in a flat voice. 'Sophie believes me, why can't you?'

'Sophie would say the sky was purple and that pigs can fly if you told her to.' Sam had raised his voice and Flora looked up in surprise.

'What's that supposed to mean?' she replied, narrowing her eyes at him.

'Just...' Sam couldn't meet her gaze. He picked up an orange from the fruit bowl and began to toss it from hand to hand, studiously concentrating on the trajectory of the orange. 'Just that she tends to agree with whatever you say.'

'Well that just shows how much you know about Sophie. If you actually bothered to get to know her, you'd know that she always tells me the truth. Whether I want to hear it or not. She's the only person I can rely on.' Flora got off her chair and went to leave the room, fed up with the conversation.

Sam swept her into his arms before she could reach the door. He held her tightly, kissing the top of her head. 'I'm sorry, Flo. I don't think you are crazy. I don't know what happened to your cards. But I promise you, it wasn't my mother. She would never hurt you. I swear it. Let's just put this whole thing behind us. Remember I'll always protect you.' He took her face in her hands and kissed her on the nose. 'Whether that's from flying cows.' He kissed her nose again. 'Meteors.' Another kiss. 'And anything else.'

She looked up into his sea blue eyes and chuckled despite herself. He always said the strangest things to make her laugh. He was right. She was overreacting. She needed to let it go and stop seeing danger in the shadows.

11

From the very first day that Sophie started at Cavendish & Sons, she had realised that she was going to have to battle for her right to stay. Greg may have given her a job, but it would be up to her to keep it. Most would have turned tail and run when they realised just how unevenly matched the sides were. It was Sophie versus Cecelia and Alistair.

But Sophie relished the challenge. She had been brought up by and survived Lily Moore, after all. Outwitting an alcoholic and social services and the teachers at school had been a full-time job. It had taught her how to manipulate and stay one step ahead of the game. Having to hide and endure her mother's neglect and her drinking problem was actually a blessing as it taught Sophie to overcome emotion. She had learnt to weaponise her emotions. Sophie knew when to cry and when to mask her feelings and become unreadable.

Sophie also knew how to make money. Her mother would drink all the child support and jobseeker's allowance money before she even got home on payment day. When Sophie's school uniform no longer fit and she could no longer cope with the comments from teachers about her inappropriately short and shabby skirt, Sophie had started her first business. Flora had offered to help her, but she didn't accept handouts unless she had to. Plus, she didn't want Flora's parents getting involved. Although there was every chance Flora's mum, Rebecca, already knew. Each sleepover, she'd find something of Flora's that was too big for her or the hole in her skirt she thought she'd hidden so well had been miraculously sewn up overnight.

With a little help from fate, something she firmly believed in, she had found a ten-pound note blowing across the pavement as she walked home from school. It was creased and dirty, obviously having fallen from someone's pocket and been trampled. Her mind raced with the possibilities. All she wanted to do was go and buy all the things that had been denied to her due to her mother's self-inflicted poverty. She wanted the fancy pencil case and the new trainers to show off in the classroom, instead of having to pretend that she didn't care. But she had to think clearly.

A plan soon formulated in her mind and that morning, she visited the off-licence. Ayaz, thinking she had been sent once more for some alcohol for her mother, went towards the shelf that held the Stella, but Sophie called him back. He turned back towards her, curious. Ayaz had been Sophie's friend since she had learnt to walk. He had brown skin and she had never seen him without a huge smile on his face. Everyone who came into the shop couldn't help but be charmed by his infectious joviality.

'How many sweets and chocolates can I get for this?' She held out the ten-pound note with trembling hands. It was the most money she had ever had in her life. Money that was her own, to do with what she wanted. She didn't really want to let it go and pulled it back, hugging it to her chest and clutching it tightly between her fingers.

Ayaz gave her a confused look but helped her to load her

rucksack with as many sweets and chocolate bars as it could fit. Ayaz had always treated Sophie with kindness. She had always thought it was because her mother was his best customer, but the gentle way he had helped her today made her think he felt a bit sorry for her. Especially when he gave her back a five-pound note in change. His face creased into a warm smile, his white teeth sparkling against the background of his dark skin. He was a lovely man and Sophie felt tears rise. The amount of chocolate and sweets in her backpack was almost tipping her over backwards... there was no way she should have that much change.

She put the money back on the counter. But he opened her hand, placed the note into it and then closed her fingers around it, holding her small hand in his large hands. 'Spend it wisely,' he said and then ushered her out of the shop.

Sophie tried hard to act normal when she walked past the teachers counting in the students. Her heart was racing, and she swore everyone was looking at her differently, that they could sense she was bringing contraband into the school. Thanks to recent government changes trying in vain to solve the obesity crisis in children, the school meals were now junk-food-free and the children were subjected to vegetables and more vegetables with a side of fruit. Even those with packed lunches had only healthy snacks, any contraband would be confiscated by the lunch lady.

Sophie hung up her rucksack on her peg with great difficulty. Sitting at her desk, she had watched in agony as the clock slowly ticked away the minutes until their morning break. Surreptitiously, Sophie had filled the lining of her skirt with sweets from her bag. Outside in the playground, with Flora at her side, she took a deep breath and walked straight over to Melissa. Melissa was the richest child in the school – as she told anyone that would listen almost every day. She would bring money to school and buy food from the canteen and the vending machines for her select group of friends. This wasn't as much of a bonus anymore now that the vending machine held only fruit bars and packets of carrot sticks.

'Oi, Melissa.'

The queen bee was sat on a bench, flanked on each side by her two most loyal disciples, Lisa-May and Jennifer. They rose as Sophie and Flora walked up to Melissa, like very skinny bodyguards.

'I've got something for you. I know you could afford it and no one else could.'

Melissa visibly preened at the mention of how much money she had. She leaned forward. 'What is it?'

Melissa's gang surrounded Sophie and looked at her with interest.

Sophie slowly pulled out the bars of chocolates and sweets and there was an audible intake of breath. Chocolate and sweets hadn't been seen in this playground since the plague of the health kick had swept through the school last year. Sophie pulled out Snickers, Mars Bars, Galaxy as well as bags of Skittles and Maltesers.

She drank in the shock and awe on the faces in the group. Melissa's eyes were hungry, and she stood up.

Sophie remarked, 'I just knew that there was no point offering them to anyone else as I knew you had enough money to buy the lot. I've got more than just this.' She was taking such a risk, there was every chance that Melissa could go running to the teacher and the plan would be ruined. She just had to pray that the queen bee's greed would outweigh her spite. Sophie could almost hear the cogs turning in her head as she decided what to do.

'How much?'

~

It took all Sophie's restraint not to jump and shout all the way home. Fate had smiled on her. From that day on, she became a believer in fate. If she was meant to succeed at anything, fate would give her a sign. Melissa had been her sign from fate. She had bought all of the sweets and chocolate for £20. All day, Sophie had watched her bestowing chocolate on her chosen people, buying loyalty and cementing her control over her existing followers. Sophie didn't care, she had more money than she had ever had in her life.

Instead of spending it on herself, she invested it in things that she knew people would want and slowly she became known as the 'go-to' girl who was the only person brave enough to bring things into school. Finally, she had found the one advantage of not having eagle-eyed parents to pack her bag and watch her every move. For once, her mother's neglect was a reason to celebrate.

It became a stable income and Sophie replaced her school uniform and bought the pink sparkly pencil case and the scented gel pens. No longer did she have to rely on handouts from Flora. She was given respect by the other pupils instead of ridicule as she shed her second-hand clothes and washed her hair.

When Flora's parents died, she was able to help Flora with things she couldn't get because of her aunt. Slowly, Sophie realised that she was good at business. She branched out when she reached secondary school and could spot like-minded kids that she could trust to work with her. Soon she had a network of sellers all reporting back to her. She could sense the trends before the other kids and was supplying a vast array of yo-yos before they even became cool. She manipulated teachers and situations to stop the teachers from tracing anything back to her.

Sophie liked to think dealing with the tantrums of the kids that worked for her had made it easy to deal with the tantrums of adults in the business world.

Alistair was like a child, really. He was the female version of Melissa, thinking that his money gave him a power and status higher than everyone else. He thought he was the top dog and that he could not be manipulated. But his money was his weakness.

Coming from nothing, Sophie had had to struggle and fight to get to where she was. She had earned every penny that she got and that gave her skills and strengths that Alistair would never have. His money had been handed to him on a plate simply because he had the luck of coming down the birth canal of a woman who belonged to a family that had done the graft and hard work already. Alistair didn't work because he needed the money, he worked because he enjoyed the power of lording it over everyone; of playing with the lives of those who didn't have money.

If there weren't laws against it, she knew he'd have gladiators in a ring fighting to the death for his entertainment. Alas, he had to make do with the tame, modern-day version where people vied for positions within the company, sabotaging other colleague's business deals as they battled to impress him.

Her first day, Sophie had become a new player in his games. Egged on by Cecelia, he had called her into a business meeting along with seven other new starters and announced to the group that he wanted to invest in a company but that he needed to have at least an eighty per cent share for it to be worthwhile. Whichever person got him the best deal would be returning to work tomorrow. Everyone else was fired. He smiled around at the graduates who had gone pale and shaky at his words. No wonder, as no entrepreneur would give up eighty per cent of a company that had cost them blood, sweat and tears.

Thankfully for Sophie, after years of convincing greedy school children to give her four pounds of every five pounds that they made and have them think it was a good idea, she was not worried. All it took to get by in business was to find what made people tick. Make them think you had a connection and then they were putty in your hands.

The owner of this particular business had, like her, come from a broken home and worked hard to get himself to where he was. He also happened to have a daughter with severe autism. This was fate once again, giving her a helping hand. Using some of the sob stories Flora had told her, he really believed she understood the condition and the strain he had faced. Stroking his arm gently, she promised him that the company would provide his daughter with a year's worth of classes at Flora's art centre as a goodwill gesture whilst the business was still growing. Squeezing his leg gently, looking up at him from beneath her lashes, she assured him that once they were done with the company, his ten per cent share would be enough for him to open his own autism centre if he wanted to.

The only sign of Alistair's true feelings was the pulse of the vein in his temple as he congratulated her.

Cecelia and Alistair had both done their hardest to bring about her failure; to make her give them cause to get rid of her. When that didn't work, they tried to drown her in work so that she would want to leave. They could have fired her easily enough with the right ammunition, but Sophie was exactly where she wanted to be. When you've lived in a house with no running water and vomit filling up the broken toilet, the office was a place of luxury and she did not mind spending every minute of her day there.

Sophie had created relationships with almost everyone in the company, made herself known to everyone, garnered respect from her colleagues, to the point that her absence would be noticed. When Cecelia and Alistair realised that they weren't going to find cause to legitimately fire her and that Sophie would not go quietly, they had given up and watched begrudgingly as Sophie rose through the ranks.

Greg had soon lost interest in her. His delight at their mutual ambition had afforded her his attention temporarily. He used to play this game with Sophie: they'd show each other the contracts that they had signed and the revenue they had generated, sitting in his office with a glass of wine. She'd be wrapped in his arms on the leather couch, until they both couldn't resist tearing the other's clothes off. The high of business success an aphrodisiac.

But with Alistair setting her what he thought were impossible tasks, the opportunities were getting bigger. Tasks engineered to exhaust and overwhelm her were causing her to outshine Greg. Funnily enough, after her third win in a row, he no longer had time for 'childish games' anymore. It was a 'family business' after all, so really 'anything she did' was helped by his 'family name'. According to him, she'd get nowhere on her own.

He didn't have a clue. Did he really think she was here because he made it so?

Having risen as far as she could, Sophie now had her own fancy office and a bunch of assistants. She could realise her ambition and passion for making money. Any attempts that Alistair and Cecelia made to de-throne her were just like batting away an irritating fly.

Today, she had cancelled her appointments. She was not in the mood for dealing with other people. Her mind was racing with everything had had happened in the last few days.

Sophie brought up Flora's 'new' house on Google maps. She stared at the house that had once represented nothing but pain and suffering for Flora. Even now, all these years later, she could picture the walk from her mother's house to Flora's.

She could still picture a teenage Flora, waiting outside on the wall, kicking her legs against bricks and chewing on the end of her braid as she waited for Sophie so they could walk together to school. Sophie knew that the loss of her parents was a weight that Flora carried around her neck. She had always done what she could to help her bear it. But the loss had come to define Flora and made her crave love and a family of her own.

Although Sophie had not lost her parents in the traditional sense, she may as well have. Sophie was an accidental by-product of Lily Moore's never-ending search for a 'good time'. Booze and men were her way of life and that did not change when she became a mother. Lily had decided that six was a perfect age for Sophie to gain her independence and start to look after herself and gave herself permission to return to long nights at the pub with a different man to share a 'good time' with each night.

On Google maps, Sophie was only able to look at the front of the house. But she didn't need a picture to remember the inside. It had become a refuge for Sophie. Especially in the years before Flora's parents had died. They always welcomed her as if they she was one of their own. It was a house that did not have the heady scent of booze and vomit; where she did not have to put her mother in the recovery position; or try and block out the animalistic grunts coming from her mum's bedroom. It was a house full of laughter, where she was asked how school was going and people actually listened when she spoke.

Then, in the Pauline-era, after the car crash that killed Flora's parents, it was a place to sneak into to be with Flora. She could almost hear the end credits of *Emmerdale* playing in her ears as she thought back to sitting outside of Flora's house waiting for the tune that was the customary signal that Pauline would now be asleep on the sofa with a cigarette in one hand

and an empty bottle of wine in the other, and it would be safe to creep into the house.

Sophie's mother was neglectful and powerless to her addiction. But she was never vicious. Flora's Aunt Pauline was the embodiment of cruelty. When she had taken custody of Flora and moved into her sister's house, it was like she had also adopted the task of terrorising Flora like an evil spirit.

Flora eventually admitted to Sophie that the bruises on her hands were not because she was clumsy but from the walking stick that Pauline pretended to the authorities she needed to keep the disability payments coming, but only seemed to need it to whack Flora for some perceived insult or disobedience.

The physical violence was nothing compared to Pauline's love of psychological torture. Sophie's blood turned to ice once more as she recalled the night Flora had turned up on her doorstep wrapped only in a bed sheet. The frost in the midnight air had been vicious and Flora's whole body had been icy cold and turning blue. She was shaking violently, but Sophie couldn't tell if it was from the cold or fear.

Through hysterical tears and hiccups, Flora told a horrific tale of how her aunt had decided that she dressed like 'a common tart' just like her mother. She'd walked into her bedroom to find her aunt there, cutting all of her clothes to shreds, switching between laughing manically and shrieking insults about her mother at the top of her voice. Pauline had even ripped off the clothes Flora had been wearing until all that was left in the room was a bed sheet.

Flora had stayed with Sophie for a whole week. They'd managed to get by sharing a school uniform and Sophie had given Flora some of her clothes, but they were completely different sizes. Sophie had a stick-thin pencil-shaped figure whilst Flora had feminine curves and breasts that seemed to grow each day. Using the precious earned money from selling at school, she bought Flora new clothes and a new uniform of her own. It was a while until Flora had built up the courage to return home. Her aunt appeared not to have noticed that she'd been gone or that she had replaced her clothes.

Sophie would have loved Flora to stay with her forever. However, Lily's drunken rampages were becoming more frequent. Three times Sophie had only just managed to intervene when Lily, convinced Flora had stolen her beer, tried to evict the girl forcibly from the house. Soon Flora began to feel that the wrath of her aunt was easier to stomach than Lily's. This was just one more reason for Sophie to hate her mother. On the face of it, it had probably been a good thing: the two girls could not risk going into care.

Top and tailing on Sophie's blow-up mattress – her mother had sold her bed for a bottle of vodka from Jimmy up the road – the girls had discussed what going into care would be like. They both agreed that it was probably worse than what they were going through now. Plus, they wouldn't have each other. Sophie smiled as she pictured the pinkie swears that they used to make. *Make friends, make friends, never, never break friends. There is nothing I can't do as long as I have you.*

Lost in her reverie, Sophie had not heard Alistair enter the room. 'So that is the house in which my son will be living, I presume.'

Ice trickled through Sophie's veins, freezing her in place.

'Not the grandeur we Cavendish men are used to,' he added.

'Not everyone is as conceited as you, Alistair. Some people realise there is more to life than money.' Her voice came across cold and flippant, but inside she was quaking with fear. This man was dangerous and should be avoided at all costs. She had thwarted his attempts to break her. But the things she had recently discovered about him put his psychological games in a whole new light. Just his presence triggered her survival instinct and like all prey, she was overwhelmed by the desire to run. He chuckled at her words and left the room.

She began to relax and she was about to return to her computer when Greg charged in. The door slammed against the walls and the windows in her office quivered. Unlike Alistair, Greg could not hide who he truly was. And what he truly was at that moment was furious. Anger pulsed from him so fiercely that she couldn't help but shrink away.

'What the fuck have you done, Sophie?'

12

'But it's our wedding anniversary,' whined Flora, pouting.

'I know.' Sam smiled at her through the mirror as he adjusted his tie. 'Do we have to have this same discussion every time something important falls on a Friday?'

'I just don't see why we have to go every Friday. We didn't sign a contract.'

Sam chuckled. 'Obviously you weren't listening the first hundred times I told you this, but tradition is important in my family. We have never missed a Friday Night Dinner.'

'Never? What if you were really sick and unable to get out of bed?'

'Nope, not even then.' He grinned at her look of disbelief.

'But Sophie and Greg aren't going.'

'Yes, well, that's Greg's affair.' He frowned his disapproval. 'I made a promise to my mother as you well know and I'm a man of my word.' Tie perfect, he turned away from the mirror to look at her. 'Look, we are booked in your favourite restaurant of all-time tomorrow. You know, the one that plays the cheesy seventies music and sings everyone happy birthday every five minutes. I've also got you a really special present.'

'Is it a get-out-of-Friday-Night-Dinner pass?'

He turned and grabbed her, wrapping her in his arms so hard she could barely breathe. He began to tickle her sides and she squealed trying to escape. 'Dearest Flora. You knew when you married me that you were agreeing to attend Friday Night Dinners for the rest of your life. Now stop moaning and get dressed.' He released her and got up, smoothing down his rumpled shirt and re-straightening his tie. 'If you make it snappy, I might have time to give you your anniversary gift. It will be waiting downstairs for you with me.' Swinging his jacket on as he went, he left in a cloud of delectable aftershave.

Flora dressed quickly, taking one last look in the mirror to check that her outfit was 'Cecelia-proof'. The Cavendish family lived in a Downton Abbey era where clothing was a uniform that denoted your status. The one time that Flora had worn the same dress twice, Cecelia had spent the whole night making references to people that didn't dress properly and how much she detested people that couldn't put effort into their appearance. Flora had left embarrassed and chastised, especially when Cecelia bade them goodnight and offered to send some dresses to Flora's house.

It had taken a few days for Sophie to help her overcome her mortification. Since then, Flora made sure she always wore something different, but took satisfaction in getting her dresses from charity shops. The silent rebellion made her feel better. Tonight's dress was a beautiful red dress with tiny spaghetti straps. A mere £2.50 at the local Oxfam, Flora had paid £5 as it was so beautiful. She laughed as she recalled Sophie's expression of disgust at the smell as they walked into the Oxfam. She refused on principal to buy anything. Sophie viewed it as a step back: they had been in a situation where Oxfam was all they could afford, and she did not like to be reminded of that.

As they drove to Cavendish Manor, a mere ten minutes from

the house, Flora revelled in her husband's kindness. He had taken the only picture she had of her parents and had had it blown up and put on a giant canvas.

Flora only had one photograph of her parents. All the rest of her family photographs had been destroyed by her aunt. Flora had come home from school to find her aunt in the back garden, stood in front of a bonfire, cackling like a witch. An assortment of items lay at her feet and she was chucking them into the flames one by one. Photographs, picture frames, Flora's mother's clothes – anything personal to her parents was being burned. The pile included the things that Flora had squirrelled away in the attic and in her room during the first few days of her aunt's 'renovation' when she moved in. They were all being tossed into the fire like garbage. Realising what was happening, Flora had raced to her bedroom and just managed to hide one photograph of her parents in her underwear before her aunt had burst in the room and purged it of the last of the items that Flora cherished. Although badly creased, the precious photograph had pride of place on her bedside table at Sam's house. The picture was a close-up of her mother and father and Flora as a baby. Her father, Daniel, tanned and smiling broadly had his arms wrapped tightly around her mother. Her mother was beaming down at the baby in her arms.

Seeing it in canvas form was incredible. The things they could do with technology these days. The photo on her bedside table was worn, creased and the colours faded. But with this canvas, she could make out more detail than she ever had before. She could see the different shades of blonde in her mother's hair, the 'R' on the necklace she always wore. Her father's moustache looked thicker and she could see the crow's feet framing his twinkling blue eyes, and his hair the exact same shade of hazelnut brown as her own. Flora saw that her eyes were the same distinct amber colour as her mother's. She had always thought they had similar eyes but now it was possible to see that she had her mother's exact eye colour.

It had taken her a while to compose herself. Sam had looked aghast when she had begun to ugly cry, but she assured him they were happy tears.

She gripped his hand as he drove, never wanting to let go. Her love for him now was overwhelming. Like a tangible thing inside of her that made her want to cry and laugh at the same time. She wanted to tell Sam how she felt but how did you explain the indescribable. The loss of her parents had tainted her whole life. There was a hole in her heart where they should have been. Not a day went by when she did not wonder what they would think of her or what they would be doing right now had they still been alive. Flora had studied that same photograph hungrily since the day they died. She had wanted to stare at the canvas all night, relishing this magnified view of her parents. It made them feel more real to her, no longer just the fading images in her mind like a worn-out film reel. Here they were, sharp and in focus. Real people who had wrinkles and eyes just like hers. How had she not thought to do this herself?

Sam had torn her away from them with kisses and promises that she could spend the whole weekend staring at it if she wished. He would hang it wherever she wanted in the house. It was so large it would cover one of the walls.

The car came to a stop and before she could even reach for the handle the door was opened by Sam. He took her hand, helping her out of the car, pressing a kiss to the back of her hand with lustful eyes full of promise. She blushed and followed him into the house. Reginald appeared from nowhere like the resident ghost, making her jump as he requested their coats. Flora felt a momentary pang of sympathy for Reginald as Sam strode away without even glancing in his direction, not even a thank you. But that feeling soon subsided as she caught the look of disdain that he gave her coat as she handed it to him. He took the grey jacket and held it far away from his body as if it had fleas, his nose turned up as if she had just handed him a dirty rag.

Following Sam into the greeting room, she found him deep in conversation with his mother. As usual, Cecelia had her hand resting on Sam's arm as they sat on the chaise longue together. At first, Flora had found it sweet that whenever Cecelia was near Sam she was always touching him, needing to be close to him. But then she began to catch the territorial looks she would fling at Flora. She may as well have put up a sign saying, 'this man belongs to me'. This used to bother Flora and she would find a way of touching Sam as well. They would be locked in a silent battle of possession, finding excuses to touch Sam and divert his attention to them. It became like a game of table tennis and Sam was the ball.

Cecelia had once turned an angry shade of purple when Flora, in an unusual display of bravery fuelled by the three glasses of sherry she had consumed and egged on by Sophie, had taken Sam's face in her hands and kissed him passionately. From the corner of her eye she saw Cecelia choking on her sherry and excusing herself from the room. Flora had revelled in the glory for a whole thirty seconds, until Cecelia had called them into the dining room and announced that they were having seafood for every course that night. She gave Flora a huge smile, well aware that Flora hated seafood. Over dinner, Cecelia announced to Sam that she had booked the two of them a weekend retreat to a winery for some mother/son bonding time, looking pointedly at Flora to make sure she got the message that she was not invited.

Tonight, Flora realised that the dinner table and chairs had been replaced. Flora marvelled at Cecelia's display of frivolity: everything was dispensable in her world. She couldn't imagine how much the last wrought-iron table had cost, let alone this new one that was made of thick glass that glistened in the light.

She felt apprehensive, as always, when she sat down, like she was eating with the queen and was bound to make a fool of herself. It never got any easier being around Sam's family. She would always be the weed in the flower bed of elegant roses.

Cecelia's voice penetrated her thoughts. 'There's a new bistro opening tomorrow, a close friend's son. Trained in Paris, don't you know? I've got us the best table in the house. Can you be there for 7pm?' said Cecelia.

Flora held her breath. Sam coughed and looked down at his plate. *Don't you dare, Samuel Cavendish*, she thought.

'Sorry, Mother. We already have plans tomorrow night.'

'What plans? Just rearrange them. I've already said we will go. This is much more important.'

'I can't, Mother. It's our anniversary.'

'What anniversary?'

'Our wedding anniversary.'

'Ah. Well, what better way to celebrate than at a restaurant with a Michelin star chef? I bet it is much better than what you were going to do. Anyway, it's not like it's a special anniversary.'

Flora was not surprised that Cecelia was being so dismissive. She had tried everything in her power to stop the wedding from going ahead. Along with her joyful memories of the day, there would always be the memory of Cecelia's last-ditch attempt to stop the marriage.

Flora had been sharing a bittersweet moment with Sophie, wishing with all her heart that her mother and father were there. Staring into the mirror intently, like if she stared hard enough she could conjure their image, standing and trying to see their faces either side of her in the mirror.

'They'll be watching, Flo. Don't doubt that,' said Sophie assuredly.

Relinquishing her melancholia, Flora had focused on the fizz of excitement when she thought about becoming Sam's wife. Belonging to someone finally. Starting a family of her own. She twirled in her dress, a huge smile on her face. Sophie perched on the bed, her happiness seemed to match Flora's own.

It had been the perfect moment. Unadulterated, pure happiness. One of those moments that happen so rarely. Where the heart fills up, like it might burst from your chest and your smile is so wide it hurts your face. Her happiness was intense and overwhelming. A feeling that would lodge in her mind forever. The joy of the moment never fading, no matter how much time passed. She had thought nothing could spoil it. That was until Cecelia had burst through the door.

She did not stop to acknowledge Flora's wedding dress, she only gave Sophie a cursory glance as she strode into the room, a woman on a mission. She sat down on the chaise longue at the end of the bed, regal in a royal-blue dress, her pearl-white hair coiffed to within an inch of its life. Not even a hurricane would dislodge a strand.

'Can we help you?' asked Sophie, not one to be intimidated by uncomfortable silences.

'I've come to stop this mockery of a wedding. I can't see another son of mine trapped into marriage by some two-bit harlot.'

Flora's mouth fell open in shock. Cecelia's words knocked the breath from her body.

Sophie leapt to her feet, shoulders pulled back, a look of outrage and shock on her face. 'Excuse me?'

'You heard me. I've had enough. We all know what you girls are really after. I will not play these games anymore. Not when it comes to Sam.'

Flora reached out to the chest of drawers for support. She knew that Cecelia did not approve of her, but she had thought she could see that Sam was happy, so she was grudgingly putting up with Sophie and Flora, content to play her games. But to come here, on her wedding day, calling her a money-grabbing harlot... Flora blinked back the tears and bit down on her tongue to control herself.

Sophie replied, 'I think you need to watch what you say, Cecelia. If I hear you say one more bad word about Flora, I will not be held responsible for my actions.' Her voice was ice cold.

'Oh, like I'm scared of you.' Cecelia laughed and threw her a look of utter disdain.

Sophie had moved towards Cecelia, standing over her, looking fierce. Even though anger was pulsating off her, it did nothing to ruin her beauty. Wrapped in a blush-pink bridesmaid dress, she was elegant and sophisticated with her blonde hair in a chignon. She also looked ten seconds away from punching Cecelia in the face. 'You should be. You have no idea what I'm capable of.' Sophie's voice was low and menacing.

'Oh shush, you pathetic child.' Cecelia stood up and walked around Sophie, moving next to Flora. 'Look, what's it going to take? We both know you just want the money. I was too slow to stop Greg from making the biggest mistake of his life, but I won't let that happen again.' Cecelia opened her clutch bag and pulled out her cheque book and a pen. She looked at Flora expectantly. 'Go on. Name your price.'

Flora shook her head. 'I... I love Sam. I don't want anything.'

'Oh, come now. Do you really think this relationship is going to last? What can *you* possibly offer him?' She sneered at Flora. 'An orphan with no money or standing. At least she–' she nodded at Sophie '–has a business head and can contribute something of value to the company. But you? You have no ambition, no talent and nothing to offer my son except embarrassment and eventually heartbreak. Now. Name. Your. Price.'

Flora shook her head. Cecelia scribbled on the cheque, ripped it out and thrust it into Flora's hand. She glanced down and saw the cheque was for five million pounds.

Sophie moved swiftly across the room and placed herself in front of Flora, blocking Cecelia's view of her. 'How dare you speak to Flora like that! Sam, rightly so, worships the ground Flora walks on. She is kind, loving and beautiful inside and out. You should be thanking your lucky stars that Sam has someone like her in his life. Do you really think that Flora would marry Sam if she didn't love him? Why on earth would either of us marry into this family, knowing it meant we had to spend time with you?' Sophie raised her hand and poked Cecelia in the shoulder to emphasise her point. Then she grabbed her mother-in-law's arm and marched her towards the door. 'Now get out of here, you old bat. Go back downstairs, take your seat and use those incredible acting skills of yours to make Sam think you are the happiest you have ever been. You will not spoil this day for Flora.' She pushed Cecelia again, so hard that the older woman stumbled out into the hallway.

Cecelia looked at them both, ashen-faced and shaking with rage. 'Well, I–'

'Get out!' shouted Sophie. 'Leave now and we will never speak of this again. I don't think your precious son would like to hear that you tried to pay off his bride-to-be.'

Cecelia didn't move.

'Flora. Where is your phone?' asked Sophie. Looking around the room, she spotted Flora's phone on the bed. She picked it up and began to tap on the screen. She started reading out the words she was typing, 'Hi honey, I've got your mum here. Look what she just gave me if I promised not to marry you and leave.' Sophie turned, snatched the cheque out of Flora's hand and snapped a picture of it with the phone. She then took a picture of Cecelia, holding the cheque up so they were both in the picture.

'He won't believe you.' The quiver in her voice betrayed her doubt.

'But, Cecelia, why else would you write Flora a cheque for five million pounds?'

Cecelia looked at Flora, the hatred emanating from her was almost tangible. 'You will regret this,' she spat at her and then finally she turned and left.

Flora would have sunk to the floor, but Sophie was there, holding her up and making soothing noises. 'Do not let that woman win, Flora. Nothing that makes us happy comes easy. You can't have the light without the darkness. If we don't have to struggle how can we appreciate happiness? You love Sam. Sam loves you. Cecelia is just an irritating spider. She looks scary but at the end of the day, she's just an insignificant pest and you can easily stamp on her.' Sophie released Flora and straightened her veil. Stroking her face, she looked Flora in the eyes. 'You look so beautiful.'

Flora smiled and swallowed back her tears.

'Please don't let that woman ruin this day for you,' begged Sophie.

'I won't.' Flora took a deep breath and tried to settle her emotions and return to the feeling she had before Cecelia came into the room.

Sophie took her hands. 'Flora, you're getting married.' Her smile lit up her face. She pulled Flora around in circles. 'Flora's getting married, Flora's getting married.'

Flora laughed as they jumped around the room. She felt like they were twelve years old again.

'That's better.' Sophie tucked an escaped hair back behind Flora's ear. She looked almost as happy as Flora felt.

'Thank you. For what you said to Cecelia.'

'Ah don't worry about it. Stupid bitch. Now, we aren't wasting any more time on her.'

'I love you, Soph.'

Sophie turned away and moved across the room to get Flora's wedding shoes, but not before Flora saw tears in her friend's eyes.

Sophie returned, shoes in hand. 'Love you too. Now let's get these on.'

Alistair's voice cut through Flora's memories. 'Cecelia darling, you remember what it is like to be young and in love. Leave them to do their own thing.'

Cecelia threw Alistair a furious look. It was nice to see her mad at someone else for a change. Then she turned to Sam, defeated. 'Fine. I'll just have to try and find two other people to go. It's very short notice, though.'

Flora glanced at Alistair, intending to give him a grateful smile but he was staring into space like he'd never even spoken. He often tuned out of the room, like he was bored and would rather be anywhere else. She found it uncomfortable to be around Alistair. He was too mercurial for her liking. His ability to turn on and off his charismatic personality like a computer was unnerving. At least Cecelia was transparent in her dislike of Flora. Alistair was so capricious that she did not know how he really felt about anything, especially her. He would either be the life and soul of dinner or he'd be lost in a reverie so deep he often forgot to eat.

'Sorry, Mother. We'll go another time if you like, just the four of us.'

'Or maybe just you and I could go for lunch?'

'Sure.'

Cecelia beamed and stole a sly look at Flora who let her have her small victory. She no longer worried about Cecelia meeting up with Sam alone. After this many years she had yet to do any damage to their relationship. She was sure that Cecelia would be bending his ear about them moving away, after her unsuccessful conversation with Flora she would most likely be plotting another way to stop them from moving.

'How are the plans for the move coming along?' asked Alistair, suddenly coming alive again.

Cecelia looked as though she wanted to throw her plate in his face. 'Darling, they aren't even a hundred per cent sure they are moving yet. They may change their minds.'

'Mother.' Sam reached for her hand and smiled at her. 'You know that we are moving.' He turned to his father and answered his question. 'We're just waiting on the renovations and then we can move in. Flora's aunt left it in bad shape, so it needed a lot doing.'

'How are you dealing with your aunt's passing, Flora? It must be a really difficult time for you. The last member of your family gone.'

For some reason, Flora had a sense that Alistair's sympathy was insincere. Her knee-jerk reply was to say that she hoped her aunt rotted in hell, but she did not think it was an appropriate response. 'I'm a little sad, but we weren't close. I'm just so looking forward to living in my parents' home again. It's going to be amazing.'

Cecelia raised her eyebrows and tutted. 'Well, who knows what the future holds. Apart from dessert.' Cecelia clicked her fingers and like magic Reginald appeared out of thin air like a genie and began to clear the dinner plates.

Sam excused himself to use the bathroom and Flora was left with Alistair and Cecelia, neither of whom were looking at her. Alistair had his hands steepled together, his head resting on the fingertips, his face vacant and expressionless once more. Flora hated silence, it made her feel like the room was closing in on her. Words bubbled up inside her fighting to escape. She tried to fight the compulsion, but she wasn't strong enough: the empty silence of the room was excruciating. It felt like there were ants climbing up her legs and someone had told her not to move. It got too much, and the words broke through. Stupid, idiotic words.

'Cecelia, I could show you the new house if you would like?' *What? Why would you say that?* Desperation to break the silence had obviously scrambled her brain.

Cecelia's face broke out into a sinister smile, there was no warmth in her face. She leaned closer to Flora from her position at the top of the table. 'I think you'll find I will never be setting foot in that house. And neither will my son. If it's the last thing I do.'

Her tone was so menacing that Flora felt a frisson of fear descend her spine. Flora looked at Alistair, hoping he had heard what Cecelia had said and would interfere. He was looking at them both with a broad smile on his face. Like the whole situation amused him. He stood up and left the table, quietly chuckling to himself as he went. Flora did not dare to look at Cecelia, she wished with all her heart that Sophie would appear out of nowhere like Reginald. But Sophie was not there, and Flora could feel Cecelia's gaze burning into her, raising the hairs on her neck. The only sound was the ticking of the grandfather clock in the hallway which became louder with each second, filling up the silence as she waited for her husband to come back and rescue her from her evil mother-in-law.

13

It made Sophie's skin itch to know that Flora was at a Friday Night Dinner without her. Sam took his obligation to attend these dinners as seriously as a blood oath. Being the apple of his mother's eye had caused him to place a disproportionate amount of importance on the traditions she tried to create. Not being his mother's favourite, Greg found it perfectly acceptable to shun the dinner when he was offered something better. Tonight, he was at a football game, best seats in the house apparently.

Sophie had gone to order a pizza and found all her cards had been taken from her purse, replaced by a scribbled note from Greg that read, 'ha ha'. The irony that Flora had had her cards taken and replaced by someone and now she had had hers confiscated by her husband was not lost on her.

Sitting on the sofa, she flicked through the latest issue of *Vogue*. Her subscription was just another way of confirming that she had 'made it', she was not really interested in the pretentious twaddle they peddled. She couldn't focus, distracted by a gut feeling that Flora needed her. Cecelia was a vicious viper and Sam had his head in the clouds: he wouldn't be able to help Flora. He wouldn't stop Flora from taking Cecelia's words personally. Flora's sensitivity was endearing but it made her an easy target for Cecelia.

But it was Alistair Sophie was more worried about. She tried to take heart in the fact he had never shown much interest in Flora, at least not in the way he had begun to take interest in her.

The door burst open. She started. The magazine slipped from her fingers as Greg all but fell into the room, the stench of alcohol joining him. He held himself up using the back of the sofa. Sophie stood up, warily moving away, trying to judge what type of drunk he was this time.

Before Flora had announced they were moving, she had been keeping everything under control. But things were starting to get out of hand, including Greg.

'Hello, bitch,' he said. A wolfish smile playing on his face. Ah, he was a nasty drunk tonight. A throb of fear pulsed through her. It was so hard to deal with him when he was in this mood. She may be able to outsmart him but she would never be physically stronger than him. He was blocking the exit. This was probably the first and last time that she would wish that they had gone to Friday Night Dinner.

Greg charged at her. 'I should never have married you!' he roared.

Finally, something we agree on, she thought as she danced out of his way. He stumbled to the floor, clutching the air where she had just been. She tried to edge towards the door, avoiding his flying fists.

'Stop ruining my life,' he shouted at her from the floor, watching her as she escaped into the hallway, running to the safety of her bathroom. She had already stored blankets and pillows in there so she could sleep in the bath at a moment's notice, when she needed the locked door to keep her safe.

14

Flora shut the front door, wishing, not for the first time that week that she was anywhere hot and sunny. The weather had turned particularly vile that week. Which was why, at first, Flora was too preoccupied by the invasive October wind, nipping at her fingers, stealing down the back of her coat and whipping at her jeans to realise that when she tossed her keys in the bowl that stood on the sideboard next to the front door, they actually crashed to the floor.

Blowing hot air into her hands and stamping to bring back the feeling in her feet, she finally registered the clinking sound. She turned and saw her keys on the floor.

The sideboard was gone.

Wait. No, it wasn't. It was on the other side of the front door.

The hairs on the back of her neck prickled. She looked around and could sense that this was not the only thing out of place. The world looked off kilter. She walked gingerly into the living room. The armchair had been moved. It was no longer on the right of the sofa but to the left of it. Even the pictures had changed places. There had been three garish paintings that Cecelia had chosen especially for them. The ugly fat cupid was now in the middle of the three paintings when he used to be on the left. The picture of Sam and Flora on their wedding day was no longer on the mantelpiece but on the coffee table.

She turned to leave the room, intending to look around the rest of the house when the front door opened, and, along with a gust of blisteringly cold air, in came Sam. Flora almost ran to him in relief. 'I'm so glad you're home! The weirdest thing has happened.' Not giving him chance to reply, Flora tugged him by his coat sleeve and dragged him into the living room. 'Look!'

Sam looked around the room and then looked at her, his brow furrowed. 'Look at what?'

Flora laughed in disbelief. 'You're not serious?'

Sam looked around the room once more, more slowly this time. He turned to her again. 'Erm... you've redecorated?'

Flora grabbed his arm and walked him over to the armchair. 'This has been moved. It used to be over there.'

Sam looked down at the armchair, his face screwed up as if trying to remember what the room had looked like the last time he had been in it. 'It was?'

Flora was exasperated. 'For god's sake, Sam! Do you walk around this house with your eyes closed? Look at the paintings. You must remember the paintings.'

Sam looked up, perplexed. 'What about the paintings?' he asked in a small voice.

'Seriously? All of our things have been moved around and you are honestly telling me you can't tell. There's also a weird smell.' She sniffed the air, unable to work out what it was.

Sam looked around again. 'Are you sure, Flo? It looks exactly the same to me. Maybe you should go and have a lie down. We both know you haven't been sleeping well since that mix-up with your cards.'

She bristled. It was not a mix-up: someone had taken her cards she wanted to say. Although, the more time passed the less certain she felt. But this was different. He had to realise that everything had been moved. She couldn't be the only one that noticed. Grabbing his arm again, she dragged him back into the hallway. She pointed defiantly at the sideboard. The sight of it in the wrong place jarred her. Sam tried to hide his confusion, but she knew him too well.

'You're kidding.' She looked at him, shaking her head. 'Sam, every day for however long, you have come in from work and put your keys in the dish on that sideboard. Every morning you pick them up from the dish on your way out the door. Are you seriously telling me that you don't remember where that sideboard has stood for the last however many years?'

'Oh yeah. It was on that side, wasn't it? What's it doing over there?'

'Finally, it dawns on him.' Flora stormed off to the living room. She automatically walked to where the armchair used to be and then realised it was no longer there. She let out a grunt of frustration and flung herself down onto the sofa.

Sam followed her into the room. 'Flora, please calm down. I'm sure there is a reasonable explanation.'

'Are you not sick of saying that to me yet. I'm sure as hell sick of hearing it. There *is* no explanation for my cards vanishing and reappearing. And now all our stuff has been moved around the house!'

Sam moved towards and her and pulled her into his arms. She nuzzled into him despite her irritation with him. Damn him and his irresistible touch. As it did every time, her head sank into the crook between his neck and head, and as she did every time she thought, *I fit here.* All the stress flowed out of her as he gently caressed her hair, brushing kisses on the top of her head.

'I'm sorry,' she said. 'I overreacted. I guess I'm just anxious after that thing with my cards.'

'It's okay, sweetheart. I understand. I'm sure there is an explanation. Maybe my mother had something to do with it.'

Flora jerked upright and turned to look at him. 'You mean, you think she is trying to scare me? By taking my cards and now moving around our stuff. Trying to make me think I'm crazy. That's what me and Sophie were wondering as well.' Her heart swelled at the thought that Sam had finally begun to see through his mother.

His face clouded and he stood up, pushing her off him. 'Actually, that wasn't what I meant. I just thought that she might have organised the cleaners to come in and do a deep clean of the house. She knows that we both work and she may have been trying to do something nice for us. But it's nice to know where your head is at.' Before he left the room, he stopped and looked at her, his eyes so sad it made her heart ache. 'Are you ever going to stop thinking of my mother as the enemy? Have you ever thought that this whole time it has been you projecting your own insecurities on her and thinking she doesn't like you? All I can see is her treating you as part of the family and trying to show you in her own way that she cares.' He left the room shaking his head sadly.

Flora felt awful. It wasn't Sam's fault really. His mother was too clever with how she masked her insults around Sam. If only he knew everything his mother had put her through over the years. She told herself that Cecelia was just one of the crosses she had to bear. You could not choose your family; her aunt was proof of that. If Cecelia wanted to play stupid mind games, then let her. She was made of stronger stuff than this. Her parents' death was the worst thing she had ever suffered. Cecelia's stupid tricks were nothing compared to that.

She walked over to the armchair and heaved it back, intending to move it to its rightful place. It had only budged a centimetre when a rotting smell hit her nose and she caught sight of some black fur. Flora screamed and fell back onto the floor.

Sam's feet thudded on the stairs and he skidded into the room. His shirt was undone and he was only in his boxers. 'What's wrong?'

Flora couldn't speak. She dragged herself back until she hit the skirting board, trying to put as much distance between herself and the armchair as possible. With a shaky hand, she pointed.

Sam moved around the armchair and reeled back when the smell hit him. 'Oh god. What *is* that?' He pushed the armchair further out of the way, revealing a large black rat, stiff as a board and obviously dead.

Flora ran from the room. She waited in the relative safety of their bedroom.

Eventually, Sam came upstairs to find her. 'I got rid of it.'

'What's your reasonable explanation for that?' she asked, sarcasm lacing her words.

He sat on the bed next to her, rubbing his face with his hand. 'Well, the poor thing obviously got trapped in the house and died. Maybe from natural causes.'

Flora looked at him, incredulous. 'A rat just happens to die in our house on the same day as all our furniture got moved around?'

'Maybe the furniture moving dislodged it from where it had died. Not everything is a conspiracy against you, Flora. I know you are sensitive right now. But seriously.' He must have seen the hurt in her expression, because he leaned over to her and stroked her face, his voice gentler. 'Look, the most obvious explanation is normally the right one. It obviously was in the house already and died here. We just happened to find it today. Come on, why don't you get some sleep. You look shattered.'

Flora's mind was racing. There was no way she would sleep

now. Was Sam right? Or was the campaign to scare her stepping up a gear? Was it Cecelia? Questions spun in an endless vortex in her mind. Sam mistook her silence as an agreement and he eased her into the bed, wrapping his arms around her, holding her tightly. 'Everything is going to be fine, sweetie. Don't worry.' She fell asleep to the feel of his fingers running through her hair.

15

In her memory, her parents' house used to stand proud and tall. It had stood out for all the right reasons, the tallest and biggest house on the street. It was also the first house that greeted you when turning onto Trelawney Close. In her parents' day, most of the street parties and celebrations were held in their spacious front garden with all the neighbours invited. It used to be the envy of everyone on the street but now it screamed of neglect, like the embarrassing relative no one wants to admit to knowing. The front door was a faded green, flecks of paint peeling off, a panel of glass replaced with a square of cardboard. The lawn that was once bordered by bursts of colour was now an unattractive jungle of weeds and bracken. The house appeared smaller to Flora, like it had shrunk itself in embarrassment.

The inside of the house had not fared much better under her aunt's reign. Pauline's disregard for her sister was reflected in the way she had treated the house. It was stripped bare and scratches, stains and holes littered the walls.

The competing smells of tobacco and alcohol assailed Flora's nostrils. But she closed her mind to that and focused on what she knew this house could be. This way she could refill the house with the images of how it had been when she was younger and her parents were alive. She made her way through the hallway, her mind replacing the holes in the walls with pictures that her mother had drawn and her father insisted had to be displayed.

The echoes of her parents' laughter followed her through the house as she walked into the living room that had once housed an ostentatious yellow sofa that clashed with the deep blue walls. She could picture her parents sitting there, arms around each other, beaming at her. Flora swallowed the lump in her throat and took some steadying breaths.

Sophie's arms came around her from behind. She always had a sixth sense when it came to Flora's feelings. 'Maybe this isn't the right thing to do, Flo. Isn't it going to be too painful to live here surrounded by memories and thoughts of what could have been?'

It had been a difficult decision that had kept her awake for many nights. But it was the fury towards her aunt – a fury matched only by that she had for the hit-and-run driver who had left her parents on the side of the road to die – that had finally convinced Flora she was going to live in that house. Flora had always considered herself a glass half-full kind of person. Whenever she discussed her past, she would finish by stating that everything she had been through had led her to the best things in her life. That she wouldn't have met Sophie or Sam if she had not been forced to stand on her own two feet. But she was struggling to retain that positive attitude when she considered her aunt's betrayal. Too much of her future had been stolen from her.

To counteract this, she had an unshakeable need to restore the house to the happy, family home it used to be, in honour of her parents. She had been gloriously content here before their car accident. It was only right that she take back some of what had been stolen from her.

Another compelling reason was that she could finally escape from Cecelia. Surprisingly, Sam had taken little convincing. He may not see how his mother treated Flora, but he was by no means under the thumb. Sam had a sensitivity she had always been told did not exist in men. Whilst he was not expressive with his feelings, the fact he did not mind uprooting his life to move into this house demonstrated a depth of their connection. It showed her that he genuinely understood the gaping hole left by her parents' death.

Flora had never had closure; it didn't help that the person who killed her parents was never caught. Sam had recognised that she felt that living in this house would help restore her connection to her family. So, when she had asked him what he wanted to do, he'd merely wrapped her in his arms and asked where he needed to sign. She had never loved him more than in that moment.

Flora turned into Sophie's hug and then stood back so she could look her friend in the eye. 'I've thought about it, Soph, non-stop. But I feel closer to them here. I think they would want me to be here. To remember them and restore this house and make it a home again.'

Sophie looked away quickly but not before Flora saw the tears in her eyes. Sophie had always seemed to share Flora's loss keenly. All those nights she had cried on Sophie's shoulder when the grief overcame her, Sophie would hold her and cry with her. Although Sophie's mother hadn't died Flora knew that Sophie grieved for the mother she should have had. The one who wouldn't try to convince her to steal bottles of wine from the shops. Sophie didn't even know who her dad was. At least Flora had precious memories of being loved by her parents. In some ways, Sophie had it worse out of the two of them.

'But we've always been by each other's side. This is all the way across town. What if you need help and I'm not able to get here in time?'

Flora grinned. Sophie was so overprotective. 'Oh, Soph, don't be so dramatic. Why would I need help?' She grabbed her hands and pulled a funny face. 'Is the bogey man going to get me?'

Sophie's face paled. Flora pulled her into a hug, concerned. 'Sophieeee, I'm all grown up now. A married lady, even! I'm not that little fourteen-year-old girl with the psycho-aunt anymore. I'll be fine and so will you. This is a good thing.'

Sophie pushed her away gently, not hiding her tears anymore. 'But what about me? You're leaving me alone with the Dragon Lady.'

The sick feeling in her stomach flared at these words. It was their friendship that made Cecelia bearable. Without Flora next door, they would no longer be sharing the burden of being an inappropriate wife as evenly. Sophie would get the full force of Cecelia's resentment. But the pull of this house where her parents had lived and breathed was overpowering. Plus, Flora reminded herself, Sophie was the only one who could stand up to Cecelia.

'I'm sorry, Soph. I've got to do this. It is time to move forward. Me and Sam are ready to start a family and I want to do that here. Somewhere I know that Cecelia can't breeze through the door whenever she wants. Please understand.'

Sophie's shoulders slumped with what appeared to be resignation. 'I do. I do understand. Ignore me. I'm just going to miss you, that's all.' She pulled Flora into another hug. 'Come on then, give me the rest of the tour.'

16

Sitting on rusty garden furniture in the back garden, Sophie had to admit that she could see why Flora wanted to live here. Without Pauline's ominous presence the house seemed to have reverted to what it once was before a dark and evil soul inhabited it.

Flora had practically floated around the house talking ten to the dozen about all the changes to be made and once she had breathed life back into the place it was evident that it would be a proper home.

Sophie had never had a proper home. The closest she had come was the one-bedroom studio flat she had shared in university with Flora. They were both so excited to have their own place away from Pauline and Sophie's mother, Lily. It prevented them from noticing the mould on the walls that triggered Flora's allergies most nights. It stopped them from moaning when they had no money for the heating and had to wear most of their clothes to stop their teeth from chattering. It was not a proper home in the traditional sense, but it was the best she ever had.

There wasn't anything she wouldn't give to have the vision

that Flora was painting for her. Flora and Sam living in this house, raising their children together. Flora pushing her little girl on a swing set whilst Sam kicked a ball around with their son.

Pain lanced through Sophie's chest as she remembered, once again, that she would never have that. Greg had seen to that. Just another sacrifice she had made. Flora did not know the half of it.

Flora believed that the future she had always wanted was within her grasp. But she did not know what Sophie knew. There were no 'happily ever afters' when you were married to a Cavendish. A flash of anger pulsed through her causing her hands to shake. She got up and went to the bathroom before Flora could notice. Did Flora walk around with her eyes closed? Did she not realise what type of people the Cavendishes were? Did Cecelia's never-ending assault not make her question what type of people she was tied to?

Did she really think that the powerful Cavendish family were going to let a member of their family make their own decisions on where they lived and what they did? She wanted to tell Flora everything she knew, explain the danger that they were both in; tell her that announcement had been the final straw that broke the donkey's back. For so long Sophie had been holding their world together to ensure Flora and Sam were happy. But it was out of her control now. The tide had turned, and all Sophie could do was find a way to make sure Flora was not swept away. She needed Flora to see that Sam was just as bad as the rest of them. But she couldn't bring herself to trample Flora's happiness. The whole situation made her so angry she could barely breathe. She clutched at the sink, trying to regain control. Why could Flora not wake up and realise what was going on? Her naïveté was going to make Sophie the bad guy, the one who stole her future; when in fact Sophie was the one trying to ensure she had a future.

Taking some deep breaths, Sophie looked at herself in the bathroom mirror. Anger had reddened her face and she stared into her ice-blue eyes and watched until her colour faded back to its normal pale shade. Returning to the garden, she felt the chilly wind wrapping around her. The sun was out but it was no protection against the arctic breeze whipping at her, trying to penetrate her clothes, to steal her body heat. Her coffee cup was by her chair, but it barely had any residual heat left to protect her hands from the biting cold. She clutched it to her anyway.

'How did it go with Linda?' Sophie asked.

The whole situation fascinated Sophie. In her world, she had to make twenty ruthless decisions before breakfast. She had lost count of the number of people she had told that they would not receive an investment, knowing that this would likely mean that they would lose not only their livelihood but also their homes. Yes, it was sad, but she had not worked her way up from nothing to lose it all by giving it away. Sophie could not see why Flora did not take the Cavendishes's money and use it to her advantage. It was the only benefit of actually being a Cavendish. With the sort of money that they had, Flora could open a chain of centres and there would be no need to be wracked with guilt the way she was.

Flora blushed scarlet red and could not meet Sophie's eyes. 'I took the coward's way out and called her on her mobile. She didn't answer so I left a voicemail.'

Inside Sophie was laughing. *Oh, Flora.* This was her all over. She could not bear to let people down or hurt their feelings. But her thoughts sobered when it suddenly occurred to her that Flora did not mind letting her down or hurting her feelings.

'She's tried calling me back, but I haven't answered. Soph, I'm such a coward.' Flora covered her face with her hands.

Taking pity on her, Sophie asked, 'Do you want me to talk to her? I can lie and say I'm your business partner?'

'Would you? That would be amazing. You are so much better at things like this than me.' Flora beamed at Sophie. It was the type of smile that reminded Sophie that the sacrifices she had made and the danger she was about to face were worth it.

Getting Linda's number from Flora's phone, Sophie called and organised to meet with her later that afternoon. She didn't tell Flora that Linda's voice was eager and that she obviously believed it was good news. They spent the rest of the time before Sophie had to leave discussing Flora's cards going missing. It seemed such a trivial thing, but the more they talked about it the more freaked out Flora was becoming. It was a relief to see the rose-tinted glasses with which her friend viewed the Cavendish family slipping away. But as Sophie drove up the motorway on her way to meet Linda to have the conversation Flora was unable to have, she pounded the accelerator and brake, venting her anger that the Cavendish family were responsible for causing Flora pain. She pictured the fear and confusion on her face when she found her purse returned to normal. How dare they do this to her? The speedometer was creeping towards 100 miles per hour and she was driving almost as fast as the thoughts racing in her mind.

17

The October half-term was over. Next week, the children Flora supported would be reduced to coming to see her during weekends or evenings as they had to go back to school. For many of her children, this meant going back to a place that did not understand them, where they were belittled and teased relentlessly. Many of the teachers had no patience or empathy and would discipline them before attempting to actually comprehend their autism. It also meant that Flora would have a wonderful reduction in her workload. Only the most severely autistic children would continue to come during the day as they were usually home-schooled or just flat-out refused to go to school. Meaning Flora would have more free time to spend sorting the renovations on the new house. The sooner they could move in the better.

The impending new term was making the classes today particularly challenging. Six-year-old Jeremy, a scrawny boy with curly black hair had become overwhelmed by the girl he was sat next to. Megan, who had a cold, kept sniffing and Jeremy, unable to cope with the repetitive sound, had tipped a pot of red paint over Megan's head and screamed at her to shut up. His meltdown was infectious and disturbed the other children in the class, and it had taken Flora a while to calm everyone down. Eventually she had called Jeremy's parents. She had just cleaned up the last of the red paint from the floor, when Charlotte came over to her.

Charlotte was a brown-haired angel sent from heaven. The same thought went through Flora's mind each time she laid eyes on her. Charlotte had a friendly face, lovely green eyes that – on the rare occasion she looked at you – sparkled with intelligence. Before Charlotte had come to work for Flora, she used to hate the back office at the centre and it hated her. Things would move of their own accord, just to spite her. And no matter how neatly she tidied the room, as soon as her back was turned, paperwork would appear from nowhere. It didn't help that she was dyslexic which put her at a disadvantage when it came to anything related to literacy.

When Charlotte, who used to be a student at the centre, approached her a year ago looking for work, Flora had hired her on the spot. Until then she had been reluctant to employ anyone because she didn't feel that there was someone out there who would match her passion for what they did at the centre. But she'd known Charlotte since she was eleven years old, had seen her grow from an angry and uncommunicative child into a polite, intelligent young lady. Her angry meltdowns that had been driving her family apart were a distant memory. She could still be a little too blunt at times but she had a penchant for numbers that Flora would never have.

She was now as much the business's lifeblood as Flora was. She kept control of the finances and the day-to-day administration and also helped with the children on occasion. After all, she could relate to how they were feeling. Charlotte also had a superpower: she made the most incredible cup of tea.

'Thanks, Charlotte!' Flora beamed as Charlotte, studiously

staring at the cup in front of her, focused on making sure not a drop was spilled. It was not until Charlotte's first day that Flora realised she had been making tea wrong her whole life. No matter what she tried, she was unable to replicate the magic formula that Charlotte must use to make normal Tetley tea taste like liquid heaven. She would just have to ensure that Charlotte was always in her life. Taking a sip, Flora made appreciative noises as it slid down, warming her insides and brightening her mood.

'I keep telling you, Char, you should be running your own café. You are so talented.' Charlotte's cheeks reddened and she looked down, examining the floor. After the class ended, they moved into the office together. Charlotte took the seat next to Flora and began flicking from screen to screen on the computer. It was always strange watching her symbiotic relationship with the computer considering every time Flora tried to use it, she was treated to a cacophony of error beeps and warnings.

'Flora, there is a woman staring at us across the road. I think she has been there all day.' Charlotte said this in a level tone, as if she had just told Flora the sun was yellow.

Flora went over to the window. It was an unsettled day, the sun was sharing the sky with dark clouds casting an array of dark and light patches across the street. Linda was standing directly opposite the centre, staring in through the windows. The busy road meant that Flora was only seeing Linda in snatches between cars. But Sophie had talked to her. Questions flooded her mind. *Why is she here? Why wouldn't she come inside? How long has she been there?*

'Is she homeless?' Charlotte moved next to her. It was obvious why Charlotte would think that. Linda looked more unkempt than the last time Flora had seen her. Her short black hair was pointing in various directions, and even from this distance her clothes looked shabby and dirty. Flora could see people arcing around her, some walked into the road, so strong was their desire to avoid getting too close to the dishevelled woman.

'No, I don't think she is. How long did you say she's been there?'

'I can't be sure exactly. I saw her this morning, I thought she was waiting for a bus or taxi. Then I saw she was still there a while ago and meant to say something to you as she was staring in at the window. It wasn't till I saw her again just now that I remembered to tell you.'

The intensity of Linda's unwavering stare unsettled Flora. Her instinct was to run and hide, pretend she had never seen her. But she knew she had to deal with this. Obviously, Sophie's chat with Linda had not had the desired effect. She turned to Charlotte. 'You stay here. I'm going to talk to her.'

Flora put on her coat and taking a deep breath opened the door. She was about to cross the road when she realised Linda was no longer there. There was no sign of her anywhere. It was a good job Charlotte had seen her or Flora would have thought she was going insane.

18

The man quailed in his chair. Sophie suppressed a groan. Duncan Lockwood was her client and he was making her look bad. She knew his business was solid and was going to be extremely profitable. Whilst she had benefitted from his lack of confidence when she negotiated a sizeable equity stake, she was embarrassed at the beads of sweat running from his bald head down his face. To most people, sitting in front of a board of directors was terrifying, but Duncan looked like he was sitting opposite his executioner.

Alistair may as well have been a vulture circling the poor man, never one to pass up a chance to make Sophie appear incompetent. Cecelia would be devastated that she had missed it.

'You have still not explained why exactly you have not delivered on the forecasts that you made, Mr Lockwood. As you can understand, I am a busy man. I do not have time for excuses.'

'Well... The thing is... What you have to understand...' Duncan trailed off under Alistair's glacial stare. Greg was lounging back in his chair looking at Duncan but not really seeing him. Unless it was his investments that they were discussing he was as inanimate as stone.

Duncan looked at Sophie with desperation in his eyes. Sophie sighed inwardly. She despised men without a backbone but not as much she despised being made to look a fool.

'Mr Lockwood, weren't you telling me just yesterday that Tesco was ready to place a big order. Over 60,000 units at a substantially higher price than we had forecasted. So, when that contract is signed, you'll have doubled your projections and also superseded our anticipated return on investment.'

Duncan took the life raft she had flung at him and regained his composure. Having one person in the room on his side seemed to remind him how to speak in full sentences. 'Yes, yes, exactly. You see, Mr Cavendish, it is just taking a little longer than I had planned but within a couple of weeks I will have repaid your investment and then some!'

Alistair threw Sophie a look that filled her with dread. He did not like to be undermined. The last time she had done this to him, he had buried her in so much paperwork she slept at the office for a week. Although this time she was sure he was more annoyed that she had spoiled his fun. He loved nothing more than to torment the clients they invested in, knowing he had the power to make or break their future. Sophie's interjection had deprived him of another victim whose soul he had not yet crushed.

'Very well, Mr Lockwood. We will meet again very soon. I expect much better financial reports next time.' Alistair strode from the room.

The instant he was gone, both she and Duncan began to breathe easier. 'You can leave now, Duncan. I will call you tomorrow.'

Duncan tossed her a quick smile and nearly ran from the room, tripping on his chair in his haste.

Greg sneered. 'Honestly, Soph, what were you thinking? He's an idiot.'

'That may be, but he is going to make us a lot of money. So, I would say it was a small price to pay.'

Greg shook his head and walked out the room. She wondered if he realised that his suit was becoming slightly too small for his growing stomach. His appetite for money was second only to his appetite for food these days, and he was no longer making the effort in the gym to keep his body toned the way he used to.

There was no doubt that Sophie had been attracted to Greg when she first met him. But it was more the smell of money and the clothes that screamed wealth that had caught her eye. Flora and Sophie had been at the bottom of the food chain for too long and Greg was their ticket out. She had met him at a networking conference she was attending in the hopes of securing a position. Under-utilised and underestimated in her role, she was always on the lookout for her big break. She just needed a sign from fate, which she got at the conference.

Greg's height made him stand out from the crowd. He parted the crowds like he was Moses walking through the Red Sea. He was impeccably dressed, with a voice permanently raised to ensure everyone was aware that he was there and visibly preened under the attention that was lavished on him.

Although intrigued, she thought nothing more of him before fate intervened, forcing her to recognise her future. She turned a corner, hurrying to a seminar she should have been at five minutes ago when she body slammed straight into him. She apologised profusely and offered to buy him a drink at the bar. It was there she discerned that one on one, Greg was more than just a rich boy. He had an ambition that matched her own.

'Can I ask why you aren't drinking?' asked Greg. 'The free bar is the only reason I let my father send me to these events.'

'Long story. The short version; my mother was a raging alcoholic and I have no desire to be anything like her.'

'Yikes. That's rough.'

'No, it's fine. It gave me the determination to make something of my life. I will be a successful businesswoman and run my own company and when I earn my first million, I will know that I did it all myself. Plus, I don't need alcohol to have a good time.' She shot him a sly wink.

He chuckled and moved closer. 'I respect that. I am trying to do the same thing. It's hard though, as my family have this successful empire already. I can't really branch out on my own as I'm expected to take over the reins once my father is ready to retire. My brother is useless in business so I'm the only one that can do it. But I'm just spending each day proving to my father that I can grow the business on my own. That I don't need his help.' He looked at her with a bemused expression, his cheeks reddened. 'I'm not sure where that came from. I'm not normally this open with someone I've just met. In fact. I'm not normally open at all.'

They looked at each other, sharing a smile. Sophie felt a connection with him. She could sense in Greg the same drive and determination that coursed through her veins. An idea was starting to formulate in her mind. 'So, you have a brother? What's he like?'

'Sam? Yeah, he's my younger brother but we are complete opposites. He works in the family business as well, but he isn't ruthless enough. We use him mainly to maintain relations with our clients. He is the one keeping everyone happy and smoothing out any interpersonal issues. Sam's problem is that he is as soft as they come. No drive or determination to earn money. He just cares about the people.'

Sophie knew someone exactly like that. Yes, this would work very well. Greg was perfect.

Theirs was a whirlwind romance. They spent as much time together as possible and most of the conversation was about making money. Shared ambition and drive were an aphrodisiac, and to her delight, she found that not only was he hungry to succeed in the business world, but he was just as hungry in the bedroom. Within a few weeks, Greg had offered her a job in the family business. It was not the high up position she knew she was capable of, but he assured her she would work her way up the ladder.

After meeting Sam, Sophie knew he would be perfect for Flora. She knew Flora as intimately as she knew herself therefore she felt qualified to make this decision. She just had to get Greg to agree.

'Please!'

'But we never socialise outside of family obligations and work commitments. It would be awkward.'

'No, it won't. He'll be with Flora. Then I can give you all my attention without having to worry about Flora.' She gave him a sultry look and saw his eyes dilate.

'Fine. I'll sort it. Now come here, woman.' And with that he swept her off her feet and laid her down on the floor, peeling off her clothes.

If Sophie needed a sign from above that her idea was the right thing then she was given it only a month or so later. Flora had been reluctant to like Sam.

'It's weird though. You're dating his brother.'

'Why is that weird? We aren't related, Flo.'

It was annoying Sophie that Flora was being so obstinate. It was obvious that Flora and Sam were meant to be together. They were both trusting, gentle and had the same optimistic outlook on life. In the beginning, Sophie had engineered meeting after meeting, desperate to make them see what she could. But it turned out she needn't have bothered. Fate was on her side once more. Flora's battered, unreliable Corsa broke down on her way to the centre and as 'luck' (also known as fate), would have it, Sam was driving past and saw her on the side of the road. He gave her a lift to the centre and the rest was history.

It was going perfectly. Flora and Sam were happy. Sophie and Greg were the power couple. When they weren't working together on securing lucrative equity deals, they were making passionate love in whichever room they happened to be in. She had everything she had ever wanted.

Until she fell pregnant.

It was the beginning of the end. Greg did not want children. Ever. They had only been together for a year and had not had any deep conversations about emotions. She didn't even know how she felt about it, let alone how he would react. Deciding that the place where he was happiest would be the best place to tell him, she knocked on the door to his office. His fingers whizzed across the keyboard and he merely glanced in her direction, not stopping to look at her properly and what she was holding.

'I'm pregnant.' She brandished the pregnancy test in shaking hands, holding her breath in anticipation.

'Oh shit.' He stood up abruptly, his face leached of all colour. 'But– But we were careful. You are on the pill, right?'

'Yes, but nothing is a hundred per cent safe,' answered Sophie.

Greg sat back down hard. His chair creaked in protest. 'Well, we will just have to take care of it.'

For a minute, she did not understand his meaning. She

opened her mouth to say as much, but he carried on talking. When it hit her, her legs weakened. She had not even considered an abortion. To be honest she hadn't thought about anything apart from telling him. This was never something she expected to happen to her. But hearing Greg say it so nonchalantly made her feel sick. Did he even realise that there was an actual human being growing inside her?

'I'm quite far along. I didn't recognise the signs until my clothes started getting tighter. I'm not sure if that's possible anymore. It might be too late.'

'Nothing is impossible when you've got money. Don't worry, sweetheart, I'll sort it for you.'

Sophie moved and sat in the chair opposite him. His colour had returned to his face and he flashed her a quick smile and stared at his iMac, typing away as if she wasn't there, dismissing her as if she was a lowly intern.

'But don't you think we should talk about it? Discuss our options?'

He looked at her, incredulous. 'What options? You're not keeping it?'

'But why not? I'm not saying I want to, but I'd like to consider it. This is a human life we are talking about.' Tears pricked her eyes and she rubbed them away.

'Sophie, it is a clump of cells. Nothing more. I do not want children. I thought you knew that. My work means more than anything to me and nothing is going to get in my way. I am going to make Cavendish & Sons the giant of venture capitalism and I can't do that with a baby.' He said the word 'baby' scathingly.

'And what about what I want?'

Greg leant back in his chair, he sighed heavily. 'I thought we were on the same page. I thought we both wanted the same things. Look, I don't want to be a jerk, but I know what I want from life and I want a partner that wants the same things.'

'So, what you're saying is, I have an abortion, or we break up?'

'Well, you make it sound so crude. There is more to it than that. I don't want to raise a baby. Don't you think it would damage the child to have someone in its life that resents it? If you want to keep the baby you can. But I can't be a part of it.'

She got up and left the room.

She wandered down the hall to her office in a daze. She saw no faces and registered nothing, so lost was she in her turmoil. Sophie had never considered becoming a mother. Her own childhood had never instilled any maternal desires. For her whole life her only focus had been her own survival and making a place for herself in the brutal, suffocating jungle of a world.

In her earliest memories she was self-sufficient, looking after herself with no one to help her. She had never contemplated bringing life into the world when it was a daily struggle to get by. But now, she was thinking about it. She had money, a home and a stable relationship. Why shouldn't she bring a child into the world? What better way to heal the wound of neglect by giving her child everything she never had? Her child would want for nothing. *Her child.*

When she got back to their flat, Flora was practically bouncing off the walls with happiness. Her face was flushed and her eyes sparkled.

'I'm engaged!' she shouted thrusting her hand in Sophie's face. A large diamond ring glinted in the sunlight. Before Sophie could congratulate her, Flora had flung her arms around Sophie, holding her so fiercely she could barely breathe. She relaxed into the embrace and took comfort from her friend's warm body wrapped around her. Tears welled up and she let them fall. Let Flora think she was crying with happiness at her engagement. Not at the awful decision she was about to make. Flora pulled back with matching tears in her eyes. She wiped away Sophie's tears.

'Sophie, I'm so happy, and it is all down to you. You knew Sam was right for me from the start. Now we are going to be a proper family. You and Greg, me and Sam. It is going to be perfect.'

Greg had taken Sophie out for dinner that same night. She took it as a good sign. She thought that he was going to apologise for his knee-jerk reaction and they would talk properly about this. She could not have been more wrong.

'Have you booked an appointment yet? I've been thinking it over and if you do decide to keep it, you'll have to move away. I don't want to risk anyone looking at it and thinking it's mine.' He talked to her as if discussing the finer details of a contract at work. Not the most life-changing decision she could ever make. To end the life of a baby or not. Her baby. His words poured cold water on the fledging idea she had had to raise the baby alone with Flora's help until Greg changed his mind. Surely once he'd seen the baby, he'd change his mind. She should have realised that Greg would have thought everything through. Ever the businessman.

She was reminded of a night, early on in their relationship, when Greg had had a bit too much to drink and admitted that his father had gotten a girl pregnant. When she refused to terminate or move away he bought the building she was living in and had her evicted. Alistair had used every tool at his disposal to make her life hell until she had no choice but to take his handout and leave the area, never to return. This must be what Greg was planning.

'Don't you care about me at all? How can you talk about this so callously? I thought you loved me? Why aren't you more upset about this?'

Greg shushed her. 'Calm down. Of course I love you. But I love the real you. The one that is driven and career-focused. I do not want a housewife whose only conversation is about children. If you continue to act like a different version of Sophie then I will act like a different version of Greg. Only the real Sophie gets my love and devotion.'

He took her hand in his. 'Look, if you stop with this baby nonsense and be my Sophie again. I'll marry you right now.' He stroked her hand gently. 'We are the dream team. We are good for each other. Together we can take on the world. I want to marry you and have you as my wife. We don't need children. We are better than that. I don't want children. Ever. Is that something you can accept?'

Sophie thought about the alternative. She would have the baby, be driven from Manchester and would most likely turn to drink like her mother with nothing and no one to support her. She would not be able to see Flora. If she did see her it would not be the same, knowing that Flora was married to Sam and living the life she used to have, that they no longer lived next door to each other. She had spent most of her life seeing Flora every day. Could she picture a life without seeing Flora all the time? Or worse, Flora might choose to leave with her, and they would try and raise the baby together. But then Flora would not be with Sam. Could she really risk the happiness of her best friend? She thought of the way Flora's eyes danced as pure, unadulterated happiness poured from her. Sophie knew if she were to have this baby, that unequivocal happiness would be tarnished. After everything Flora had been through, she did not deserve that.

'I mean, look at your mother. She turned into an alcoholic. Do you really want to take that risk?'

'Okay.'

Greg's handsome face lit up. He moved around the table and got down on one knee, pulling a small black box from his pocket. The other diners in the restaurant clapped and cheered as Greg swept her into his arms and kissed her when she said yes to his proposal. Just as she did with Flora, she let Greg think her tears were of joy. Not devastation and grief. She reasoned with herself that she could always try and change his mind. Okay, she just wouldn't have *this* baby. That didn't mean she couldn't have one in the future.

Greg organised everything. He came to each hospital appointment, whether to support her or make sure she followed through with the termination she wasn't sure. But she was glad he was there. She had gone numb inside, unable or unwilling to acknowledge the gravity of what she was doing. Greg was on first name terms with her doctor, so she sat there mutely. She signed the consent form shoved into her hands. The words 'dilation' and 'evacuation' leapt out at her, but she was paralysed inside, unable to speak or question anything.

The next thing she knew she was in an operating theatre with doctors and nurses milling around her. It was like she was watching the world through a broken television. She could see and hear the people around her, but the sound wasn't working properly and everyone was blurry and unfocused. This had happened ever since the proposal. She was a co-pilot in her own body, no longer fully in control.

When she woke up from the operation it felt like only five minutes had passed when Greg helped her get dressed and bundled her back to his house. She stayed in bed for a whole week, unable to function or focus on anything. Greg had decided that now they were engaged they were moving in together and so her stuff appeared around her.

Flora came to visit. Greg had must have come up with a lie as to why she was ill because Flora never mentioned anything. Just brought her soup and stroked her face. She could hear Flora talking but only a few words actually processed. 'Moving in with Sam', 'neighbours', 'fever'. But her consciousness was too fragile to process anything, because to engage with the world would mean acknowledging her loss.

She slept fitfully and barely noticed whether it was night or day. Time was no longer a concept she bothered to acknowledge. Her mind was empty and she only moved when Greg or Flora came in to feed or wash her. A strange man entered the room, but Sophie did not attempt to move. She presumed he must be a doctor as he used various instruments to check her temperature and blood pressure. She could hear the buzz of his voice but could distinguish no sounds, like her brain was out of practice and no longer understood the English language.

She was in the hospital. That was the first thing she realised. Someone must have fixed the broken TV that was her mind. The world around her came into focus again and she now recognised words and sounds. Time became a construct she understood and she felt time passing once more. She heard the doctor's word's, 'womb infection' and 'damage to the cervix'. She put a pillow over her head to block out the sounds, to try and avoid hearing the rest of the doctor's words. But the pillow was an ineffective barrier and the word 'infertile' struck her like a knife in her heart. She would never have a baby.

The only reason Sophie was able to work through her grief at the future she could have had was because of Flora. Seeing her and Sam thriving together and living next door to her made the pain lessen each day. There were days that she wondered whether she should tell Flora. At the moment, she thought that Sophie had had a nasty infection. Well in a way that was true, she had been infected by the Cavendish family poison.

19

Flora was starting to hope that her life would become normal and drama free. She and Sam were slowly breathing life into the house at Trelawney Close. Before she went over to check on the progress, she decided to have a quick swim. Sophie liked the regiment of a gym but Flora liked her exercise a bit more laidback and less intense.

There were only a few things Flora could remember with clarity when it came to her parents. It was getting difficult to remember the sound of her mother's voice or the feel of her father's bear hugs – but one of the few things she did remember was regular trips to the swimming pool. She could hear the echoes of her parents' laughter as they tried to coerce her into leaving each time. If she concentrated hard enough, she could just about recall her dad's voice. 'Come on, Flora. I swear you must have been a fish in a previous life. It's time to go.'

Now she liked immersing herself in the water and the memories it brought. She had also grown to love the swimming pool politics.

The water caressed her skin, small waves lapped at her, churned by the other swimmers. A cacophony of noise echoed around the space: shrieks of joy, the admonishments of parents and children shouting instructions at each other. The sounds were like a balm to her soul, drowning out any thoughts and allowing her to just be in the moment.

As Flora swam up and down the slow lane, she was particularly enjoying the tuts of displeasure aimed at a busty older lady with winter-white hair, swimming in their lane. Her watery blue eyes didn't appear to have noticed the signs informing swimmers which direction she should be swimming in the lane. To the disgust of the regular swimmers, this older lady had the audacity to swim in the middle of the lane. Flora smirked as each judgemental middle-aged woman, one after another, aimed a thinly veiled look of disdain at the oblivious elderly lady. Everyone had to swim around her, but she didn't seem to notice, or simply didn't care.

Flora was not perturbed as she just slowed her pace and kept behind her. But she laughed inside at the contempt and frustration bubbling in the other swimmers. She could almost hear the diatribe they were longing to launch but couldn't because of some unwritten English code of conduct that insisted on politeness at all times. Flora bet that if they were any other nationality, the older lady would have most likely been told, unceremoniously, to 'get the hell out of the way' or perhaps even pushed out of the way. But that was not the English way.

Being the only pool for miles around and given the fact the lockers, changing rooms and showers and the pool were all in one space, it would feel busy with only a handful of people in it. But Flora preferred it busy, there were more people to observe and noise to quieten her thoughts. She needed that more than ever today, given the stress she had been under lately.

The lifeguard was waiting at the end of her lane and Flora watched in anticipation for the woman to be told off. Balance would be restored, until the next faux pas was committed. Flora slowed her speed so she could enjoy the uncomfortable conversation that was about to take place between the spotty lifeguard and the clueless pensioner.

Water.

She barely had time to acknowledge the hand on her head before she was thrust underneath the water. Cold, chlorine-tasting water filled her lungs and flooded her mouth and nose. Her blood pounded behind her eyes. She thrashed her arms and legs, but she couldn't reach the surface. Terror like she had never felt before rose within her. Her lungs screamed in agony. An unseen force was holding her down. Bubbles clouded her vision. *Help me.* Her eyes searched desperately for someone to help. Was that a leg? All she could see was air bubbles and smudges of pink, white and splashes of colour. The chlorine burned her eyes and nose. An intense pain surged within her ribs. Her lungs were burning. She fought hard to resist the urge to open her mouth. Her legs began to tire from frantically kicking and fighting the insurmountable pressure keeping her held under the water.

Without warning the pressure from her head was gone and she was able to propel herself upwards. She broke through the surface and gulped in glorious mouthfuls of air.

Flora looked around, disorientated. She trod water wearily as she tried to stop hyperventilating, her eyes wild with fear, looking for the person who had held her under the water. There was no one there. The other swimmers were at the opposite end of the lane, no one seemed aware that anything had happened to her.

She groped for the side thankful she had chosen a lane at the edge of the pool. Her body and hands were shaking so much it took her two attempts to gain a proper grip. She clung to the wall and tried to wrap her mind around what had just happened. Her body felt heavy and her lungs, nose and throat still burned painfully. Coughs wracked her body as her lungs expelled the pool water she'd swallowed. She couldn't hear anything above the hammering of her heart. Looking around again, she could see that the lady she had been swimming behind wasn't that far away. It had felt like an age that she had been under the water when apparently it had only been a few seconds at most.

No one seemed to notice that anything was amiss. The wayward older lady was at the other end of the pool now, keeping to the rules this time and swimming on the right. All around her the water churned and lapped against her skin as people made their way up and down. Men in the fast lane tore their way through the water like a shark was chasing them. The orchestra of noise and splashes of the water echoed around the room, overwhelming her overwrought senses, when only moments ago, she'd embraced the noise and loved the atmosphere. She needed to get out, but she didn't trust her ability to move.

Someone had been holding her under the water, stopping her from surfacing. She looked around, feeling vulnerable. Looking for... what was she looking for? Everyone in the lanes around her were focused on their task. No one was watching her. Were they? She met the eyes of a man who had stopped for a break next to her. He peered at her curiously. *Was it him?* she thought. Did he hold her under the water? Why was he looking at her?

'You going, love?' he asked, motioning to the lane.

Relief flooded through her. She must have looked like she was about to swim again and he was being polite and letting her go first. 'No... No. You go,' she stammered, her voice hoarse from the coughing.

Her body trembled uncontrollably. She had a desperate need to escape, to get somewhere safe. Unsteadily, she pulled herself along to the ladder at the end of the pool. She had an urge to run to the changing rooms, but she was still weak and shaky. It took two attempts just to summon enough energy to pull herself out of the water. Her body was heavy, like she was now made of stone. Timidly, Flora made her way back to her locker. Every step was difficult due to the heaviness of her limbs. Her side ached and her nose and throat still burned each time she took a breath. Nausea threatened with each step she took, her stomach rolling, repulsed by the pool water. There was a very real possibility she may vomit.

Paranoid, she felt the eyes of everyone in the pool boring into her back like pinpricks on her skin. She tried to make herself smaller, hunching her body in.

When she had grabbed her bag, fled to a changing room and locked the door, she slumped on the wooden bench and finally gave way to tears. She had been so scared. Had she imagined the hand on her head, like she'd imagined her cards disappearing? Was there something wrong with her? One minute she was staring at the back of an old lady's head. The next minute, water was everywhere. She shuddered at the memory, reliving the pressure in her lungs, the desperation for air. She was sure there had been a hand on her head. But there was no one there when she came back up. Surely if there was someone holding her down under the water, someone would have noticed. *Wouldn't they?* she wondered. *Oh god, I am actually going insane.*

The tears seemed to soothe her. With a shaky breath, she began to get changed and head back to Sam's house. Fear was exhausting.

20

Sophie had been on the phone to Duncan, coaching him for their meeting with Tesco, when Flora's message came through on the iMac in front of her.

Someone tried to drown me at the pool. Need to see you.

'Sorry, Duncan, I've got to go. I'll call you back.'

She didn't wait to hear his reply. Instead, she picked up her bag, threw her phone into it and left her office. Sophie pulled up outside her house ten minutes later, having broken every speed limit on the way. She ran out of the car and let herself into Flora's house.

Flora was on the sofa, wrapped in both a blanket and Sam's arms. Sophie gave herself a moment to absorb how utterly adorable they were before she swooped into the room. At the sight of her, Flora burst into hysterical tears.

Sam moved away, displaced by Sophie who took Flora in her arms. He hovered over them awkwardly, watching as Sophie rocked Flora gently and made soothing noises. It triggered flashbacks to all the nights she had done this when they were children and Flora was crying in tormented pain at the loss of her parents. She raised her eyes questioningly at Sam.

In a low, gentle voice he explained. 'I came home and found her like this. Wrapped in a blanket, hair still damp, crying her eyes out. She said she went to the swimming pool and someone pushed her head under the water and held her down, but when she resurfaced no one was there.'

His eyes said what his words didn't. That he did not believe Flora. He thought, like with the cards and the dead rat, she was being oversensitive and latching on to the worst-case scenario. Sophie could see why: in her experience, most men only saw in black and white. Also, it did sound a bit ridiculous to think someone would hold Flora's head under the water. Poor Flora. She must have been so scared.

'It's okay, Flo.' She rocked her friend until she began to calm.

Wiping her face on her sleeve, Flora looked up at Sophie with a small smile that slipped off her face quickly. 'Sophie. What's happened to your lip?'

Sophie brought her hand to her split lip. It was still tender but not as painful as it had been. 'Oh this. It was stupid, I slipped in the shower. I looked a right state in my meetings today, I can tell you.'

Sophie moved closer to Flora and manoeuvred her until Flora's head was lying in her lap. She stroked her chocolate-brown hair slowly until Flora's breath evened out. After another five minutes, Sophie moved Flora's head, got up and placed a cushion underneath. Flora didn't even flicker, she looked catatonic. Sophie motioned to Sam and they both crept out of the room.

Sophie made them both a cup of tea and they sat facing each other across the kitchen island. It felt strange to be alone with Sam. It had only ever happened a handful of times.

'Sophie, I don't know how to handle this. It doesn't make any sense: first the nonsense with the cards and now this.' He shook his head slowly, seemingly at a loss for words.

Sophie was almost as hurt as Flora would have been had she heard this. There was always a part of Sophie that prayed Sam was different to the rest of the family. That he had absorbed all the decency that was sorely lacking from his parents and sibling. But no, he was just as bad as them. How dare he make it sound like Flora was going crazy. 'Sam, she's not crazy. I've known her almost my whole life. If she says these things are happening, then they are happening.'

'But why would someone take her bank cards and money and then put them back in her purse? It is just so ludicrous. Who would even have access to her purse to do that?'

'I think we both know the answer to that.'

'Oh, for Christ's sake. Not you as well.' Sam got to his feet suddenly and started pacing up and down. 'My mother is not evil. She does not hate you and she does not hate Flora!' His face flushed red. He drew a deep breath in before continuing. 'You say you've known Flora almost your whole life. I've known my mother all of my life. She would never do something like that. It wouldn't even occur to her.' Sam ran his hands through his hair. 'She doesn't even own a purse. My father buys everything for her and everywhere she shops she has an account.'

Sophie stayed quiet, not trusting herself to speak.

'It makes much more sense that Flora lost track of her cards; and she bumped into someone swimming which caused her to panic. That makes much more sense than someone vindictively trying to scare her and drive her crazy.' He slumped back down in his seat. He looked up at her with sadness in his eyes. 'Please, don't misunderstand me. I love Flora. I love her so much it overwhelms me sometimes. I would never want to hurt her, but I can't lie to her and agree with her when I know in my heart that it is not true. My mother is not terrorising her. No one is. You have to see that.'

Sophie got up, intending to go back and be with Flora, more determined than ever to stop this family from causing her any more pain. Sam had proven he was not worthy of Flora. Loving someone meant being there for them no matter what the circumstances, even if what was happening couldn't be fitted into a neat little box. It meant withstanding the uncertainty and putting that person's feelings and needs first, not your own desire for everything to make sense to you. Flora was better off without him. Sophie just wished she had seen it long before now. Then maybe she would have kept her baby and vanished with Flora after all. The thought caused physical pain in her heart.

She turned back to Sam, hand on the door handle. 'I think we just have to agree to disagree. Some of the most poisonous people are disguised from us by the love we have for them.' As she closed the door behind her, she couldn't quite pinpoint Sam's expression as he watched her leave.

21

Setting the table was soothing. Lining up the cutlery and putting out the glasses helped to take Flora's mind off Linda. Even though Sophie hadn't seen her, Flora was convinced that she had seen Linda at the garden centre that morning. Looking around the Joules section at things she could never justify buying, there was no doubt in her mind that she had seen Linda's gaunt face looking at her from the seeds section at the other side of the shop.

It was her, Flora was sure of it. But with Sam doubting her sanity she was losing confidence in herself.

Flora had shrugged off the sighting with Sophie and hadn't even mentioned it to Sam. There was no point. She could quite easily recall his expression of disbelief: she didn't need to see it again. Flora tried to push down the sense of foreboding circling around her stomach like a slithering snake. She just felt that things were going to get a lot worse. The doorbell rang and she raced to answer it. A night with Sophie was just what she needed. She had begun to think of Sophie as her reset button. Spending quality time with her always calmed her down and all the stress and anxiety that she felt ebbed away. It was just a shame that Greg was part of the package.

One look at Sophie's face drove all thoughts of Linda out of her mind. Sophie's greeting was over-friendly and forced. Her face was tight, and her smile was exaggerated. There was something very wrong. Tensions fizzled between Sophie and Greg even though they weren't looking at each other. Their bodies giving voice to the words they could not say in polite company. The echo of their argument pervaded the room.

Greg took Sam's seat at the top of the table, giving him a challenging look, daring him to say something. Sam backed off and walked to the other side of the table leaving an awkward silence in his wake. It had taken a while for Flora to accept that Greg was a part of her life. They had absolutely nothing in common. On the rare occasion that they found themselves alone, she could not think of a single thing to say to him. They would sit in an uncomfortable silence that made her skin crawl.

Flora often felt that she and Sam were a different species to Sophie and Greg. Their lives were different in every way. Even their houses spoke to this: Sam's house was painted in colour (much to Cecelia's disgust) and had a lived-in feeling. Sophie and Greg's house looked like it was a show home. Nothing was out of place and everything was a neutral black or white. It was sophisticated and elegant; but not homely.

As Flora passed the gravy boat to Sophie, she saw a flicker of frustration escape her friend's face before she could hide it behind a smile. Greg had been drinking more wine than usual and his voice, already louder than a normal person's, was bouncing off the four walls. Manners were never his strong point, but even Sam looked shocked when he snatched the gravy boat out of Sophie's hand before she'd even started pouring it on to her plate. He emptied the entire thing over his plate, drowning his roast beef and Yorkshire puddings. The gravy swam close to the edge of the plate, the slightest shift would have it spilling over onto the table. He smiled sweetly at Sophie. 'Sorry, darling, did you want some?'

Whether he didn't notice the awkward atmosphere and shocked faces around the table or he was choosing to ignore them Flora wasn't sure. He began to eat his food with the gusto of a starving man, gravy inevitably splashing over the tablecloth. It was the only time that Flora wished Cecelia were here. Flora would have liked to see her face at the etiquette – or lack of – being displayed.

Sam raised his eyebrows at Flora, puzzled amusement on his face. Sam and Greg spent a lot of time together but it seemed this was only because they were related. Sam once confessed that he didn't understand his brother but felt bound to him in a way Flora could never understand.

Sophie's face was like a stone wall. The only indication of how she might be feeling was the unnecessary force she used to cut into her roast beef. Flora was worried. She had been seeing far too many cracks in Sophie's marriage. Was she overreacting, like she was with the swimming pool incident and her cards? Could she even trust her judgement anymore? Sam seemed to think she was seeing danger where there wasn't any. Was this the same thing?

Greg had always been almost reverential in the way he spoke about or to Sophie. His jests were always about her being 'too perfect', 'too sophisticated'. He had never in the five years she had known him treated Sophie as anything less than a princess. It was sickening at times. Flora shook her head. She was overthinking things, too on edge after the last few days. It was clouding her judgement. No one could be on their best behaviour all the time.

All couples had their ups and downs. She smiled at the thought. She would never admit this to anyone but occasionally she deliberately instigated an argument with Sam. She would offload all her negativity in that fight and then revel in their reconciliation. It was true what they said about make-up sex. Mind made up she decided to overlook 'gravy-gate' as Sam would later call it.

It seemed the rest of the evening would pass without incident. Sophie asked Flora how the centre was going, a strategic move if she was trying to instigate a long conversation as they all knew that Flora could wax lyrical about the centre. She began to tell them about a quiet girl who had not spoken a word her whole life, but who, it turned out, was an incredibly talented singer. She wouldn't talk to anyone but could sing with the most beautiful, angelic voice. It was her way of communicating. Flora's eyes welled up once more as she recalled the haunting beauty of the girl's voice and the look on her parents' faces when they walked in to see their daughter, singing, communicating for the first time.

Greg interrupted Flora mid-flow. 'Why don't you do that, Soph?' It was blatantly obvious from his glazed eyes that he had not really been listening.

Sophie looked up at him with a confused expression.

'Help people instead of being so selfishhh and money-grabbing.' His words slurred together thanks to the copious amount of wine he'd consumed. Unspoken words were flying between Greg and Sophie as they stared at each other. Flora felt indignant. Greg was the most materialistic person she had ever met. When had he ever helped someone? She opened her mouth to speak but Sam put his arm on hers and shook his head.

Sophie jumped up. 'I think that is our cue to leave. Someone has had a little too much to drink.' Like a whirlwind she ushered Greg to the door and supported him as he stumbled across the driveway back to their own house.

Flora had to take a deep breath before she could put her hands in the water to rinse the plates to make them ready for the dishwasher. Just the feel of water on her skin caused her pulse to race. Her throat would close as if she was drowning in that swimming pool all over again.

Showering was even worse. Usually she would spend hours luxuriating in the powerful spray of the shower, letting the warm water wrap around her like a warm hug. Now she was in and out as quickly as possible. The first few times had left her a quivering wreck on the floor. Not that she would admit this to Sam.

'Sam, can you bring in the rest of the plates so I can put them in the washing machine.'

He came through chuckling, plates already in hand. 'It's a good job I know you. I think you mean dishwasher.'

She pretended to whip him with a towel. 'Don't be mean! You know I always get them mixed up.'

Sam carried on bringing the rest of the pots into the kitchen, stopping to kiss her when they passed. It was a task he had eventually gotten used to once she had moved in and fired his housekeeper. It was bad enough that they had four bedrooms and four bathrooms just for the two of them. They did not need a housekeeper as well.

'I wonder what's got into Greg. Do you think I should have a word with him?' Sam asked.

'It might be a good idea,' replied Flora, loading up the dishwasher, 'I've noticed a lot of tension between them lately. I'm really worried.'

'Hasn't Sophie said something to you?'

'No, I think she's probably not wanted to burden me when I've been so stressed,' replied Flora. But that was going to change. She would talk to Sophie later. She would welcome the distraction from feeling like someone was trying to make her think she was crazy. She would instead focus on making sure that Sophie was okay.

Moving out of Sam's arms, she went over to the living room window, intending to shut the blind. Darkness had blanketed the world, the street lights battling to keep it at bay. In the beam of one of the lights she saw a shadow flicker. Was that someone standing, watching the house? Stumbling into the armchair in her haste, she dashed into the hallway and outside. There was nothing there. The street was silent apart from the occasional hoot of an owl. Nothing moved, as if the street was holding its breath. The cold pierced her skin and she shivered. But whether it was from cold or the fear she wasn't sure.

22

I t was the hole in his sock that started it. Greg's hairy big toe was peeking through the hole and Sophie couldn't stand it.

'You need to throw those socks out,' she said, barely concealing the disgust in her voice.

He didn't even look up at her.

After how he spoke to her in front of Sam and Flora last night, he should be grovelling for her forgiveness. She continued to stare at his big toe, and it seemed to magnify under her scrutiny. The curly hairs on it revolted her. The more she looked at it the angrier she became. When they had first met, she had been seduced by Greg's effortless sophistication. His Calvin Klein suit was impeccable, he was well-groomed and took pride in his appearance.

Fast-forward five years and she was sat staring at him as he lay spreadeagled on the sofa, dishevelled, shirt mucky and half the buttons undone with a great big hole in his sock. She felt conned. A fierce anger began to bubble within the pit of her stomach. Her body was shaking, and she wanted to scream.

The frayed edges of the sock burned into her retinas. It was like the hole in the sock represented his contempt for her. When had he stopped respecting her? Hadn't she proven to him time and time again she was an equal in every way? Her life was not meant to be like this. He had promised her a life of excitement and power; not one where she would be sitting in an armchair reading a magazine on a Sunday night, with her unkempt husband barely exchanging a word. Her feeling of impotence at how her life had turned out forced her into action.

She stood up.

Greg didn't seem to notice.

'Take. Off. Those. Socks.' Her voice was icy cold.

He didn't even seem to hear her: too engrossed in the paper he was reading.

Her whole body vibrated with anger. She could hear her pulse in her ears. Unfiltered rage fizzed and before she knew what she was doing, she had leapt on to his legs and was pulling at the sock. She couldn't get it off easily because his jeans were in the way.

Greg's arm reached around her. 'What the hell are you doing?'

'Taking off your bloody socks,' she screeched at him. She was like a harpy, completely out of control. She didn't even recognise her own voice. She pulled and ripped at the sock, simultaneously batting away Greg's large hands that were desperately trying to control her.

He tried to buck her off his legs, but she would not move, fury giving her a strength she didn't know she possessed. He roared at her, trying to get her to stop. But she couldn't even if she had wanted to. She had started pulling at the hole in the sock, making it bigger and scratching at his foot as she tried to rip it away.

A sudden pressure around her throat knocked all the fight from her. Her hands clawed at Greg's as she tried to pull his hands from her throat. Her lungs screamed for air and black lights danced in her eyes. Sophie scratched at his hands and then the pressure was gone. She fell off his legs onto the floor, holding her neck as she greedily gulped in breath after breath. Sophie lay on the floor, dizzy and weak. Unable to move. In her peripheral vision, she saw Greg's hairy toe walk away from her and out of the room.

What. The. Hell. Just. Happened.

23

This Friday Night Dinner was going to be different. Flora had a reason to celebrate and finally a reason to make Cecelia respect her. After all, not everyone gets approached and asked to write a book about what they do for a living. It was not a natural process for her, putting her thoughts and ideas down on paper. Having dyslexia also made it hard as she spent a long time staring at her computer not knowing how to transfer the ideas in her mind into written words and she couldn't even spell half of the words that she wanted to use. Writing a book that people would read and judge made her feel vulnerable.

But Luke, one of the fathers at the centre had approached her. He was an editor at Education Press and he had convinced her people would want to read what she had to say; that other people deserved to know about the work that she did; that with this book she would be able to reach more people, to give them hope for their child's future.

Now, at last she was holding her book in her hands. *Her book!* Hardcover, a beautiful picture on the front of Flora leaning over Isabel – Luke's daughter – whilst she held a paintbrush over a piece of paper. It was a lovely photo and perfectly encapsulated the work she did at the centre. The concentration and focus on Isabel's face was captivating. Flora didn't look too bad either: her hair must have been photoshopped as it was never that glossy chocolate-brown colour in the mirrors she looked in. Flora kept stroking the cover of the book, unable to believe she had created something so professional.

Sam reached over and took her hand. 'I'm so proud of you, Flo.' He beamed at her. 'My talented wife is now a famous author.'

Flora blushed with pleasure. Sam was her number one fan. He had patiently helped her fix the errors in her book, not once laughing at some of the crazy mistakes her dyslexic brain had made, not even when she had used the word *incestuous* instead of *incessant*. They pulled around the circular driveway. Flora was no longer overwhelmed with awe when she saw the manor. Cecelia's malevolence had tarnished it. There seemed to be a correlation between how appalling the owners were and how attractive their house appeared. Flora had no respect for Cecilia so had no appreciation for anything she owned.

Reginald was there to greet them as usual, a silent spectator of the Cavendish family. Flora wondered at the secrets he must know. He took their coats and led them into the greeting room.

'Samuel, darling.' Cecelia flung her arms around Sam as if they'd not seen each other for years. 'We'll go straight through: your brother is already here.'

'Is Sophie not coming?' asked Flora, her heart racing at the thought of not having an ally at dinner.

'Oh yes. She's here too,' replied Cecelia and she led the way into the dining room.

Alistair did not acknowledge either of them. She felt a pang of sympathy for Sam, as Alistair rarely spent time with him. She got the sense that Alistair felt Sam was beneath him. Sam did not share his ruthless thirst for business and was therefore not worth his time. If only Cecelia thought that, Flora might get some peace. Maybe Alistair resented the fact that Cecelia worshipped Sam like he was her only son. It was the only time Flora felt sorry for Greg. It was obvious to all that Sam was her golden boy. Alistair could be charming if he wanted to, but only if he thought you were worth the effort apparently.

Sophie rushed over, radiating excitement. 'Is that it?' She took the book from Flora, holding it like she would a painting by Da Vinci. She turned the pages delicately. 'Oh, Flora,' she breathed. 'It's amazing.'

'Shall we eat?' came Cecelia's bored voice behind them.

Sam took the book out of Flora's hand and walked over to his mother. 'Mother. Flora's brought you a present. A first edition of her book.'

Cecelia took the book from Sam, gave it a cursory glance and passed it straight to Reginald who, as always, appeared from nowhere. 'How lovely,' said Cecelia disingenuously. 'I won't read it of course. It would be simply awful if I didn't like it. Could you imagine.' She chuckled but there was no laughter in her eyes.

Flora's face heated up. How foolish of her to not realise that this was exactly how Cecelia would react. It would take more than this to gain Cecelia's respect. She needed to stop seeking it. Flora looked down at the floor, not wanting to give Cecelia the satisfaction of seeing tears pricking her eyes. She rebuked herself: many people would have the same reaction and she would have to stop taking it personally. Not everyone was a published author. Plus, no one cared that she had poured her heart and soul into that book. No one knew that she had struggled with literacy her whole life and the thought of publishing a book was so ludicrous she would have laughed if someone had suggested it. Still, she couldn't help it, to see Cecelia completely dismiss it like it was nothing at all was painful, no matter how much she tried to remind herself that Cecelia was just being her usual mean-spirited self.

Flora sneaked a look at Sam, waiting to see what he would say.

'It's really good, Mother. I've read it and thought it was brilliant.'

Cecelia changed the subject to her new favourite topic: houses they have seen for sale that Sam might want to buy. Flora tuned her out. There was no way she was buying another property and she knew that Sam felt the same. It was getting boring now.

Sophie caught her eye. 'Waste of a book, really. You should have given it to someone else. You should have bought her a book on dragons instead. Much more relevant.'

Flora choked down her laugh, glancing at Cecelia to check she hadn't heard.

'How are you?' asked Sophie. 'Really.'

It took a while for Flora to answer. The truth was she didn't know. She was convinced that someone was trying to scare her. Just this evening, she had arrived at the car park after leaving the centre and could not find her car anywhere. She finally found it on the top floor of the multi-storey she had parked in. There was no way she had parked it there because she didn't like the tight turns coming down the car park so she always parked on the lowest floor she could find when using the multi-storey. She cringed at an echo of the panic she had felt running around the car park like a crazed person, convinced her car had been stolen. She almost wished it had. It would make much more sense to other people that way. She hadn't told Sam. There was no point: there was no way he would believe someone had moved her car. He would just think what everyone else thought:

that she had forgotten where she parked it. Just another stupid, ditzy woman.

She wondered whether to tell Sophie. But Flora still hadn't talked to Sophie about Greg's behaviour at dinner the other night. It was obvious Sophie was not confiding in her because she didn't want to burden her when she was so wound up. Telling her this was only going to make Sophie even more reluctant to share anything that was worrying her. So she swallowed it away. It was her secret. Plus, telling someone would trigger that fear all over again and she was not going to let whoever was doing this get away with it. So what, they moved her car. They were obviously just trying to mess with her mind. She would rise above it. Flora also tried to ignore the small voice in the back of her mind that reminded her that no one but Sam had a key to her car.

Flora jumped as a hand touched her arm. It was Sophie.

'Hey, where did you go?' Sophie laughed. 'Away with the fairies?'

'Sorry. I'm just going to nip to the loo.' Flora needed to compose herself, eradicate all thoughts of today and convince Sophie and more importantly herself, that she was fine. She had just left the room when Cecelia's shrill voice pulled her towards the kitchen.

Her anger was palpable. 'She will not get away with this! Taking my son away from me. *My* son.'

Unable to stop herself, Flora peered around the kitchen door, just in time to see Cecelia throw her book into the kitchen bin. Not satisfied, Cecelia turned and grabbed a saucepan off the stove and poured its contents into the bin, covering the hardcover book in thick brown syrup.

Flora could see Cecelia's side-profile and could just make out a malevolent smile. She was breathing heavily.

Reginald stood to attention next to her. 'But what can we do, madam? Master Cavendish loves her.' Reginald sounded devastated.

'You'll find, Reginald, that there is nothing that money cannot solve. That includes love. We will just have to work harder to get rid of her. If I have to, I'll ensure that little orphan Flora goes exactly the same way as her parents.'

24

'You'rre so pretty,' slurred a drunken Flora.

Sophie smiled affectionately. 'Someone is feeling better,' she replied.

Drunk Flora was hilarious. She'd been known to steal traffic cones and people's hats. Sophie did not drink; she did not like anything that took away her control. She had also seen first-hand what it did to her mother. But she was happy to be the sensible one looking out for Flora, fending off the wandering hands of drunk men who seemed to think it was their right to touch whatever came in their vicinity. A swift jab to the nether region always put them in their place.

Flora was only tipsy tonight, so she didn't need much looking after. For the first time in months, Sophie was enjoying herself. It was like the old days before they had got married. Flora was letting her hair down, drowning her fears with alcohol. Sophie couldn't believe the nerve of Cecelia. The things that she had said about Flora confirmed what Sophie had known all along. The Cavendish family were dangerous.

Sophie had been so certain that marrying into the Cavendish family was the right path for them both. When she realised that Greg had a brother, it had felt serendipitous. But now, spending some time with Flora alone, she wished more than anything that she had never met Greg Cavendish. She fingered the bruise along her arm, pressing at the place where it was the most painful. It was her punishment for bringing these men into their lives.

'Cheers,' yelled Flora. She attempted to clink her glass with Sophie's on the table. But Flora's vision wasn't quite what it had been before she began drinking and the next thing Sophie knew her blouse had been drenched by the 'mocktail' she had been drinking. Flora began to apologise profusely and urgently searched for a napkin. Once she found one, she moved over to Sophie's side of the booth and began to rigorously scrub off the wine from Sophie's arm. She hissed in pain before she could stop herself. The silk of her shirt had become translucent from the drink. The angry red and black bruise that snaked up her arm was plain for anyone to see, even in the dim light of the bar. Sophie looked up to see Flora's eyes wide and fixed upon her arm.

'The Macarena' began to play, and before Flora could say a word, Sophie reached for her and dragged her onto the dance floor where a clumsy circle of people had formed. Taking advantage of the cheesy music, she began to complete the dance moves of her youth, acting like she was having the best time in the world. She ignored Flora's stares, hoping to avoid a conversation about the marks on her arms. She was not ready to share that story yet. It seemed to work, as Flora appeared to be seduced by the drunken joy and happiness in the room. Thank god for alcohol clouding her friend's brain.

Her phone beeped and she pulled it out of her pocket and despite the stifling heat in the bar, her blood ran cold. Alistair.

We need to talk. You can't avoid me forever.

25

The world was spinning. Flora couldn't get out of bed without her stomach lurching dangerously. Why oh why did she drink so much? It was all Cecelia's fault. If she hadn't been so evil then Flora would not have had to drink away her sorrows. She felt unsettled, like something had happened last night that upset her, but her memories were blurry. All she could remember was drinking and dancing. Picking up her phone, she began to text Sophie, hoping she could convince her to bring her a McDonald's breakfast. It was the best hangover cure in the world, something she'd learnt at university. An email popped up as she was typing, it was from Polly, one of the mothers at the centre.

'Thought you ought to see this...' a link to the *Manchester News* website was underneath. Clicking on it, Flora saw the title 'Mother of Autistic Child Denied Support because of Poverty'. She read through the article and before she knew it, she had thrown up on the floor.

~

Whilst she was scrubbing her sick off the grey carpet, she received another copy of the article from Cecelia along with a demand for an urgent meeting.

Linda's words in the article reverberated around her mind.

'The woman, Flora, couldn't wait to get rid of me. She looked at me like I was scum of the earth. The whole place was packed with rich kids. It breaks my heart that my Ethan is being denied the therapy other children have because I am a single mum that can't afford their prices. She didn't even have the guts to tell me to my face that she wouldn't help my son. Sent one of her lackeys to meet me and give me the brush off.'

Linda. How could she do this to her? It was all her own fault for not explaining everything properly to Linda. Why did she let Sophie talk to her? She should have explained that she had to make ends meet.

According to the article they had tried to contact her for comment, when? If they had, she could have explained that she did not take money from the Cavendish family and that the centre was not doing well. Flora felt guilty not taking the Cavendish money to expand her centre and it was something she thought about every day. When she looked at her Excel spreadsheet and extended the limit on her business credit card, she had to stop herself wondering how much easier her life would be if she just accepted the money. How many more children could she help if she opened more than one centre? But she just couldn't do it. Not for Ethan. Not for anyone.

Travelling into work, the words of the article kept reverberating in her mind. She could no longer control her guilt at not helping more children. At not helping Ethan. Linda had taken her guilt and exposed it to the world. She could no longer deny that she was turning her back on money that could help a lot of people. What sort of person did that make her? Under the scrutiny of the world, would her desire to remain independent and ensure the business remained under her control stand up in the light?

She unlocked the centre and tried to give herself a pep talk. This centre was hers. She had opened it before she met Sam and named it after her parents. She had built it from nothing. It was part of her identity.

Flora was scared that once she started dipping into the Cavendish pot of money she would lose what defined her. She was also not stupid. Nothing in life came for free. She would be beholden to the Cavendish empire for the rest of her life. Cecelia would claim an input into what she did and how she did it. Up until now, she just had to secretly struggle to manage her guilt and live with the fact that this would reduce the number of children like Ethan who she could help.

In the office she was met with another three emails with the article attached. One parent had withdrawn their child, but most of the parents had known her long enough to realise that she was not a money-grabbing bitch like she was portrayed in the article. A few had sent her messages of support.

But the ones that came from money, for whom reputation was everything, would not brook the whiff of a scandal. She wondered how many more would contact her by the end of the day.

Flora's head thumped onto the table. She was unable to hold herself up under the weight pressing down on her.

She jumped when a hand gently stroked her head.

Charlotte jumped as well. 'Sorry. That's what I do to my cat and it seems to cheer him up.'

Immediately Flora's mood improved. It would have taken Charlotte a lot to touch her. She had never liked to be touched or touch other people ever since she was a child. Flora felt like her heart had grown a few inches and she just wanted to sweep Charlotte into a hug. But she didn't; instead she took some deep breaths and smiled warmly at her assistant. 'It did cheer me up. I just wasn't expecting it, that's all.'

God, I just can't catch a break, she thought. It was bad enough someone had tried to drown her in the swimming pool; now Linda was trying to ruin her reputation. Flora couldn't let that happen. People like Charlotte depended on her. She knew what she did here was a good thing. She wasn't going to let anyone tear it down.

26

Sophie walked through Flora's new house in astonishment. Considering they had only been working on the house for less than a week, it was like a whole different place. It was alive with the melodic sounds of building works and workmen covered every inch of the house, plastering, painting and sanding.

Sophie went upstairs, lugging her bag with her and trying to avoid touching anything lest she be covered in the wet paint, the smell of which was assaulting her nostrils. Entering Flora's old bedroom, she gasped. It was unrecognisable. The last time that Sophie had been in here, the pink wallpaper with white balloons on it was peeling and ripped. There was only a small bed and a bedside table that had seen better days and a wardrobe that had barely any clothes in it. Now, the room had been painted a stylish navy blue on one wall and the rest of the walls were a dazzling white. New carpet had been laid and the room felt inviting.

Sophie moved curiously over to the room that had once been Flora's Aunt Pauline's. She had never been in here; she would not have risked Pauline's wrath as it was Flora who would have suffered. There was a scruffy man in white overalls painting the back wall a gorgeous shade of green. As she entered, he downed tools and left the room. 'Coffee break,' he mumbled.

Sophie took it in and smiled. This was going to be Flora's room, then. Most of her clothes were green – why not her bedroom too?

Arms came around her and held her tightly. 'What do you think of the green?'

Sophie grinned. 'I wouldn't have expected anything else.' She turned and appraised Flora. 'You look happy, feeling hungover?'

'I felt rough this morning but nothing a day working with my kids couldn't fix.'

'Good. Feeling better about the whole article thing?'

'Yeah. Especially here. It's hard to be worried when I'm here. It's as if the house soothes me. When I'm at Sam's house, I feel so on edge. But I walk through this door and the outside world just melts away.' Flora's smile lit up the room. 'I sound silly, I know.'

Sophie's heart warmed as saw that the sparkle had returned to her friend's eyes.

'Anyway, what brings you here?' asked Flora. 'You said you needed a favour.'

Sophie's smile died. All her life, she had had to be in control. She was the one that took care of herself and her mother, made sure the bills were paid and that no one had any reason to call social services. When she had met Flora, she had assumed the mantle of responsibility for her welfare too, including getting them their own place together as soon as they could afford to. She always knew what to do, always had a clear plan or ambition to follow.

Now, though, she was completely out of her depth. It pained her to admit it, but she was scared. She did not know what the future held. And she did not know how to escape from the danger she had inadvertently put herself and Flora in. Sophie wasn't just scared, she was consumed by a stifling terror that followed her around all day, every day. She was scrabbling for a plan and that did not sit well.

'I need to ask you a favour. But I need you to not ask me any questions and just do what I ask.'

Sophie could see that Flora was swallowing back her questions. In all their time as best friends, Sophie had never asked her for anything like this. It seemed Flora understood the gravity of the situation and merely said, 'Anything.'

Pulling her bag off her shoulder, Sophie withdrew a large and heavy bin bag. She passed it to Flora, who opened it and gasped. 'Sophie, what the hell are you doing with all this money?'

'Flora, what did I say?'

'But there must be thousands of pounds in here.'

'Five hundred thousand pounds to be precise. Listen, can we find somewhere to hide this. No one can know about it. Please, don't ask me why. Just hide it, Flora. It's really, really important. Now, you need to do this quickly, I've got to go: I've got a client waiting for me.'

She walked out of the room leaving an open-mouthed Flora standing stock-still with the bag of money in her hands.

27

I t took Flora ages to get to sleep that night. They had hidden the money in one of the new kitchen units. With no furniture in the house she had had limited options as to where to hide a sack full of cash. She kept panicking that one of the builders would find it. But the kitchen had been completed so they would have no reason to go through the cupboards. *Right?*

She'd felt like a thief, panicking and trying to stash the loot before the police caught up with them. Maybe she'd move it again tomorrow. Find somewhere more secure. Questions buzzed like flies around her mind. Why on earth had Sophie given her a bag full of money? None of the reasons that she had come up with so far made sense. Unless Sophie was planning on leaving?

Flora turned over, putting a pillow over her head trying to quash the worries pervading her mind. She missed Sam – he'd been away on business in London since Monday. There was too much room in the bed, no one to wrap her arms around and keep her warm in the night, his gentle snores were always enough to soothe her. She needed that more than ever, when she managed to bat off her worries about Sophie, she was then treated to flashbacks of being held down in the pool or reminded of the humiliation of not having any money in the coffee shop. She did not know what was worse: wondering what was going to happen next or worrying about who could be doing these things to her.

Her life had gone downhill ever since she had announced they were moving. Was it Linda? Had she moved on from following her and was now trying to scare her into submission? Did she think if Flora was scared enough she would want to help Ethan just to make it stop? Flora hit the pillow in frustration. That made no sense. Nothing made sense anymore. Eventually she fell into a fitful sleep.

The cold and slime drew her back into consciousness. Her eyes were heavy with sleep. Her mind was trying to find its way back into the sweet oblivion of her dreams, but it was like there was a little person in her head urgently clawing at her, battering at her consciousness to tell her something wasn't right. That was when she felt something slick with slime making its way across her cheek. She swiped at her cheek but couldn't feel anything. Putting it down to a rather vivid dream, she turned on her side and her hand, instead of landing on the soft cotton of the duvet, fell amongst a mass of moving wet and slimy bodies.

Her eyes flew open and she looked at her hand with growing horror. In the moonlight streaming in through the gaps in the curtains she could see a mass of worms wriggling to escape her hand.

She whipped her hand away, staring in abject horror. Screaming at the top of her lungs she dived off the bed. As she moved, she realised that there had been worms on her pyjama top and one on her face. They tried to cling to her, but she flicked them off, screaming even harder. Hysterical, she pulled off her top and flung it onto the bed. It landed on the mound of glistening, twisting worms that had made their home in her bed.

Flora stood there in shock, naked to the waist, breathing hard. She kept scrubbing at her body, convinced there were more worms clinging to her. Stepping out of her pyjama bottoms she threw them on the bed and ran from the room. Her heart was racing and tears were running down her face. She was nauseous and could not escape the feeling of slimy phantom worms all over her body.

In the bathroom across the landing she got in the shower, unable to face going back into her room to use the en suite. She needed to scrub every inch of herself and get rid of the feeling of worms wriggling across her body. Half a bottle of jasmine-scented shower gel later, she finally felt clean enough. It seemed her fear of the worms had managed to help her overcome her fear of water. Her face was red raw when she looked in the mirror. Her skin burned from the vigorous scrubbing. But despite the fact her body was burned and sore from where she had scrubbed at herself repeatedly, she could still feel the wet slimy body of the worm on her cheek. Each time she blinked, she saw their cavorting bodies twisting in the sheets, clinging to her clothes. It was like a nightmare, but she knew she was awake.

Pulling a T-shirt of Sam's out of the wash basket on the landing, she made her way back to her room, fervently wishing it was all a bad dream. But she could just make out the pile of worms, spreading out more in her absence, making themselves at home. She shut the door firmly and slumped back against the wall in the landing. *What the hell?* How did hundreds of worms end up in her bed? Was this a practical joke? Was it Sam's idea of a prank?

What was she going to do about the worms? There was no

way she could go back in there. But Sam wouldn't be back until Friday. She could stay in the other bedroom. A bubble of maniacal laughter burst from her. It was so crazy. Things like this just didn't happen.

She made her way downstairs, shivering involuntarily as her body kept reliving the feel of the cold, wet worms on her skin. She picked up the house phone and stared at it. She scrolled down the list of programmed numbers, stopping at Sam's name – Cecelia's was first, obviously.

She couldn't quite make herself hit the call button. She remembered the dubious look he had given her when she told him about the incident in the swimming pool, and the way he accused her of being sensitive. Also, it was 3.35am. She could picture him, blond hair sticking up at all angles, reaching blindly for the phone, cursing violently at the person that dared to wake him at this ungodly hour. He did not do mornings, not even for her. Did this even qualify as an emergency? She didn't think so.

No, there was only one person she could call for any reason and they would always be there. Trying to take deep breaths to calm herself, Flora fumbled with the phone and dialled Sophie's mobile.

'What do you want?' asked a gruff male voice.

'Greg?'

'Yeah.'

'Where's Sophie?'

'Why?'

'I want to talk to her.' Her voice breaking in her desperation to hear Sophie's voice.

'Why?'

'I just do. Please.' She sounded so pathetic, like a child. But she had just been lying in a bed of worms. The thought made her shudder once more.

'Whatever. Don't know why you'd want to talk to that crazy bitch anyway.' Greg sounded like he had been drinking. The venom in his voice was shocking. Flora didn't know what to say. There was a crackle and then Sophie's voice came down the phone.

'Flora. What's wrong?'

'Sophie.' Flora came undone, unable to talk anymore. The terror at what had just happened had overcome her.

'Just give me a few minutes to deal with Greg and I'll be right there,' said Sophie.

'So how do you think they got in here?' Sophie asked whilst she picked up the worms with a ladle and scooped them into a bin bag. Too focused on making sure none of the worms came near her, Flora could hear Sophie's voice but could not process her words. With the light on, the worms looked more menacing, their pink and brown bodies vibrant against the bright white duvet cover. The veins on their bodies rippled as they expanded and contracted in a disgusting convulsive dance that made her chest feel tight.

'Flora, you've gone green. It's only a bunch of worms, not snakes!'

'Sorry?' Again, she wasn't really listening to Sophie. Sophie scooped up the last of the worms and shook out the duvet cover. Flora screamed and ran into the bathroom, honestly believing she would pass out if she had to experience another cold, slimy worm on her body. Flora heard Sophie moving around, then the front door closing and opening again a few minutes later.

'They're gone now!' shouted Sophie. Flora got up from the edge of the bathtub where she had been deep breathing to return her heart rate to normal. She opened the door and stuck

her head out first, needing visual confirmation before she would
risk leaving the safety of the bathroom.

'Oh come on. I've said they are gone,' snapped Sophie.

Defensive, Flora snapped back, 'You know my history with
creepy-crawlies!'

Sophie wrapped a conciliatory arm around Flora. 'I know,
but they are gone now. Sophie to the rescue, remember?'

'Okay, but can we just go downstairs? I can't stay in here
anymore.'

In the kitchen, Sophie ordered her to sit down. 'I'll make us a
drink.'

Obediently, Flora sat at the kitchen island, head in her
hands. She could hear Sophie pulling out the cups from the
cupboard and turning on the hot water tap. The cutlery drawer
opened. Sophie let out a screech, jumped backwards and hit her
back against the worktop. 'Oh my god!'

Flora jumped to her feet. Sophie was staring at the cutlery
draw in horror, hand over her mouth. Flora gingerly moved
around the island to see what Sophie could see. Inside the
drawer, there were worms crawling over the knives and forks
leaving trails of slime and crumbs of dirt in their wake.

Flora let out a scream, fled into the living room and jumped
onto the sofa. She remained standing there listening to Sophie
swearing in the kitchen.

'I'll sort it. Don't worry!' Sophie shouted through to her.

Knowing Sophie was dealing with the worms, Flora sat
down on the sofa and started rocking backwards and forwards,
trying to keep her panic in check.

She had never had a problem with creepy-crawlies until her
aunt had punished her by making her sleep in the pitch-black
attic among the spiders and mice. The whole night she was
terrorised by the feel of little legs as they scurried past her or

sometimes over her. Ever since then even money spiders had her pale and shaky.

Why the hell are there worms inside the house? Her skin crawled at the phantom slime of hundreds of worms all over her body. She was close to a mental breakdown.

Who is doing this to me?

28

Worms were disgusting creatures. She knew that every creature had a place, but worms – seriously. Ugly, pink contortionists that gave her the creeps. Sophie chucked the last of the worms into the bin. They were everywhere in the kitchen, in most of the drawers and cupboards. It was foul. She wasn't scared of them, just grossed out.

Grabbing the bin bag, she walked out of the front door and tossed it into the black bin. It reminded her of all the times she had had to clean up her mum's vomit after another drinking binge. She wasn't sure which was the more disgusting. She shuddered and went back into the house and washed her hands twice, desperate to cleanse herself of the slime and dirt she was sure was sticking to her.

She found Flora rocking backwards and forwards looking demented, her arms hugging her body, face pale and sweaty. Ever since they were young, Flora had hated bugs and creepy-crawlies. She'd freak out if an ant went near her, let alone long, slimy worms. Sophie sat down next to her and began to rub her back, making the soothing noises like she would with a baby. It worked like a charm, as always, and Flora sank into her. Sophie wrapped her arms around her.

But then Flora pulled away, frowning, her face tinged green. 'You washed your hands, right?'

'Yes, stupid. Of course I did.' She pulled Flora back into a hug and rested her head on her friend's. Every inhalation brought with it the subtle scent of jasmine. They sat there for a while, both trying to process what had just happened.

Flora spoke eventually. 'It's Cecelia, isn't it? It has to be.'

'It looks that way,' Sophie agreed.

'But how? Sam said she was away in France this week.'

'Oh, Flora.' Sophie kissed the top of her head, holding back a chuckle. It never ceased to amaze her how naïve Flora could be. 'Cecelia has a lot of money. Do you really think she wouldn't find someone to do her dirty work?'

Flora was quiet as she absorbed the fact her mother-in-law hated her enough to hire someone to torment her. 'But it just doesn't make sense. What does she think? That I am going to be scared into leaving Sam? The worms are disgusting. But not scary enough to make me want to leave. She'll have to do better than that.'

They sat in companionable silence, Sophie slowly stroking her hair. She could feel Flora start to unclench and relax. 'Do you think we should go to the police?' asked Sophie eventually.

'And tell them what? Excuse me, mister policeman, someone put worms on my face and in my bed and I didn't like it,' answered Flora sarcastically. 'They will think that I am crazy.'

'You don't know that. Anyway, it's not just the fact that there were worms. It's also the fact someone broke into the house.'

'But did they, though? There is no sign of a break-in. So, it must be someone with a key. I know we think it is Cecelia, but I can't very well go reporting my mother-in-law to the police.

What would Sam think?' Flora sat up quickly. 'That's it. That's what she wants. She thinks she can either scare me so that I'll leave. Or that I'll go to the police and accuse her and it will destroy my marriage. I bet that is what she is banking on.' Flora got up and began to pace up and down the room. Restless energy exuded from her. 'Well, she isn't going to win, Sophie. I won't let her. She thinks she has the upper hand but two can play at that game. I am going to move house with Sam and I'll do everything I can to cut the strings between us. It's time Sam became a grown man and started to focus on his future with me. These petty games aren't going to accomplish anything. I won't let her win.'

Sophie was shocked to see her normally quiet and sensitive friend growing a spine before her very eyes. Flora was holding herself stronger and taller than she ever had before. The transformation was breathtaking.

If only it wasn't too late.

Flora had no idea what was coming for them both. That the danger was a lot worse than a bunch of worms.

29

October was her favourite month. Sophie sat in the car and watched the window blowing the branches of the barren trees. A few brown wilted leaves brushed the floor on their journey to decomposition. It was such an atmospheric time of year. The wind was cleansing and sharp in contrast to overheated houses and offices. It was the time of year you could wrap yourself up in layers but still enjoy the refreshing blasts of cold air that made you feel alive. Sophie loved it.

When she used to live with Flora, they loved those months. They spent days watching old movies on Freeview and drinking cheap sachets of hot chocolate that they would kid themselves tasted just like a Costa. They'd take walks in the park, huddled together, crunching their way through the fallen leaves of brilliant yellows and oranges, feeling red-faced and happy.

Sophie was waiting for Flora in the car. They were going out for dinner, determined to cheer themselves up after the stress of the last few days. It was cold in the car as the small heaters tried to tackle the frosty chill in the air. Luckily, the seat warmers were quick, and the back of her body was nice and warm. Anything was better than the frosty atmosphere in the house. The rage in Greg's voice was still ringing in her ears.

Flora opened the door to the BMW and Sophie was hit with a blast of cold air that took her breath away. 'Sorry! Sorry!'

'You look tired.'

'Oh, thanks. Hello to you too.'

Sophie didn't laugh: the dark circles under Flora's eyes and the redness around her eyes worried her. 'Did you sleep at all last night?'

'Not really. I just couldn't settle, I just kept feeling like there were worms on me every time I closed my eyes.' Flora wiped at her face as if brushing off a phantom worm. 'It was awful. I haven't had a night like that since–' Flora stopped and looked down at her lap. 'Since Prague,' she continued quietly, looking steadfastly at her lap and fiddling with a tassel of her cream scarf.

The first time either of them had left the country was supposed to be the best time of their lives. Sophie had persuaded her boss at the shop she worked at in the evenings that everyone deserved a Christmas bonus and she insisted on spending the money on a holiday for the two of them. She even got enough money for their passports.

They had settled on Prague, seduced by promises of magical river cruises and snow-capped buildings with quaint little pubs and restaurants. Plus, Ryanair had a sale on flights which gave them money left over for spending when they were there. Flora had been shaking by the time they got there. The security at the airport had traumatised her. Sophie had laughed at Flora's face: she looked so guilty going through, like she was expecting to be arrested any minute. But the minute they landed in Prague, they had dumped their suitcases in their Airbnb and almost ran into the city centre.

It was just before Christmas and Wenceslas Square was alive

with festive spirit so an explosion of colour assaulted their eyes. Every building was adorned with fairy lights. Golden lights twinkled in the night sky. The artificial lights bathed the tall buildings and enhanced their majesty. The smell of charcoal and chocolate was thick in the air. There were people everywhere bustling between the different stalls, but there was not a miserable face in sight. Sophie had to drag Flora away from a collection of hand-painted Christmas baubles after fifteen minutes of her standing there awe-struck.

They repelled the cold with a cup of velvety smooth hot chocolate and soaked up the gorgeous scenery around them. When they reached the Christmas tree near the famous clock, they both stopped and stared. There were no words, only pure joy as they watched the tree's light display matched to the Christmas song from *Home Alone*. It was magical.

That first night was perfect. The next day even better. They walked five miles to a cat café. Then they did the traditional tourist stuff, walking over Charles Bridge. Flora had once read a book called *A Year and a Day* which included a legend that if you touched a specific part of the bridge and made a wish, it would come true a year and a day later. Flora had waited patiently, but Sophie refused. She already had everything she needed.

There wasn't an inch of Prague they didn't explore. They walked for miles, stopping to look at the John Lennon wall and all the padlocks on the bridge. They left an engraved padlock on Charles Bridge inscribed with the words Sophie and Flora 2009. Everything was perfect until they stopped at a bar to try some chocolate beer. Sophie relenting on her lifelong drinking ban to try a sip. It was disgusting and not worth the extortionate price.

No matter how many times she revisited the moment in her head, she never figured out exactly why she had needed to follow Flora to the bathroom. Sophie was supposed to be watching their drinks at their table, but she had been compelled to follow Flora.

What she had found would forever haunt her memories. At first, she could not process what she was seeing. A greasy, brown-haired man was pushing Flora up against the wall in the corridor leading to the bathrooms. One hand was restraining Flora's neck, pinning her to the wall. The other was roaming around trying to undo her trousers. 'Last Christmas' was blasting out from the speakers in the pub, drowning out Flora's pleas for help. She was scratching at the man's hand, trying to break free. Without thinking, Sophie turned and ran back to the bar. Her heart thudding in her chest, she could barely breathe.

Spotting an empty pint glass, she grabbed it and raced back to Flora. Flora's top was now ripped, and the man was gyrating against her. His clothes were dirty and stained, his hair dishevelled and matted. Tears streamed down Flora's face, her eyes closed against the terror of what was happening.

Without thinking about what she was going to do, Sophie brought the glass down on the man's head. All of her strength went into her swing and he crumpled to the floor. She looked at the glass, it was mottled with blood. In her shock, she let go and watched as it bounced onto the floor and rolled away, fleeing the scene.

Flora slid down the wall hyperventilating and rubbing her neck.

Sophie stepped over the man and pulled Flora to her. 'It's okay,' she soothed, rocking Flora gently. Her fury at the man was unbridled. If she wasn't holding Flora together, she would have turned around and kicked the man until he no longer resembled a human being. Any minute, someone would come around the bar and down the corridor. She didn't want to have to explain what had happened. Who knows what the law was in this country? They needed to leave. Gathering Flora up, she helped her to her feet, and they walked quickly out of the pub, stopping to grab their coats on the way.

Back at their flat. Flora fell to pieces. Her neck was a violent shade of red and she kept clawing at it as if the man's hand was still there. They didn't leave the apartment again until their flight home the next day.

It had taken many months for Flora to 'deal' with what happened to her. They had never talked about it again. Just day by day, Flora returned to her normal self. Sophie wanted to talk about it. Sometimes she could still hear the sickening thud of the glass against the man's head. But she would not cause Flora suffering by forcing her to relive one of the most traumatic moments of her life. After all, Flora was the one who had been violated in the worst possible way. Even though he had not got far, he had still made her feel powerless and terrified. Just the thought that it could have happened was as traumatic as the action itself.

Sophie had squashed her need to talk and was slowly getting better at locking away the whole thing. It went on a shelf in her mind, where the other secrets were stored, locked in boxes that would shake and jump around as the contents fought to be released from their prison.

'I can imagine. Do you want to talk about it?' asked Sophie, hoping that this was the moment she would finally get to expunge the ghost of the man from her mind and hear the vindication she so desperately needed.

'No. I don't ever want to think about that again.' Flora shuddered and looked out of the window. 'Shall we go, then?'

Inside, Sophie screamed with disappointment. She glanced in the rear-view mirror to ensure that her face was devoid of emotion. She boxed up her feelings and all the words she had been planning to say and put it back up on the shelf with all the other boxes. She was getting quite the collection.

Flora spent the whole of the journey and dinner talking about their new house. Sophie tried to seem interested but inside, she was still trying to ignore the shaking boxes in the recesses of her mind. She was emotionally drained. The fight with Greg before she had left was ferocious. It was hard trying to keep control, prevent things from escalating, and it was getting harder to predict his moods and his actions. Her whole life was exhausting.

Trying to shake off her negativity, she focused on Flora and attempted to absorb some of her positivity. But even this did not help. Flora had no idea what was really going on. She lived in a fantasy world; and her bad mood made her less forgiving. After all, they were both in danger because of her stupid decisions. Thanks to Flora, Sophie was working tirelessly behind the scenes to fix everything, trying to guarantee their safety.

Flora seemed to sense Sophie's mood as she took her hand and squeezed it. The feel of her friend's affection melted away the dark clouds that were consuming her. Flora was like the sun that way. Her sensitivity and kindness could light up the world when it felt oppressive and dark. Sophie smiled and squeezed Flora's hand back.

'You are my best friend, Soph. Spending time with you, it's like you're my reset button. Everything builds up and feels overwhelming. Then I spend time with you and it all goes away.'

Sophie flushed with pleasure, blinking away the tears that pricked her eyes. 'Stop being so slushy. I don't remember you saying such nice things to me when I accidentally lost your S Club 7 CD all those years ago.'

'Oh god. Do you remember all those routines we used to perform to my parents to S Club 7. Mortifying.'

'For you maybe. I happen to be a great dancer.' Sophie began to wave her hands above her head, dancing to imaginary music.

They spent the rest of the night reminiscing about their childhood, then their university days.

Not for the first time, she felt guilty that she had engineered the direction that their lives had taken, they had been broke; but they had been safe. Now, they had the real possibility of their lives crumbling around them.

Sophie leaned over the table to smooth back the errant bit of hair that always fell in front of Flora's face and tucked it behind her ear. Flora sniggered as usual, used to the gesture and amused that Sophie couldn't cope with unruly hair. Flora's laughter was a balm to her soul. It made her all the more determined to ensure that her friend laughed like that for the rest of her life. It was the least she deserved and she would do whatever it took.

30

Justin was running around the room naked. Typically, he was a quiet, shy boy which was why it had caught Flora by surprise when she looked over to find him naked in the corner of the room, scratching at his skin. He saw her move towards him and began to run around in circles. As he was younger and faster than her, she was struggling to catch him.

'No, too itchy. No clothes.'

Many people with autism find their senses are easily overwhelmed, and a common trigger is clothing. Certain types of material can overload the senses and cause considerable distress and anxiety. Justin ran towards the clothes he'd piled on the floor, swiping a bottle of paint from the side as he went. Before Flora could reach him, the clothes were doused in a startling blue paint. In soothing tones, Flora eventually convinced him to come into the back room where she had some clothes that would not itch him. Justin's parents insisted he wore Ralph Lauren polo T-shirts despite the fact he could not tolerate the fabric. She had tried to broach the subject sensitively, but it had fallen on deaf ears. They were the type of people that could afford to buy a whole shop full of Ralph

Lauren polo shirts and so they just replaced the ones Justin destroyed.

She could not decide if it was a relief or not when the day was over. She was sporting a scratch down the side of her face and her arms ached from holding Alicia tightly to her to calm her down when she began to lash out at everything around her. It was not her fault: having autism meant that Alicia perceived the world differently, and the sound of one of the other girls dropping a cup on the laminate flooring had overwhelmed her. Instead of crying, or withdrawing like some of the children, Alicia would become angry and violent as she struggled to regulate her emotions. But Flora had managed to calm her down and only received a scratch in the process. She had experienced a lot worse. Besides, it had distracted her from thinking about Cecelia.

She had told Sam over the phone about the worms. Not having seen it, it was obvious he could not understand the gravity of it and how awful it was to wake up to find worms on her body. It was like he thought of it like a practical joke. She tried to explain to him, make him see the reality of the situation.

'Sam, don't you realise that for someone to have put worms in my bed whilst I was sleeping. They must have been in the house. They were standing over me whilst I slept.' Tears choked her and no amount of reassurance from Sam that they would *get to the bottom of it* would stem her fear. It didn't help that her constant anxiety was chasing away any chance of sleeping through the night.

Despite her decision not to let Cecelia get her down, as much as she told herself that she could handle whatever her mother-in-law threw at her, Flora was freaked out. She was on edge all the time, as if waiting for Cecelia's next move. Flora had not voiced this to Sam. There was no point. He would not entertain the idea that his mother was behind any of this. But didn't he see that she was the only one who would want to drive a wedge between them; that his mother was the only one evil enough to try and torment her?

Taking a deep breath, Flora tried to regain some of her determination from last night. *I will not let Cecelia win*, she thought, repeating this over and over like a mantra whilst she set to cleaning up.

Clearing up the mess left from the class was one of her favourite parts of the job. It gave her a chance to spend time looking at the creations of the children. Today, Andre had created a picture of his dog using different coloured materials. At the moment, Andre was non-verbal, and his parents weren't even sure how much he could understand. She could not wait to show his mother, Sandra, this picture when it was finished. Across the top, he had written 'Max' in large spidery writing. His first word. Swiping the tears from her eyes she continued around the room, collecting up the work and moving them carefully to the storage cupboards that lined one of the walls. Each class had a cupboard where she could store their projects until the following week.

Giving the room a last once-over, she checked for anything she could have missed. Something twinkled on the floor under one of the tables. Climbing under the table, she reached out and found it was a silver chain. She held it up to the light. Recognition stole her breath away. She stared at the silver necklace, stunned. Hanging from the silver chain was a heart-shaped pendant. It was just possible to see the 'R' engraved on the front of the heart. The 'R' stood for Rebecca. Her mother. With trembling hands, she lowered the heart onto the palm of her hand, gently caressing the 'R'. She did not know how long she sat on the floor. Tears welled from deep inside and coursed down her face.

During her bouts of insomnia, caused by the anxiety she had

been through in the last week, she would stare at her parents' faces on Sam's canvas, trying to focus on them instead of her turbulent emotions. On the canvas, it was possible to see every detail of her mother's necklace. It was an exact match for the one she was holding in her hand. The only reason she knew it wasn't her mother's was that this one was newer and shinier, whereas her mother's had been tarnished with scratches as she had worn it every day without fail.

Flora remembered asking the social worker who came to see her shortly after her parents' death where her mum's necklace was, as she would have been wearing it in the accident. She never took it off. Eventually, the harassed social worker had looked into it. 'I'm sorry, dear, it seems it got destroyed along with everything else when your parents' car caught fire after the accident.'

It was only then that Flora turned the necklace around. On the back, a word had been crudely scratched into the silver surface. 'Flora'.

31

The weather was awful. October was no longer her favourite month anymore, Sophie decided as she opened her door and was instantly slapped in the face with droplets of cold rain. It had been relentless all day and it made her mood plummet. The wind and rain battered her fiercely as she crossed the car park and entered the garden centre. It was only Flora she loved enough to leave the house for in this torrential weather.

Sophie preferred to eat in more sophisticated establishments, but Flora would insist on living off her meagre wage from the centre which meant she could not afford to dine anywhere expensive. A meal at Sophie and Greg's favourite restaurant would probably amount to the same as Flora earned in a month. She could not understand why Flora would not want to treat herself every once in a while. Did she not remember all the times they would share a 99p cone of chips from the local chippy because that was the only place they could to afford to eat? To be fair, those chips had tasted like luxury compared to their staple diet of pasta and rice. Still, the breakfast was quite nice here so she would tolerate it. There wasn't anything she wouldn't do for Flora.

Sophie spotted Flora sitting at one of the tables in the café. Once again, Flora was holding the necklace in her hands, absent-mindedly rubbing at it with her fingers. She was still wearing the same cream jumper and blue jeans she'd had on last night, albeit more creased. Her face was gaunt, her cheekbones seemed more prominent than usual. When she looked up at Sophie, her thin smile no longer met her eyes, which were dull and expressionless. Her pale skin made the dark circles under her eyes all the more pronounced and her eyelids were swollen and puffy. She looked more like the Flora Sophie had known as a child, the one still reeling from her parents' death. But it was completely understandable: seeing a locket that looked exactly like your late mother's would disturb even the strongest of people.

Yesterday she had received a gibberish voicemail from a distraught Flora. Sophie had raced straight over to find her in the kitchen drinking a glass of red wine. The bottle was already half empty and she spied another one in the recycling. A necklace was on the table and Flora explained that it was just like the one her mother used to wear. Her voice was robotic, like she was devoid of emotion. After finishing the whole bottle of wine, Flora had cried herself to sleep in Sophie's arms, the grief of losing her parents as fresh as ever. Sam hovering in the background as useful as a chocolate fireguard.

Sophie took a deep breath and sat down at the café table. She tried to ready herself for another conversation that would just go around in circles. *Who knew that my mother wore this locket, Sophie? Why was the locket on the floor in my centre? How did it get there?*

Sure enough, an hour later, Flora was still clutching the necklace and glaring at it as if begging it to give up its secrets. She looked like a woman possessed. Her hair was sticking out at odd angles as she repeatedly ran her hands through it. 'I mean, the only way someone could know about this locket was if they were in my room looking at the photo of my mum. But why would someone do that? How cruel do you have to be?'

She put her head in her hands, exhausted by the questions.

Sophie did not answer as there was nothing that she could say that she had not said already. At first, Flora had theorised that maybe it was Cecelia. But there was no way she could have got in the centre without Flora seeing. Could she?

Sophie felt sick to her stomach as she looked into her friend's bloodshot eyes. Alarm coursed through her: she had never seen Flora like this.

Flora jumped up, peering at something over Sophie's shoulder. Sophie was about to look behind her when Flora shouted at the top of her voice, 'Linda!'

Flora had dashed away from the table before Sophie had even processed what she had said. *Linda?*

Rushing after Flora, she bumped and pushed her way around people milling around the store, trying to keep Flora in sight. She caught sight of Flora's brown hair whipping around an aisle containing gourmet pet food. Increasing her speed, she was just in time to see Flora running out of the shop into the car park. Sophie followed, for the second time that day an onslaught of rain hit her in the face, driving her breath from her body. It was like she had jumped into the ocean and she was soaked through instantly. Pushing her wet hair out of her eyes she scanned the car park looking for Flora.

She was standing in the middle of the car park, hands on her head slowly rotating on the spot. Searching for something. 'Flora. What's going on?' Sophie reached out and put her hand gently on Flora's shoulder, turning her to face her.

'She was here!'

'Who was?'

'LINDA!'

Sophie tried to stop shivering but the rain was dripping down the collar of her blouse sending icy trails of water down her back. 'Come inside, we are both getting soaked.' Sophie pulled Flora forcibly by the arm, back into the shelter of the garden centre. People looked at them perplexed. She could hear what they were thinking. *What sort of nutters go outside in weather like this without a coat?*

'Sophie, Linda was in the garden centre. She was watching us.' Flora looked around again, still trying to find Linda. She turned back and gripped Sophie's arms so tightly it hurt and looked at her beseechingly. 'You saw her, right?'

'Flora, calm down.' People were shooting them curious looks. Taking Flora by the hand she led her back to their table. Thankfully their coats and bags were still there. Sophie guided Flora back to her seat and sat down herself and held Flora's hand across the table. They were both dripping rain onto the table, dampening napkins. 'Come on. You said that you weren't going to let Cecelia win. You need to pull yourself together.'

'I know. I just feel like I'm losing it. I never know what is going to happen next. Now... seeing Linda. Following me. I just can't handle it.' Fresh tears joined the raindrops trickling down Flora's face. She picked up a slightly damp napkin and dabbed gently. Flora closed her eyes and leaned into the contact, letting it soothe her.

'Well, maybe you should leave,' said Sophie.

Flora's eyes flew open. 'What?'

'Well, you can't go on like this. You just said you can't handle it. So, let's leave.'

'I can't.'

'Why not?'

'I'm not leaving Sam. My centre.'

'You can set up a new centre. And remember, it might be

Sam's mum that is doing this to you. To us. Is he really worth all this?'

Flora's mouth opened and closed with shock. 'Ye– yes. I am not leaving Sam. There is nothing that would make me leave him.'

Sophie said nothing.

Flora's eyes darted around the room. She seemed to be having a debate with herself. She wiped her face and sat up straight. 'You're right, Soph. I need to get a grip. Cecelia is not going to chase me away.' She gripped the necklace again, as if channelling it for strength.

Sophie watched in admiration. Flora would allow herself a brief window in which to break down but no matter what was thrown at her, she'd find a way to get through it, to find a positive and not let her fear win.

Little did she know, she would need that resilience for what was to come. They both would.

32

The table was set beautifully as usual. Candelabras sparkled gold in the light, the white candles giving off a delicate glow. Each setting had a gold napkin shaped into a swan. The aroma coming from the kitchens was tantalising. Alistair's watch was reflecting the light, creating a patch of rainbow on the wall. Sophie focused on that instead of looking at him. He was discussing business strategy with Greg. Sam tried to interject every now and then, but it was clear Alistair had no interest in his opinion. Sophie found it amusing that Sam knew what it felt like to be dismissed and put down by his father but did not see his own mother do the same thing to Flora.

Flora was staring down at her lap, unable to look at anyone around the table. Her face was pale and sad, and Sophie's heart ached at the sight. She hated to see Flora this desolate. It made her even more determined to get her away from this toxic family.

Sam took Flora's hand and squeezed it. He looked at Flora with such affection and love that it brought a lump to Sophie's throat. If only his actions were as authentic as how he looked at Flora. Then maybe things would be different.

As an experiment, she grabbed Greg's hand in hers. He looked at her irritably, momentarily drawn from his conversation with his father. Then he shook her off and resumed his conversation.

'Is everything all right, Flora?'

Flora's head shot up. There was warmth in Cecelia's voice, and it appeared that she was genuinely concerned. Flora's face was the picture of shock and she looked lost for words.

Before Sophie could speak, Sam answered his mother. 'Flora's been having a difficult time, Mother. Someone has been harassing her.'

'Really? Whatever has been happening?'

'We don't know, but we think some of it is to do with this lady called Linda. She came to a taster session trying to persuade Flora to let her son attend classes for free as she couldn't afford to pay. She has been following Flora ever since. But there have been a couple of weird incidents that we can't explain – that couldn't possibly be Linda. It's like someone is trying to scare her. Isn't it, Sophie?' Sam looked at Sophie waiting for her to join in the conversation.

'Yes, it appears that way. I was over at Flora's house and someone had put worms in her bed and all the cupboards and drawers. It was horrifying.'

Cecelia looked momentarily stunned and then began to chuckle. 'Worms in your house. My dear, have you lost your mind? Why on earth would someone put worms in your house?'

'It's true. I saw them, I had to clear up the horrible things. It was vile. Why would we make that up?'

Cecelia appeared thoughtful. 'But how would... this Linda... have got in the house? How strange.' Cecelia seemed to be trying very hard to hide a smile. Apparently, she was amused at the thought of someone tormenting Flora.

Sophie took her chance. 'Exactly. It would have to be someone with a key. We just have to work out who we know that would want to see Flora scared and upset, that also has a key to the house.'

Sophie looked pointedly at Cecelia. Everyone's eyes were on Sophie. Even Greg and Alistair had stopped their conversation and were watching intently. 'Do you know anyone that would want to scare Flora and make her think she was going crazy?'

Flora's mouth had dropped open. The eyes of everyone at the table were burning into her skin. But Sophie only had eyes for Cecelia.

Cecelia's face was blank. She didn't falter for one second, only stared back at Sophie with steely, unblinking eyes. 'No, I can't think of anyone.' She turned to Flora. 'Poor Flora. This must be awful for you.'

Sophie had to admit it, Cecelia was a good actor: she almost sounded sincere.

'You just need to ignore this Linda woman. Pathetic, honestly. Scum of the earth some people, expecting other people to pay their way. Bring back the workhouses, I say. Of course, this Linda has probably realised how emotional you are and decided to manipulate that. A proper businesswoman would not be intimidated by such tactics.' Cecelia must have seen Sam's face as she added; 'Not that I'm not sympathetic. It must be difficult to be forced to deal with someone like her.'

'She's just trying to help her son. It's not her fault she can't afford the classes. Being poor doesn't make her a bad person,' said Flora angrily, her face flushed red.

'Well, whose fault is it? We make our own fortunes in life, dear. Anyway, why are you defending her? I thought she was making your life hell.'

'It's not just her, though, is it. Someone else has access to my house.' Flora's voice was high-pitched and trembling. 'Someone is trying to drive me crazy and scare me. I just don't know why or who.' Flora was trying her best not to cry. Everyone around the table seemed unsure where to look and the silence was uncomfortable. Sophie wondered if Flora was going to carry on and tell them about the swimming pool and the necklace; but she seemed to have shocked herself with her outburst.

'I can't deny the whole thing is very strange,' said Cecelia. 'But I don't know why you are scared. Putting worms in someone's house is child's play. If someone really wanted to scare you, they'd do much worse than that.'

'It sounds scary to me... The thought that someone had been in my house and put these creatures in it,' added Alistair.

Cecelia looked flustered. 'Yes, I suppose I'd feel very vulnerable if it had happened to me. No wonder poor Flora is so pale.'

Sophie looked at Alistair with disdain. His fake sympathy filled her with rage. It made her even angrier to see Flora give him a small smile of gratitude. She kept quiet, not trusting herself to speak.

'Is there anything we can do, Sam? I can have some of our security team dispatched to your house,' continued Alistair.

Sam looked gratefully at his father. 'That might be a good idea. Although, I'm not planning on going away for a while so hopefully everything will settle down now.'

Typical. If only they'd known from the beginning how to stop Flora from being tormented was to have Sam around. He seemed to forget the fact that someone tried to drown Flora in the swimming pool and had broken into her centre to plant a necklace and he wasn't away when those things happened. No, the only way to save Flora was to leave this place. Leave and never come back. Sophie fidgeted in her chair, unable to get comfortable, swallowing back a wince. The dining room chairs were impressive, with gold figures carved into each of the backs, perfect for preventing people from slouching or being comfortable. A bow and arrow belonging to what looked like a golden cherub was digging into her back, stabbing at the bruise that engulfed her torso, slowly blackening with each day that passed.

33

All the way home, Flora's mind whirled. She was brimming with all the things she should have said. She had been so close, there couldn't have been a more perfect opportunity to confront Cecelia. But she had been a coward. She had felt the eyes of everyone around the table on her, burning into her like laser beams. It was on the tip of her tongue. 'I think it was you, Cecelia. I think you've been doing this to me.'

She visualised what she should have done in her mind. She should have got the necklace from her bag and slammed it on the table in front of Cecelia. She should have stood over her and yelled at her. Asked her why she would get a replica of her dead mother's necklace and then scratch her name on it. What sort of sick person was she? Did she have no soul? Everyone would be shocked and disgusted and finally see Cecelia for the cruel, vindictive person she was.

But Flora had not done that. The only thing she had done was tell everyone that someone put worms in her house. When she had said it aloud it sounded ridiculous. She was surprised no one carted her off to the looney bin. She would have checked herself in had it not been for the fact Sophie had stuck up for her and confirmed her story.

Cecelia's behaviour troubled Flora. Cecelia had a key to their house and they both knew that she had made threats because Flora was going to take her favourite son away. But she had genuinely seemed shocked and confused about the worms. To be fair, it didn't sound like something Cecelia would have even thought to do. Sophie reckoned that Cecelia had hired someone, given them the key. But still... pain lanced through her head as the unanswered questions attacked her mind, causing a tension headache. At the end of the meal, Cecelia had ordered Reginald to contact Sam to discuss setting up a security detail at not only their house but at Flora's centre. Would she have done this if she was behind everything? Was the offer just for show?

'Oi, you, come back from la-la land.' Sam chuckled.

'I'm sorry. Can I ask you something?'

'Of course.' He took Flora's hand and kissed the back of it. Flutters of desire coursed through her, which she suppressed.

'What do you really think is happening? Do you have any idea why these things are happening to me?'

Sam sighed deeply. He didn't answer straight away. She was about to ask him if he was okay when finally he spoke. 'Honestly, Flora. I have theories, each wilder than the next. I just think we need to focus on moving into our new home. I know it has been a really stressful time, but we will get through this. Together.'

It warmed her heart to know that Sam was as bewildered as she was. It made her feel less alone. She fingered the necklace in her purse. There was no doubt someone was trying to upset her, scare her. It might be Cecelia. It might be someone else. But as long as she had Sam and Sophie, she knew she could face anything. Her parents would not want her to be a quivering wreck. They wouldn't want her to play the victim, they would want her to stay strong. She would not let whoever it was trying to play stupid mind games ruin any more of her life.

34

'Where do you think you are going?' asked Greg. He was blocking the door with his ogre-like frame. Blond hair stuck up in all directions making him appear crazed and intimidating.

Sophie had her hands full with the Amazon parcel and could not easily get around him or try and push him out of the way. 'I'm going around to Flora's. I've got something for her.'

'Oh no. No, you aren't. We need to talk.'

'Seriously, Greg. Just move out of the way. We can talk later.'

'No. I want to talk now.' He moved towards her and she took the advantage and darted nimbly around and behind him before he could process what she'd done. One of the advantages of being married to a mountain man was that he was slower than her. She hefted the parcel onto her left hip and grabbed the door with her right hand.

'Please, Sophie. I can't do this anymore. You need to talk to me.' He sounded so pathetic. So far from the man she had once known.

'Soph?' Flora called out.

Once again, the benefit of living next door to her best friend showed itself. 'Flora's waiting for me,' she told Greg. 'We can talk later.'

Following Flora into her house, Sophie breathed heavily under the weight of the parcel.

'What's this big surprise?' Flora asked.

Sophie heaved the box onto the kitchen island. 'Well, open it and find out,' she said in a sing-song voice.

Flora's pale face brightened slightly. She tore into the box and then looked up at Sophie slightly disappointed. 'What is it?'

'A home surveillance system.' Sophie moved over and pointed to the pictures on the back of the box. 'See, there are eight small cameras that you can put around the house. They're really discreet so no one will know they are there. It's the best one available on Amazon.'

'I don't understand.'

'Well, it streams the footage to your phone. This way, we will find out who is coming into the house and get to the bottom of all this.' Sophie bit her lip and hesitated. 'There's one thing I want you to do that you aren't going to like.'

Flora put the box down and look up at her warily. 'Why do I not like the sound of that?'

'I don't think you should tell Sam about the cameras.'

'What? Why not?' asked Flora, incredulous.

'Let me finish.' She placed a placatory hand on Flora's arm. 'I know you want to tell him. But think about it: we don't know who is doing this and finding out is the most important thing. It could be Sam for all we know.'

Flora laughed derisively. 'Don't be so ridiculous, Sophie.'

'I said it could be, not that it was. Look, even if it isn't him, he could tell someone else about the cameras and then they would know what we were doing.'

Flora nodded grudgingly. 'I suppose.'

'It will be fine. It's only temporary and then we can take

them down.' Sophie took Flora's hands. She tucked a disobedient lock of Flora's hair back behind her ears. 'I love you and I'll do whatever it takes to protect you and sort this mess out.'

Sophie turned to the box and began to open it. 'Right, where shall we put them?'

It turned out to be a fun morning. Flora held the ladders whilst Sophie got up close and personal with the ceilings and shelving in the house. 'What would Cecelia say, dearest Flora,' choked Sophie when she inhaled yet another gulp of dust. It took them ages to hook up the cameras to the app. But by the time they were done Flora had a broad smile on her face, just as Sophie had intended. She didn't want the day to end, but they both had to go to work. She couldn't avoid Greg forever. Not for the last time, she wished she could close her eyes and rewind time to the days before her marriage had disintegrated. When the world around her glowed and everything was exciting because she was in love and had finally found a home. But there was no going back. Happiness in the Cavendish family was just an illusion.

Sophie rubbed at her temples, feeling a migraine brewing. It made the journey to work even harder, blurring her vision as the pain in her head became insistent. It was so draining, trying to put a brave face on for Flora. All she wanted to do was just grab her and run. She could explain everything once they had escaped somewhere safe. But she had to be cleverer than that. She had to duck and dive and gradually edge her way out of the tangled web that belonged to the Cavendish family. If she moved too quickly or made too much noise, she would be entangled for ever, a victim for the Cavendish family to devour at their leisure.

35

It was turning into an obsession. Every few minutes she tapped her phone to life and opened up the camera app. She toggled through the different views, her nerves settling with each swipe of her finger. There was no one in the house.

It had taken all her willpower not to mention the cameras to Sam. So many times, it had been on the tip of her tongue to tell him. Deception did not come naturally to her. The lie was filling her up until she was bursting from the seams. She prided herself on never having lied to Sam their entire relationship. It hurt that that would no longer be the case.

She was lying in their spare room. Flora couldn't face their own bed unless Sam was there. It was only his presence that could stop her thinking about the worms in their bed. When he was there, she could wrap her arms around his chest so that she felt only soft, warm skin and this would stop her imagining the cold, wet bodies of the squirming creatures. Without him, she was unable to sleep, plagued by the smell of dirt and convinced if she closed her eyes, someone would come back and put worms in her bed once more. He had said he wasn't going to go anywhere again but she had overheard Sam on the phone to a client, trying to explain why he couldn't be there for the launch. She felt so bad that it was her fear stopping him from being there. Flora had laid a hand on his arm and he'd turned to look at her. 'Just go, honey. I promise. I'll be fine.'

Covering his phone with his hand, he looked unsure. 'I don't think I should. It's not safe.'

'I'll be fine. I'll have Sophie. We can't just put our lives on hold.'

'Only if you are sure. I am only going for one night though.'

Starting to drift to sleep, Flora heard the front door open. She knew it was the front door as she could hear the familiar dragging as it crossed the welcome mat she had bought. *Friends welcome, relatives by appointment.* She had only bought it because she knew 'tacky' things like that drove Cecelia mad.

Was Sam back? Surely, he'd have told her if he was going to be back early. He'd have shouted out, wouldn't he? Maybe he had but she could not hear him over her heartbeat racing frantically in her ear. Flora wanted to call out, to check if it was him, but her fear silenced her.

Slam.

The front door slammed shut and she jumped, her phone falling from her hand. Grabbing it off the floor, she lunged toward the bathroom, locking the door behind her. For the first time, she was grateful that all the bedrooms had en suite bathrooms. Turning on the mirror light, she winced as her eyes adjusted to the brightness. Unlocking her iPhone, she stabbed at the camera app. The first picture was of the front door from the inside. There was no one there. She was about to switch to the next camera when the light went out, plunging the room into darkness. The only light was from the glow of her phone.

Looking down at the screen, the app showed an error message where there had previously been a live feed of the front door.

Cameras disconnected, please check your wifi.

Her phone was no longer connected to the wifi either. *Someone has cut the power to the house*, she thought. Irrationally, she ran to the window, even though she knew she could not jump from it, it was far too high. The window was textured for privacy and the yellow light of the street light was fractured by the pattern, but Flora was sure a black figure was walking down her driveway, away from the house. With shaky hands and a feeling of déjà vu, she called Sophie.

It didn't take long for her to hear the key in the front door, the scraping of the welcome mat and the bang of the front door. But this time there was no sinister silence.

'Flora?'

Flora didn't answer, her teeth were chattering, and she was trying really hard to hold it together. This was one time too many that she was sitting in the bathroom feeling vulnerable and frightened. Why was this happening to her? She wasn't a bad person. Did Cecelia hate her that much? Was it definitely Cecelia? The unanswered questions were overwhelming her. The light came back on, startling her.

Hearing Sophie's footsteps on the staircase, she unlocked the door and ran from the room, meeting her friend just as she breasted the staircase. Flora flung herself into her arms. 'I can't take it anymore, Sophie,' she cried. 'I'm so scared all the time.'

'Shh, shh,' soothed Sophie, holding her tightly and stroking her hair. 'It's okay, it's okay. It's all going to be okay.'

Flora let herself be led to the spare room. 'How did you know I was sleeping in here?'

'Well, first of all, I know you. Second of all, Sam's not here. Third of all, wait that doesn't sound right. Thirdly?' She nodded. 'Yes, thirdly, I don't think I'd be sleeping in a bed that had worms in it for a very long time. I would have burnt the bed, to be honest, but that's just me.'

They cuddled up in bed and the fear that had gripped Flora so tightly started to release its hold.

'Now you've calmed down do you want to tell me what happened?'

Flora pulled herself from Sophie's arms and rested her head on the headboard. Exhaustion pulled at her: being terrified was extremely draining. 'I don't really know. I heard the front door open. Then it slammed shut. Then the power went out.'

'Didn't you see who it was on the cameras?'

'No. They cut the power to the house so they stopped working. Someone was in the house again, Sophie.' Her fear, never far away now, rose up once more. The futility of her situation brought her to tears. She was at a loss as to what to do.

'I think we should call the police,' said Sophie.

'Not now. I'm not ready for that. I can't think straight. I just want to sleep and then talk about it tomorrow when I'm not exhausted. You'll stay with me, right?'

'Of course I will. I'm going to ring Sam. He needs to come back home. He said he wasn't going to leave you again.' Sophie's face clouded with anger.

'That was my fault. I told him to go.'

Sophie went into the other room and Flora could hear her voice muffled through the walls. She hoped Sophie wasn't being rude to Sam. He really hadn't wanted to leave her, she had insisted.

What was she thinking, encouraging Sam to go away when the last time had ended so badly? Look at what her determination not to let fear run her life had done. It had literally left the door wide open for someone to scare her more. Flora tried hard to fight the fatigue that was drawing her eyelids together, but the fog of sleep was descending.

Flora woke up the next morning with Sophie, fast asleep on one side of her and a fully dressed Sam, asleep on the other side, each of them cocooning her with an arm. She placed a hand on each of them and felt happier than she had in a long time. Her life was such a rollercoaster. One minute she would be scared out of her mind and then the next minute she would be filled with a determination not to be afraid. Swinging from emotions was draining but seeing both Sophie and Sam lying next to her put things into perspective. She had two people that loved her. She wouldn't let anyone take that away from her. Not even Cecelia.

She could withstand anything as long as she had Sophie and Sam. Her two guardian angels. She knew that nothing would ever change that.

36

The firing range had become Sophie's happy place. At first, it had been a means to an end, part of her plan. But now it was a place she could come whenever she needed to think. She found that training her gun on the target helped her to focus her mind. Her investments had doubled in value since she'd taken this up as a pastime. As firing a gun seemed to sharpen her sense and her mind. She was sure that she had had brainwaves that would never have occurred to her otherwise.

According to the range owner, Roger, a middle-aged, sweaty man who wore the same fleece every day, she was a natural with a gun. He kept badgering her to join a competitive team he ran, waxing lyrical about how there were not enough women with potential. She now avoided him whenever possible. She had much bigger things to worry about than how underrepresented women were in the shooting world.

She needed to get her own gun. It was harder than she thought it would be. To buy a gun she needed a licence from the police, for which she needed references from two people who had known her for more than two years. It was hard to accomplish this when she only had one friend in the world; and under the police rules her husband couldn't be a referee. *What about one of the clients?* she mused. She had known some of them for several years. *Excuse me, sir, could you just write a reference for me to help me get a gun?* It would be interesting to see their reactions to that. She could always obtain one illegally. But who did she know that she could approach without it getting back to the family?

It was when she was signing out that she saw Roger in the back office. He appeared to be putting away a camp bed. *He sleeps here?* She doubted that it was his love of shooting that kept him sleeping on a worn-out camp bed. Times were tough judging by the peeling paint on the walls and the missing 'G' from the large sign on the front of the building. What he needed was an injection of cash. The idea percolated in her mind and she realised that the answer to her problem of how to get a gun had just landed in her lap.

There went that lovely lady fate again, guiding her way by throwing the opportunities she needed into her path. Sophie pulled back her shoulders and puffed out her chest, activating business-mode. An hour later, she walked out of the firing range with one less page in her chequebook but a black, shiny new gun in her rucksack. It made her feel powerful, ready for the battle ahead. The Cavendish family had no idea what they were dealing with. By the time Greg saw the cheque clear to 'Manchester Gun Range', it would be too late.

Her phone beeped as she placed her bag in the car. She was in such a good mood, her spirits lifted even higher when she saw it was a text message from Flora. The smile soon dropped from her face when she saw what it said.

Emergency. Get to the centre now.

37

The police had left but instead of feeling comforted, Flora felt more vulnerable than ever. Now that they had actually called the police the danger was more tangible.

Flora's stomach rumbled, announcing its disgust that she had not eaten. Sam had nipped out to pick up a Chinese. She wished she'd asked him to order the banquet for four because she was starving. It was impossible to settle in the house anymore. She felt like an easy target when she was alone and couldn't shake the sense that someone was watching her.

Flora got up from the sofa but sat straight back down again: walking wasn't so easy due to the cuts on her knees. The day had been a disaster from the minute she had left the house. Gridlocked traffic had her crawling all the way into the city centre. Eventually, she'd parked at the car park closest to the centre and joined the throng of people traversing the city centre streets. She was already visualising the lesson she would be delivering, mentally checking the supplies in her inventory.

A shoulder came from nowhere and rammed into her, sending her sprawling into the road. Car horns blared and she heard squealing brakes. Her knees took the brunt of the impact.

Her hands stung where pebbles of tarmac had embedded themselves in her skin. Her breath came raggedly and she was frozen to the spot. Car horns continued to blare, the noise almost bursting her ear drums. Her mind was blank, she didn't know what to do. The pain in her shins became more prominent. Flora could hear the crunch of tyres on tarmac near her head as they manoeuvred around her. The smell of burning rubber filled her nostrils. Still she could not move. Shock had turned her to stone.

The feel of soft papery skin on her face made her jump. An elderly woman was looking down at her, watery blue eyes filled with concern, her face pockmarked with age spots. She tugged at Flora trying to get her out of the road. 'Are you all right, dear. Can you hear me? You need to get out of the road.'

'Y... yes.' Flora leaned on the lady, who was surprisingly strong considering she was around five feet tall and looked like a sharp breeze would knock her over.

'The youth of today. Bloody rotters, the lot of them. Come on, dear, let's get out of the road before we both get hit by a car.'

Flora looked around and saw the cars coming towards them were only managing to narrowly avoid her. Another car horn blared and an angry white man in a business suit put down his window and gave them the finger accompanied by some choice words. Gingerly, she moved back on to the pavement, wincing as her stinging knees protested. They walked until they were out of the stream of pedestrians into a shop doorway.

'What can I do to help, love? Can I call someone? That was a nasty fall.'

'No. I'll be fine. I'm only a few minutes away from where I work. I'll go there and clean myself up.' She took some deep, bracing breaths.

'We should really call the police, you know. I didn't get a

good look at him, they all wear hoods these days. But they shouldn't be allowed to get away with it. The hooligans.'

In that moment, Flora realised that she no longer had her bag. She looked around and opened her mouth to say something when the lady pulled it off her shoulder and offered it to her. 'Here's your bag, love. You dropped it when you fell.'

Flora shouldered the bag and thanked the woman heartily and gave her a quick, awkward hug. 'You're so kind. Thank you for helping me.'

'Nonsense. Do you need me to walk with you?'

'No. I'll be fine. Thank you again, though. You've been so kind.' Flora straightened up and swallowed back the pain in her knees and tried her best to look fine. She walked away from the woman and tried not to think about what could have happened if the cars hadn't stopped. She felt the eyes of the elderly lady follow her until she turned around the corner, out of sight.

After two cups of Charlotte's magic tea, she managed to stop shaking, grateful that she had come in early to prepare. She had not been in a fit state to teach when she arrived. As she sat on one of the small seats, the calming atmosphere seeped into her and she managed to untense slightly. Her nerves were so frayed that she panicked easily now but considering all the strange things that had happened to her that was not surprising. She was running on constant adrenaline, waiting for the next thing to happen.

Could it just have been an accident. Maybe she was just overreacting? What was the saying? Was she seeing a zebra when really it was just a horse?

Charlotte sat down opposite Flora. 'I need to tell you something. It's about Sam. He was here. He... he startled me.'

Flora let out a gasp. Whilst Charlotte had been talking, she had realised that she hadn't told Sophie and began searching her bag for her phone. As she pulled it out, a folded piece of paper flapped heavily to the floor.

Unfolding it, she almost dropped it again. Her blood turned to ice as she read the message that had been created for her from cut-out newspaper letters.

THE NEXT TIME YOU SEE WORMS IT WILL BE IN YOUR GRAVE

Sam was there ten minutes after she called him. Sophie arrived minutes after him and took charge. She called the parents to cancel the sessions that day, informing them of a family emergency, whilst Sam called the police. Charlotte had been sat next to Flora since she had got the note, she had pulled her chair close to Flora's and refused to leave her side. It took Sam a while to convince her to go home. Charlotte gave Flora a desperate look before finally being led out of the room by Sam. But Flora couldn't even bring herself to say goodbye to Charlotte. She felt if she moved or tried to speak she would break into a thousand pieces and not even Sophie could put her back together.

Sophie had seemed reluctant to involve the police initially but had quickly seen sense when she had read the note. The cut-out letters were much more sinister than a typed or handwritten note. Someone had spent time on this, carefully cutting out letters and sticking them onto the paper. Yes, a lot of effort had gone into crafting this threat to Flora, it had the personal touch.

The two police constables were extremely kind considering

Flora was a blubbering wreck. They sat at a table in the centre, uncomfortable in small chairs designed for small children. PC Wilson, a six-foot-tall handsome young man was struggling the most. Each time he moved in his chair it creaked ominously. He tried to hide his discomfort as he sat sideways, unable to fit his legs under the table.

Tears kept welling up in Flora's throat cutting off her words. Slowly, she haltingly told them about the strange things that had been happening to her. All the things that had happened before the note sounded ludicrous, but now it seemed it was stepping up.

The police officers took her statement and also one from Sophie as she had been there when the worms were discovered.

The female police constable, PC Valerie, put on gloves and took the note from the table in front of them. She pulled out a clear evidence bag and placed the note into it. 'It's unlikely we will pull any prints from it, but it is always worth trying.' She placed the note back on the table and shifted her gaze to Flora. 'Now, do you have any idea who could be doing this to you, Mrs Cavendish? Does anyone at all have a grudge against you?'

Flora shook her head hopelessly. More tears escaped and tracked down her face.

'What about Linda?' interjected Sophie. Her grip on Flora's hands was bordering on painful. Flora pulled a hand free to wipe her face. She took the tissue proffered by Sam, sat on her other side. He too had to sit sideways to avoid banging his knees on the table. In any other circumstance it would have been comical.

'Linda?' enquired PC Valerie.

'Linda has a little boy with autism. She came to one of my open days. She wanted to send her son to my classes but said she couldn't afford them. I said I'd see what I could do but, in the end, Sophie dealt with her for me. Explained the situation.'

Flora felt her face flush in embarrassment. How pathetic she sounded. 'She's followed me a few times. Stood outside the centre watching me. But I don't think it's her.'

'Why is that?'

'I think she is just a desperate woman who is trying to do what she can for her son. Plus, there is no way she could have got into my house.'

'Do you have any way we can get in touch with Linda?' PC Valerie took out a small notebook and pen and looked expectantly at Flora.

'Yes, I have her number. Her name is Linda Tugwell.' Flora got up unsteadily, wincing in pain. Sophie pushed her back down and went into the office to fetch her bag. She pulled out Flora's phone and unlocked it, searched for Linda's number and then held it out to the police officer.

'Right. I think we have enough information for now. I can appreciate this is a really upsetting time for you. We will be in touch if we need any more information or with the results of our investigation.'

They all stood up and Sophie showed the police officers to the door.

Sam turned and enveloped Flora in his arms. 'Oh, Flora. I'm so sorry this is happening to you.' She could feel his warm breath in her hair. His arm tightened around her. 'I feel so helpless.'

Sophie coughed behind them. 'Flo, should we get you home? You must be tired.'

She felt Sam lift his head from her hair to look at Sophie. She went to turn herself, but his arms gripped tighter still, holding her in place. 'It's all right, Sophie, I've got it from here. You get yourself home.'

Sophie didn't reply. There was an awkward pause and then Sam lowered his head so he was nuzzling Flora's hair once more.

'Call me if you need anything, Flora,' said Sophie eventually, sounding put out. Flora heard the door slam shut behind her. But she could not bring herself to care, and she lost herself in the strong embrace of her husband, shutting herself off from the chaotic thoughts that were threatening to overwhelm her. Instead, she focused on Sam's heartbeat thudding in his chest and his arms locked around her, strong and unbreakable. She wanted to stay here forever, safe and protected.

38

The next day, Flora felt brighter. Sam had taken the week off work and had insisted that they didn't have to go anywhere, not even Friday Night Dinner if she was still feeling unsettled by then. It was a good job she had been sitting down when he said this. Those words meant more to her than Sam declaring his love for her. It was better than that, it was a demonstration to how much he put her first in this marriage. Only days before he said nothing would ever stop him from going to Friday Night Dinner. It was a testament to how much Cecelia had put her through over the years that she couldn't say with certainty whether she'd rather be going through these awful things or spending another evening with her mother-in-law.

Sam doted on her every minute of the day, not leaving her side for more than a few minutes. It seemed he'd finally realised the gravity of the situation. He'd been away each time something had happened, and this appeared to have stopped him truly appreciating what she had been going through. But she'd never forget the way his face had drained of colour when he had read the note.

There was a tiny part of her grateful that her tormentor had stepped things up and sent the threatening note. It meant she could stop thinking she was going crazy and be taken seriously.

Instead of just saying someone had put worms in her bed and hidden her cards, she could say that she had been sent a threatening note in her bag. This note gave some credibility to her suffering. Even when Sam had seen the necklace she had found, he hadn't appeared as scared as he was now. He'd even tried to rationalise it. It had been the same with the worms, he seemed to think it was someone's idea of a joke and they would find out who it was and laugh about it later. It was only now that he was comprehending what she had known all along. Someone wanted to hurt her. Emotionally and possibly physically.

She remembered the force of the hand holding her under the water. If they'd held her down any longer, she could have drowned.

Since the threat had been made against her life, he had become a changed man and was acting the way that she had wanted him to since her cards had reappeared in her purse. She didn't hold it against him. Everyone reacted to stress differently: she was drinking more than ever and crying all the time. He had been in denial. But now, they were finally on the same page. Even better, they were facing it together.

It was a glorious week. Sam had forbidden anyone from visiting, even Sophie. He was adamant that they needed to lay low together, at least until they had an update from the police. Sam was confident that they would find out any day now who the culprit was. Flora wondered how he would react if they confirmed her suspicions, that it had been Cecelia all along. Was Cecelia at home now, terrified that they were going to work out what she had done?

As the week drew on, it became hard for Flora to feel scared anymore. Sam gave her no time to dwell on past events. He kept her constantly entertained with slushy rom-coms, cuddling under the blankets together, safe and protected from the wind howling outside. When they ran out of films, they played endless games of Monopoly and Cluedo. She had not laughed so much in a long time. Full blown belly laughs that made her face ache from smiling. It reminded her of why they were such a good match, that they had the same sense of humour and craved affection. It was impossible to get fed up of being around each other as they both revelled in being held and loved. Essentially, they were both as soppy as each other.

We should spend more time together like this, thought Flora. She cringed slightly when she realised that that was most likely her fault. She was so used to spending all her time with Sophie that she inadvertently neglected Sam. It was a hard habit to break when Sophie had been the only person in her world for over twenty years.

Luckily, Sam didn't seem to harbour any grudges as he slowly rubbed her back with soapy water in the bath. She vowed to devote more time to him. That was one positive to come out of this horrible experience, she supposed. The water was no longer scaring her like it had just after she had been half-drowned. How could it be when she was sat between the legs of a very handsome man? Instead of reliving a nightmare, all she could think about was the feel of her naked husband's body against hers. There was no better therapy.

They spent Friday night having a Domino's pizza in front of the fire, watching *Monster-in-Law*. It was a nod to Cecelia, who would be spitting with rage at the fact they had disobeyed the laws she had instituted. It was a blissful evening and Flora couldn't remember being so happy. They even talked about their future. Sam wanted to start trying for a baby as soon as they moved in to 5 Trelawney Close. It thrilled her. The note in her purse was forgotten. Everything was forgotten. It didn't matter what happened going forward: Flora had the best husband in the world and as long as she had him, she'd sit voluntarily in a bath of worms. He was worth it.

It was only when she was loading the dishwasher that she suddenly remembered Charlotte had tried to tell her something before she found the note. She resolved to ask her what it was next time she saw her.

39

It was the worst week of Sophie's life. Without Flora, she was subjected to the full wrath of Alistair, Greg and Cecelia alone. Whenever she was feeling overwhelmed by them, it took a mere five minutes in the presence of her best friend to reset and wash away the stress and strain.

A week. A whole bloody week Sam had held her hostage in that house. She was sure that Flora wanted to see her, but Sam wouldn't let her. He was controlling Flora the same way Greg had tried to control her.

Sophie couldn't help herself. She kept glancing at the house, looking at the garden, willing Flora to come into view, just to know she was okay. But the weather, like her feelings, was turbulent. The rain hadn't stopped, the gardens had turned into bogs, rivers formed as the grass could no longer absorb any more water. The wind was brutal, attacking anyone that dared to venture outside.

Sophie would sit on the doorstep of the back door, smoking. She was a stress smoker and judging by the three packets she had gone through so far, she was extremely upset. She didn't think anyone knew she smoked. It was a secret, disgusting habit. But keeping her real feelings inside, never expressing them caused a blockage. The only way she had found she could release it was to smoke. The nicotine had powerful properties that prevented her from exploding from pent-up emotion. But it wasn't working today. This was the longest she had ever been away from Flora.

How was she supposed to protect her when she wasn't allowed to see her? Sophie put out her cigarette and returned to pacing around the house. She picked up a magazine and flicked absently through the pages, not taking in a single word or picture. Wandering aimlessly around the house, Flora's face filled her mind. The fear and distress on her face the last time she saw her was devastating. She needed to be there for her. Sam wouldn't be able to soothe her the way she could. He hadn't even believed her until recently. Sophie was the only one that was really there for Flora.

The impotency eventually overspilled and she punched the wall. The agony coursing through her knuckles distracted her for a whole ten minutes. Wrapping her fist in a tea towel filled with ice, she tried to think clearly. She should be using this time to plan. If anything, this time away from Flora had made her even more certain. They needed to get away from the Cavendish family.

She went to her bedroom and began to pack a go-bag. The time was coming when she and Flora would be leaving. She couldn't go on fighting to keep Flora safe: she needed to take the next step.

From her underwear drawer, she pulled out the black gun. Just holding it made her feel powerful. She aimed it at the wall, pretending it was Greg's face. He'd no longer have physical strength on his side. Finally, she would have complete control. She jumped around and trained the gun on the other wall, picturing Alistair quaking with fear. Smiling, she lowered the gun and placed it into the black rucksack.

From underneath her bed, she withdrew the book. The book that fate had given her. The tool that would guarantee the downfall of the Cavendish family – if she was clever enough. And Sophie had no doubt that she *was* clever enough. She walked over to the window, looking down at Flora's garden.

Don't worry, Flora. I'll save you. Even if you don't realise you need to be saved.

40

Considering they had lived as neighbours for years; Flora had only been into Sophie and Greg's house a handful of times.

She had a spare key but never used it until now. She had never been comfortable in their house. Sophie and Greg's home was beautiful, sophisticated and pristine, a show home devoid of any individuality. Nothing was out of place. The black and white theme spread throughout the house. It was impossible to tell who lived here. Everything in the house was chosen for style rather than sentimentality.

Sophie must have realised that Flora was never comfortable there because they always seemed to gravitate to Sam's house. Sophie never invited her over and Flora avoided asking to visit because the house made her feel unwelcome, she felt too untidy and unrefined to be there. It also reminded Flora of a part of Sophie's personality she did not like, the side of her that was obsessed with wealth and status. This was the house of someone who had money and liked to flaunt it.

Flora tiptoed through the house. She knew that no one was home but felt like an intruder nonetheless. She was uneasy being in the house without Sophie, but she knew her friend wouldn't mind. She only wanted to retrieve the black sandals that she had lent to her.

Sam was taking her out for dinner tonight. It was the first time they would have left the house in a week. They had decided that they had hidden away for long enough and that it was time to re-join the real world. They were both reluctant: they had been in a bubble and it had been incredible. But it couldn't last, Sam needed to return to work and so did she. Sam had even bought her a new dress to wear. When he had presented her with the silky green dress, her instinct was to refuse it. She had plenty of clothes; she did not need him to waste his money on her. But he played dirty and looked at her with puppy dog eyes, pulling the cutest face that he could muster, and she smothered her protests. The only shoes she had to go with this dress, she had lent to Sophie. Why she had felt the need to borrow Flora's shoes when Sophie owned hundreds of pairs of shoes and Flora only had a couple. Sam had tossed her the spare key and told her to go and get them.

Standing in Sophie's bedroom, Flora was stunned. Obviously, the stylist for Buckingham Palace had been here. A huge bed dominated the room, soft silk curtains draped regally behind it. Gold leaf adorned every available surface, the bed, the bedside tables, the wardrobe and the dressing table. Even the walls had been decorated with matching gold-leaf designs. The gold sparkled in the room enhanced by the muted tones of the cream walls and furniture. Flora turned in slow circles, gaping in awe. Her eyes were drawn to the chandelier hanging from the ceiling, layer upon layer of crystals gleamed in the waning sunlight. She cautiously moved towards the majestic dressing table and sat down on the small stool. The mirror was framed with ornate lions made of gold, so lifelike she half expected them to turn and look at her. It was a room fit for a princess. The level of detail was astounding.

Jewellery boxes were lined up along the bottom of the mirror. Her heart lurched when she saw a battered silver box at the end. Flora remembered buying it at a charity shop for Sophie when she was around thirteen years old. She'd been so embarrassed as it was obviously used, she tried hard to clean all the smudges off it but to no avail. But Sophie was her only friend, the only one at school that would give her the time of day and she had wanted to get her something special, even though it would have been easier for her to find a golden goose than get money out of her aunt. She'd spent a whole fortnight checking under the sofa and down the sides of it for any spare change and finally scraped enough together to get something for Sophie.

I can't believe she kept it all this time, thought Flora.

The sound of a laptop notification drew her attention. Sophie's MacBook was open on what looked like Sophie's side of the bed. The bedside table held a framed photo of Flora and Sophie as sixteen-year-olds.

Curious, she went over to the laptop and saw the screen was still on. Sophie must have left in a hurry and forgot to shut it. Flora reached out, intending to close the laptop when she saw the word 'diary'. Every moral fibre she had inside of her screamed at her to shut the screen and walk away. But the temptation to peek into Sophie's innermost thoughts was alluring. Flora closed the notification that lingered on the screen – Sophie had sent herself an email reminder to transfer an important document to a client. With the notification gone, Flora could see the whole screen. She began to read.

```
I read somewhere that the best thing you
can do when you are in a situation like
mine is to write it all down. That way,
```

when the beatings become so frequent that they begin to blend into one, you have something to refer back to. Perspective they call it. So instead of a normal diary that I would look back on to see what I was doing that day, I would be able to recall whether I had been pushed down the stairs or simply slapped around the face that day. I am also writing this because if someone other than me is reading, it will mean in all probability he has killed me.

It may surprise you to know that it took a long time for me to hate my husband. I was not one of those women taken in by a nice man who then turned out to be a thug. No, I knew exactly what I was getting into from the very first time I met him. I just didn't care. He walked into my life with the confidence of someone who knew they were at the top of the food chain. And suddenly the world around me stopped being ordinary. I just knew that his ambition and drive matched mine and that together we would be an unstoppable team. That is what I reminded myself when I lay beaten on the floor the first time it happened. Even when I scrubbed at the puddle of my own blood, trying to stop it staining the carpet.

They say it takes sixty-six days for something to become a habit. It took around thirty-seven for the flinching to stop. I no longer cower when I recognise the shift in atmosphere or when I see the muscles tense and the arch of his brow, the precursor to monumental levels of pain. But the inevitability of what is to come does nothing to dull the pain. In fact, my pain is doubled because I am imagining the pain before it comes, then I am experiencing it again, the full force of it, when the blow strikes. My husband is the stereotypical wife-beater. He is sure to aim for places that can be hidden by clothing. If he becomes particularly enraged and this causes him to slip up, we sit down and rehearse my lines until I can confidently describe slipping in the bathtub or falling down the stairs. This does not happen often, as he does not want to risk his reputation.

The futility of my situation is becoming harder to ignore. I am an intelligent woman, as shrewd at business as my husband. Which means I know that I cannot escape without consequence. Cavendish & Sons is a family company built and founded upon reputation. That means my husband will not let me go. Not without a fight. He cannot risk the ripple of rumours it would cause. At the moment, his power is resolute, unshakeable. But like with everything, the higher up you are, the further you have to fall. He cannot risk questions; doubts about his character would be intolerable. As he is fond of telling me, rumours are an incurable poison to a business.

I am a rose surrounded by an impenetrable circle of thorns. There is no escape. This knowledge echoes in my head even as his fist pummels into my side, driving the breath from my body. It makes me feel angry. I ball my fists. Although I am as smart as my husband I am nowhere near as strong as him. I breathe through my anger and through the pain. Deep breath in. There is no escape. Deep breath out. There is no escape.

I think about killing him sometimes. Okay, that is a lie. I think this all the time. When we are at dinner, especially family dinners, I look at his face. The twinkle in his eyes. The way he dominates conversations. I take in everything about him and then I visualise my hands around his neck. He would look at me with amusement at first, but then when he realises I am deadly serious, he would start to look scared. He'd claw a little at my hands. His body would jerk to escape underneath my deathly grip. But my rage cannot be denied. His face would start to turn red as the blood begins to pump furiously at his temple. His eyes would lock with mine and I would watch as the little vessels in his eyes begin to burst, his eyeballs bulging in his head, trying to escape the socket. For once I would be the one in control. I would be the one inflicting the pain and fear. I shiver with delight at this image and someone offers me a jacket. I have to stop myself from unleashing the deranged laughter inside me. 'I am not cold,' I want to say, 'I am just experiencing the delicious anticipation of killing my husband.'

Flora closed down the document, unable to look at the words any longer. There was more, but nausea was threatening to overwhelm her. She'd seen enough. She was about to turn away when she saw her name. A file was on the desktop named, 'Dear Flora'. With her heart in her mouth, she double clicked and opened the file.

Dear Flora,

   If you are reading this then he has killed me. I can't believe my life has come to this. All I ever wanted was for both of us to get the happy ending we deserved. There's something else I need to tell…

41

Instantly, Sophie knew that there was someone in the house. Her arm was hurting. In fact, her whole body ached and it was bone deep. Pulling up in their driveway and getting out of the car, her eyes were instinctively drawn to Flora's house. Exactly the same red brick house as her own with elegant ivy artfully arranged to enhance the beauty of both the houses. There was no movement in the house today. Sometimes she would catch glimpses of Flora as she moved around from room to room. But today the house stared back at her gloomily, as if lamenting its emptiness.

Opening the black front door, Sophie dumped her bag on the side table and her whole body relaxed. She needed that feeling more than anything after the gruelling meeting with Alistair. This happened every time she came home. The beauty and sophistication of her home would soothe her. But the feeling was interrupted as the hairs on the back of her neck rose unbidden. Somehow, she knew that there was someone in the house. The peace and tranquillity were altered, like someone else's air was dirtying the atmosphere.

Slowly, Sophie removed her heels, not wanting to alert the

intruder to her presence any more than she already had. The hard floor was deliciously warm through her sheer black tights as she made her way around the bottom floor of the house, trying to locate the cause of her unease.

In the kitchen, she saw the smudge was still there that she had instructed the cleaner to deal with only that morning. She made a mental note to send an email requesting her dismissal.

Sophie cautiously crept upstairs, caressing the wrought-iron banister as she went. Cecelia had free rein when it came to decorating Sam's house, but Greg had drawn the line at his mother buying his house. He would choose what was in it. Surprisingly, he had a good eye for detail and the house was minimal, ultra-modern and she loved it – once she had put her stamp on it.

Upstairs, she moved towards her bedroom, a pit of dread unfurling in her stomach. Sixth sense was telling her she was not going to like what she found. Something terrible was going to happen. Reaching the doorway, her worst fears were confirmed.

Flora was perched on the edge of her bed. Sophie's laptop was open on her knees, the screen illuminating the tear tracks on Flora's face.

A wave of nausea swept through Sophie. She was not ready for this conversation. There were things on the laptop she had no doubt would devastate her friend. She had not intended for Flora to see them. Sophie had been preparing, that was all. She was rehearsing what she was going to say and how she was going to say it. But fate had intervened and forced her hand.

She tried to rally her mental faculties, willing her brain to co-operate. But she was lost for words. Unpreparedness was not something she was used to experiencing.

'Sophie,' whispered Flora, finally noticing her presence. Her face was stricken, bloodless. 'What is this?' She gestured to the laptop. 'Tell me this isn't true.'

Sophie didn't answer. She moved shakily over to the bed, words still failing her as her mind played catch-up. This was not how it was supposed to be.

'Answer me!' Flora's voice shook. She stood up suddenly, pushing the laptop away from her. 'Sophie! What the hell is going on?'

Sophie took a deep breath. It was time.

42

When she was a little girl, when the night was pitch-black, Flora would picture a land of fire and ash. Nothing grew there and the sun never shone. It howled with rain and was either too hot or too cold, torturously so. Furthermore, this land was filled with massive spiders, gigantic snakes, fire-breathing dragons and many other terrifying creatures. It was this land that housed all the evil people in the world. The first person to populate this land would be her aunt. Flora would watch in her mind's eye as she was chased by a black dragon with bulbous yellow eyes.

She would also put in the shadowy figure of the person who had killed her parents. It was only a figure without a face, but she would watch as they were eaten by gigantic spiders, only to come back to life and be eaten again. Over and over.

Flora had not thought of the imaginary hell she had constructed as a child until today. Now it would have a new member: Greg. But her imagination could not construct a creature awful enough to torment him the way he deserved. Her hatred for Greg was almost as powerful as her hatred of the person who had run her parents off the road and driven away.

She feared what she would do should Greg appear in front of her at that moment.

Flora had to allow the anger to consume her because if she didn't, she would have to face the fact that she had been so distracted that she had not seen what was happening in front of her own eyes. As Sophie got to her feet, shakily unbuttoning her dress, Flora was replaying the signs she had missed in her mind. Greg's anger at Alister's birthday party, the fight over dinner, the split lip. Flora's recollections stopped when Sophie stood in front of her, clothed only in her underwear, unable to meet her eye. But Flora couldn't have looked at her face if she had wanted to. Sophie's body was a tapestry of bruises, Greg's power and anger stamped across her body in a vivid patchwork of red, purple, yellows and grey. The differing shades revealing the length of time between the beatings. There were slashes of red where she had been cut and odd milky patches of scarring mottling her skin.

The telltale taste of acid in Flora's mouth told her she was about to be sick. Taking deep breaths, she swallowed the bile back down. She couldn't believe what she was seeing. The angry bruises were imprinted on her eyes. She swiped at tears trickling down her face. 'How long?' she asked.

Sophie wouldn't look at her. She was concentrating instead on buttoning up her dress. It was a smart black pencil dress that fitted her slender frame like a glove, hiding the evidence that her husband was a violent psychopath.

'A while.' Sophie shrugged. Fully dressed, she moved over and sat on the bed. She still wouldn't meet her friend's eye. Looking everywhere around the room, her eyes darted from place to place. Eventually, she seemed to settle at looking down at her hands on her lap, picking at the seams on the edge of her dress. 'I didn't realise what was happening until it was too late. It happened so infrequently, I didn't think it would ever become this bad.'

'But why didn't you say anything?'

For a long time, Sophie didn't answer. Still picking at the seams on her dress, she seemed lost in the recesses of her own mind. 'How could I tell you with everything that has been happening to you? You were already so stressed and terrified. I couldn't add to that.'

'That's not good enough, Soph. This has been going on for ages by the looks of it. Plus, you know that nothing would be more important to me than this!'

'But you don't understand. Telling you wouldn't change anything.'

'Telling me would change everything, Sophie! I could have helped you. I can help you!'

Sophie stood up abruptly. 'You just don't have a clue! You are so bloody naïve!' With that she stormed from the room into the en suite bathroom and slammed the door, vibrating the walls and furniture.

Flora twisted the handle but the door was locked. She could just make out Sophie's sobbing. 'Let me in, Sophie!' She slammed her palm against the door. 'This isn't going away. We have to talk about this.'

There was no reply. She turned her head and placed her ear against the door. Sophie's cries sounded muffled, like she was crying into a cloth or towel. Flora slid down the door, adjusting herself until she was leaning against the wooden frame, fidgeting, trying to get comfortable. She was not going anywhere.

43

Eventually, Sophie opened the door. Flora put down the computer. A sick need to know more had caused her to pick it up again. But it only served to confuse, sicken and revile her. How had Sophie been going through all of this and she hadn't suspected a thing? It made a mockery of their friendship. Was she really so self-centred that she hadn't noticed her friend was being beaten black and blue? She could have let herself off the hook a little bit if they didn't live so close and only saw each other weekly. But Sophie was in the house next door. They saw each other more than once a day. She felt disgusted with herself. She wanted to kill Greg. Her anger at him made her whole body vibrate.

A different person came out of the bathroom. This wasn't her Sophie. Her Sophie was bold, poised and strong. This person looked broken in every sense of the word. Her hair was bedraggled where she had clawed it at it. She was hunched over and looked like she might shatter at the lightest touch. Her face was white and gaunt, revealing what blusher, foundation and concealer had been hiding. A faint yellow bruise dappled her cheek. Where was her Sophie?

Images of Greg's fist pounding into Sophie's side arose in her mind and she realised, *This is the real Sophie.* When Sophie reached the bed, Flora stood and wrapped her in her arms. She held her so tightly, wishing she could just hug all the pain away. They had to fix this. Flora never wanted to see Sophie like this again. At Flora's touch Sophie broke down. Her body could no longer hold itself up and Flora took the weight of her friend, holding her upright. Her cries were guttural. It was like her body was forcibly expelling all the buried pain and sorrow.

Eventually, Sophie's anguish diminished, and Flora gently guided her to the bed. They lay together, Sophie clutched at Flora tightly, as though she was the only life raft in a stormy sea. Flora gently stroked Sophie's hair, making shushing noises to soothe her. It was the first time in their entire friendship that she was the one doing the comforting.

'Talk to me, Soph. Let me in.'

'I don't want to talk about it. Talking about it means I have to relive it.'

'But if you talk to me. I can help.'

At her words, Sophie sat bolt upright. She turned to face Flora, flushed with anger. '*Help.* There is nothing you can do to help. I've had years to think this through. After every punch and kick I would breathe through the pain and plot my escape.' Sophie got out of the bed. Her anger restoring her energy. She strode over to the window and pointed to it. 'I even had a whole night in the garden when he locked me out there to sit freezing cold in only a nightgown. A whole twelve hours I spent, barely able to feel my fingers trying to work out a way to escape him. To escape all of them.'

Horrified, Flora tried and failed to clear her mind of the image of a freezing cold Sophie in her nightgown shivering only a few metres from where Flora would have been sleeping peacefully with Sam's arms wrapped around her. Nausea rolled in her stomach.

Sophie pinned Flora with her gaze. 'Flora, you are not stupid. I know you have tried to keep your distance and almost ignore the wealth that we have married into. But you know as well as I do the sort of power this family has. For god's sake, Cecelia and Alistair have organised it so that any speeding tickets, the family gets miraculously vanish. They can do anything they want. Come on, Flora. Open your eyes. It's time to stop ignoring what is right in front of you.'

'Don't be like that, Sophie. I don't spend as much time with them as you do. I avoid Cecelia like the plague and I've never spent more than ten minutes alone with Greg.'

Sophie began to pace up and down the room, gesticulating wildly as she spoke. 'But you've seen the things they can do. You remember Cecelia bragging about the speeding tickets. You were there when Alistair got a restaurant to throw out all the people dining there so we could eat at a table alone, just because he didn't like the table they had given us. Greg has just as much power as them. Money is power, Flora.'

'But I don't understand what this has to do with Greg hurting you.' Flora's mind was racing. They had never talked about the darker side of the Cavendish family. Flora had ignored it and pretended it wasn't happening. Sophie had always seemed to accept that it was a part of having money. But now, the dirty washing was on the line and Flora was starting to realise that in ignoring what type of family she had married into, she had entangled herself in a mess she may not be able to get out of.

'I tried to leave.'

The words hung in the air. Flora was gobsmacked. Sophie couldn't look at her.

'I reached my limit. I just couldn't take it anymore.' She sank to the floor. Sitting in front of Flora she stared at her knees and picked at the skin around her nails.

'I knew I'd have to be clever. I'd told Greg in the past I would leave him if he hurt me again. He was eager to let me know that he would never let that happen. That I was his property.' She spat these words. 'He promised if I ever left, he would spend every minute of the day and every penny he had tracking me down.

'I knew I had to be clever. So, I booked four hotels in different names. Even I didn't know which one I was going to actually stay in. I took nothing with me except some cash I had been hiding. I couldn't take my passport as Greg had locked it away in his safe. I was so sure I outsmarted him. I chose a random day. I had meetings booked, he wouldn't have a clue.' A tear slid down her face, riding the crest of her cheek and then plummeted to the floor, splashing onto the cream carpet. 'But when I got to the room in the hotel. Greg was lying on the bed. He had this massive grin on his face. Like we were playing a game of hide and seek and he had won. I didn't dare try again after that. I knew it was pointless. The broken ribs were also an incentive.'

'Broken ribs! How did you have broken ribs without me knowing?'

Sophie looked up, her eyes so sad. 'I didn't want to lie to you. I told you I had a last-minute business trip in Barcelona. But really, I was next door, having my chest strapped up by a private family doctor.' She emphasised the word *family* in air quotes. 'She saw all the bruises on my body and wouldn't even look me in the eye.'

Sophie knelt in front of Flora, she took her hands, gripping them hard. Flora saw fear in her friend's eyes. Normally, her face was expressionless and controlled. But today her emotions were unbridled. Flora had seen more emotions on Sophie's face today than she had in the entire friendship. It was heartbreaking that Greg had literally beaten her friend's emotions out of her.

'The whole family are in on it, Flo. Alistair told me in no uncertain terms that were I to do anything foolish such as leaving the family and causing a scandal, then I would reap what I sow. Those were his exact words.'

Flora's mind was reeling. She could just about get her head around Greg being a vile bully but the whole family knowing about it and letting it happen... Her hesitance must have shown on her face.

'Flora, after the way Cecelia has treated us, the things she has said to us... Look at what she did on your wedding day. Is it really so hard to believe that she could know that her son was an abusive bully and not do anything about it? Reputation is everything to Cecelia. Look at all these ridiculous parties she throws and insists we wear designer dresses to protect the family name. Reputation is everything to all of them. If I leave Greg it will cause rumours and if the truth were to come out, it could ruin everything for them. Who would want to invest with a company that employs a wife-beater? They can't risk it.'

'But Sam isn't like that.'

Sophie looked away, as if choosing her next words carefully. 'I know you love Sam. I know you think he is a good man. But he isn't.' Flora opened her mouth to deny it. But Sophie waved her words away. 'Let me finish. Sam seems like he has a moral compass. Like he's different from the rest of them. But he is worse as he lets them get away with it. He turns a blind eye to the bad things they do. I've been in meetings where they have coerced honest, hard-working people into signing their businesses, their life's work, over to the Cavendish Group. Threatening their families if they don't. Sam was in those meetings. Staring resolutely at the wall. Doing nothing to stop it.'

Flora shook her head. Sam wouldn't do that.

'You don't believe me.'

'Sam isn't like that. He would probably do something behind the scenes. He wouldn't let that happen.'

Sophie smiled at her, but it was a joyless smile. 'Just think about all the awful things that Cecelia has done and said to you. Think about how resolutely Sam has either denied it or explained them away. He has never accepted that his mother doesn't like you. If he doesn't believe what you say when you tell him what his mother has done, do you think he would believe you if you told him what his brother has done? You, his wife, have told him on multiple occasions about the way you have been treated. He always has an explanation. An excuse. He makes it your fault or makes you think you are too sensitive.'

What could Flora say to that? There was no denying the truth. 'I guess. But there is a difference between not wanting to see the worst in your mother and knowing that your brother was knocking ten bells out of his wife.' Sam wouldn't stand for that. It wasn't as if Cecelia had been physically violent. Not that her cutting remarks about Flora's parents weren't wounding in themselves.

Sophie's head slumped onto Flora's lap. Flora stroked her blonde hair, the colour of champagne. 'Listen, Soph, the main thing is, there is no way you can carry on living like this. We have to get you away from Greg. There must be something we can do.'

Sophie looked up at Flora, her eyes desolate. 'Haven't you listened to anything I've said?'

'What if we go to the police?'

Sophie let out a growl of frustration. 'Do you remember that dinner we had a couple of years ago. The one where Alistair invited a friend to Friday Night Dinner, Thomas Doyle?'

Flora thought back. Friday Night Dinner was strictly a

family affair. Which is why it had shocked everyone to find a portly gentleman with salt-and-pepper hair and a wide smile, sat in Alistair's place at the table. Even Cecelia had looked momentarily perturbed.

'Er... yes. I remember.'

'Alistair introduced him as a family friend. He has known the family for years.'

'So?'

'You didn't let me finish. He's also the Chief Constable of Greater Manchester Police. Who do you think sorted out their speeding tickets, parking tickets, basically anything they want?'

'But surely he can't interfere in something so serious.'

'Are you willing to take the risk?' Sophie's eyes filled with horror at whatever she was thinking. 'I'm certainly not. I don't know what Greg would do to me if I tried to leave again.'

They sat in silence for a while, Sophie's head resting on Flora's lap. Sophie appeared lost in thought. Flora just didn't know what to say. She had been transported into a different universe where nothing made sense anymore.

'This is ridiculous. You can't stay with a man who does this.' Flora gestured to Sophie's body. Her mind was still imprinted with the image of the watercolour of bruises across her body. 'There has to be something we can do.'

'There is one way out for me. But I don't think I can do it.'

'What is it?'

'There is only one way for me to escape and that is to squirrel away enough money and then leave. Vanish this time. I can't stay in Manchester. I'd have to go somewhere else. No hotels. Completely off the grid. If I could get enough money together, I could be smarter this time. Run and never stop running.'

Something clicked in Flora's mind. 'That's why you gave me the money to hide.'

Sophie nodded. 'Greg was getting suspicious. I had to find somewhere safe to keep it in case I had no choice but to leave.'

'You were going to leave?' Flora's throat filled with tears and there was a sharp pain in her heart.

'I wanted to.' Sophie looked her in the eyes. 'But I just couldn't leave you.'

44

The pain Flora's eyes mirrored the pain lancing Sophie's own heart. A lone tear fell from Flora's eyes, quickly followed by another as realisation dawned. She took Sophie's hand and squeezed it, and Sophie knew that Flora had understood the magnitude of it: that the only reason that Sophie had not left her abusive husband was because of her love for her best friend. Flora seemed to be struggling for words. But what could you say when you realised that your friend had been enduring violence and mental torture because she loved you and wouldn't leave you?

'You stayed... because of me.'

'How could I leave you? We've been best friends since we were four years old. Could you honestly say that if you were in the same situation, you would have left me?' Sophie held her breath. Despite all their years together she was still insecure about their friendship, always feeling that Flora would one day stop needing her, stop wanting her. Her own mother had never wanted her, which made it hard to believe someone like Flora would want her. Your relatives were supposed to love you no matter what, friends did not have the same obligation. If her own mother could not love her, then what was there to say Flora would always be there? After all, they were not bound by blood.

Flora looked at her with such sadness in her eyes. 'No. There is no way.' She wrapped her arms around her, pulling her close.

Sophie inhaled the delicate scent of Flora's jasmine perfume. She breathed in the love and reassurance like it was air.

'What are we going to do, Sophie?' whispered Flora.

'There's nothing we can do. Not unless you run away with me.' Sophie chuckled and Flora pulled away as if she'd been stung.

'Leave? With you?' She looked aghast.

'Hey, hey. Don't worry! I would never ask you to leave Sam and everything you've worked for.' She took Flora's hand, gently rubbing the back of it with her thumb. 'I'm sure I'll find another way. I'm very smart, don't you know.' She smiled broadly at Flora, intending to reassure her.

But Flora was looking away into the distance. 'Running doesn't sound so bad, to be honest. With everything that's been happening. Someone trying to drown me. The worms. A fresh start away from this madness sounds amazing.'

Sophie laughed. 'Yeah right. Like you could ever leave Sam.'

Flora looked at her, stern faced. 'Stop laughing, Sophie. This is really serious. Do you seriously expect me to just carry on as normal knowing that next door you are being beaten black and blue? We have to do something.'

Sophie breathed hard, annoyed that Flora still was not grasping the reality of the situation. 'I've told you. Greg does not want me to leave. He has enough money to ensure that doesn't happen. He has the support of his father and god knows how many millions of pounds behind him.'

Sophie could see the cogs turning in Flora's mind,

desperately seeking a way out of this problem. She may as well have shot Sophie in the heart. If this was the other way around, Sophie would have dropped anyone and anything to keep Flora safe. But Flora was not prepared to leave her life, that much was evident from the way she was wracking her brains for a solution when the only solution was obvious.

Sophie faked a yawn. 'Listen, I've had a long day at work and I'm exhausted. I just want to get into bed and sleep.'

'I can't just leave. We haven't sorted this out. We need a plan,' said Flora.

'I've told you. The only way I can get out of this is to leave. But that's not going to happen.'

Flora looked stricken. Sophie stood up and turned pulling Flora to her feet. 'Flora, I will be fine. It's not like it happens all the time. I'm made of strong stuff. I've survived this long. Plus I'll be fast asleep before Greg gets home and he doesn't even sleep in this room.' She tried to lead Flora out of the room, but she would not budge. 'Come on. I just want to sleep. You don't need to worry. I'm like his play toy. I don't think he'd ever try to kill me.' She laughed callously.

Flora still wouldn't move. She was looking at Sophie with a strange expression on her face. 'If I can't think of anything else to do, I'll leave with you.' Flora's voice was quiet, so quiet Sophie thought she might have imagined it. But the determined expression on Flora's face confirmed she had heard correctly.

'Don't be daft. You'd never leave Sam. You're just emotional and not thinking straight.' Sophie turned towards the door, intending to open it so Flora would go. She just wanted to be alone.

'I will, Sophie. To save you from Greg. If it really is the only way, I will leave Sam and go with you.'

Sophie turned and stared at her open-mouthed. Tears

sprang into her eyes, an unusual experience for someone who had only cried a handful of times in their life. 'Are you serious?' A kernel of hope flaring within her.

'Yes.'

45

Flora faced yet another night with no sleep. She didn't know why she even bothered trying. She had left Sophie's house miserable and sickened. The distress of the threatening note in her bag paled into insignificance in the face of Sophie's pain. Everything that had happened to her was child's play compared to what Sophie had been suffering. Images of the cigarette burns in the shape of a G on Sophie's stomach filled her vision, making her stomach heave. Here she was lying in a luxurious super-king-size bed with Sam's arms wrapped around her knowing full well that her best friend was in the house next door with an evil bully.

Flora tried a visualisation technique to empty her mind, needing respite from her discordant emotions. Picturing herself on a secluded beach, she breathed in and out to the sound of waves lapping gently in front of her. She almost felt the gentle breeze brush at her hair. But then the waves swept Sophie's dead body to her feet. The pale face was covered in blood that turned the sea a deep shade of red. Sophie's dead body opened its eyes. 'Help me,' she asked in a croaky, terrifying voice.

Next, Flora tried to count sheep but instead of jumping over the fence they surrounded her. Hundreds of sheep with Cecelia's face, all screaming at her that she was a money-grabbing tramp.

Creeping out of bed, Flora was flirting with the idea of taking sleeping tablets, but instead she walked around the house like an unsettled ghost, fingering her necklace. Stepping in front of the canvas of her parents, she gently stroked her mother's face, wishing more ardently than ever that she was there to tell her what to do. But her parents were gone and all she'd ever had was Sophie. Beautiful, brave, strong Sophie who had never let her down. Her guilt devoured her once more. She found PC Valerie's card on the kitchen island and wondered if she should call and tell her about Sophie and Greg. Would she be able to help?

But then she remembered the PC's words the last time she had called with an update. 'The Chief Constable has taken a personal interest in this and will be following the case closely. So please try not to worry.'

If Sophie was right, the police would not be an option. Flora sat in the living room surrounded by things that Cecelia had chosen, allowing herself to remember all the insults, cruel jibes and general hell that Cecelia had put her through. If she channelled that it was easy to want to give it all up. To leave everything behind and start again somewhere else. But then walking back into her bedroom, her heart contracted painfully. Sam slept so peacefully. Arms open wide, welcoming her back into bed. His laugh floated through her mind, how his eyes had brimmed with tears on their wedding day. The pure, unadulterated love they shared stole her breath. How could she leave him? She wanted to wake him up and tell him everything she knew, to beg him to help her.

But he couldn't even see through his mother. Did she honestly think that he would believe her? That he would see through his brother and do the right thing? Sam was a good man, she believed that. But his family were his Achilles heel. Could she balance Sophie's future on his love for her?

She watched the sunrise and although she felt sick, the beauty of watching the sun emerging, lighting up the world eased the ache in her heart. Slowly, she got dressed and ready to leave for work. Sam was singing *I'm a believer* in the shower and rather than face him, she slipped out of the door and drove to the centre. Her first session wasn't until 9am but there was always plenty she could do. Distracting herself with menial tasks was a blessing for her whirling mind.

Her insomnia soon caught up with her and to get through the day she had been surviving on Charlotte's cups of teas, heavily dosed with sugar combined with a bottle of Lucozade every hour. But that had not stopped her snapping at Thomas. Her addled brain had forgotten that he could not stand anything that was the colour red and she had squeezed red paint into a pot and put it on his desk without thinking. Immediately, he started rocking backwards and forwards, a persistent humming signalled his distress. He began to pull at his ginger hair, strands coming out in his fingers. The humming got louder and Flora's headache escalated in response.

'For god's sake stop it, Thomas!' she shrieked.

The room went deathly silent as ten shocked faces turned in her direction. She never raised her voice. Thomas stopped dead but then he spotted the ketchup once more and continued to meltdown. She had shocked herself and stared dumbly at him, unable to move or think straight.

Charlotte marched into the room and picked up the plate of food and took it into the kitchen. She came straight back out with a fresh plate and sat next to Thomas.

Flora took advantage of Charlotte's intervention and dashed into the back room. She shut the door and leant back against it. Her breath came quickly and tears leaked from her eyes. She felt awful. She was the one supposed to advocate for these children, to lead by example, to give them the patience and understanding that they deserved. She had never lost her temper before. Shame leached her strength and she collapsed into Charlotte's chair and put her head in her hands. She cried until there was nothing left, she was emotionally barren.

Sniffing, she stood up intending to go into the bathroom and splash water on her face. She stopped in her tracks when she realised Charlotte was standing there, her head down, making no sound.

'Sorry, Charlotte. I didn't see you there.'

'Flora. I need to tell you something. It's important.'

'Not now, Charlotte. I can't. Not now. Can you watch the children for a little longer.' She strode from the room and locked herself in the bathroom, needing to be alone to compose herself.

Washing her face in the sink, she finally felt strong enough to face the world again. Flora went back into the classroom and spent the rest of the day trying to make amends for her behaviour. She was furious that she had let her personal life impact her treatment of Thomas. He got enough of that from the rest of the world; this was supposed to be his safe space and it was her job to ensure it remained that way. Flora breathed a sigh of relief at the end of the day when she waved goodbye to Charlotte and shut the door on the world.

The silence was tangible. It quieted her mind and she allowed herself to sink into the office chair and think of nothing. It did not last long.

She felt devastated when she contemplated the fact that if she really did leave with Sophie, if she could not find another way, she would have to give up her centre. How would she even do that? Flora shook her head and locked the door and tried to lock in the faces of the children she would be letting down if she never came back.

Her stomach was tossing and turning, just as unsettled as her mind. Would she ever feel normal again? It was painful being around Sam at the moment. It felt like she was living a lie. There were all these feelings bubbling inside her and she could not share anything with him. What was she supposed to do? Risk telling Sam about Sophie and hope that he took their side? What if Sam talked to Greg about it and Greg took it out on Sophie? They had discussed this at length before she left yesterday and Flora would never forget the fear in her friend's eyes. Eventually, Sophie had admitted she was worried that Greg would end up killing her. That there was a chance he could go too far and accidentally kill her. Flora would have laughed in any other situation but having seen the evidence of Greg's rage imprinted across Sophie's body, was it really that farfetched to think he could take it too far?

Thankfully, fate blessed her and for the next two days – despite his promise to not leave again, she had convinced him to go away for a couple of days as nothing had happened in so long – Sam would be in Cardiff helping one of his start-ups launch their vegan food range. So far, she had kept the conversations on the phone light, making him promise not to give in and come home a vegan. There was enough stress in her life and never being able to eat a cheeseburger again would only make things worse.

Sophie was coming over tonight, taking advantage of Sam's absence and Flora hoped they would talk more. She had played so many scenarios in her head. But even if they could get Sophie away from Greg, Sam would have to choose between Flora and his family. She wanted nothing more to do with them. Greg was a nasty piece of work and Cecelia was even worse. According to Sophie, both Cecelia and Alistair knew Greg's dirty little secret. How could she cope knowing that Sam was still seeing people that had hurt her best friend? She understood he was related to these people, but surely his principles would make it hard for him to want to be around them?

The whole situation made her head and heart hurt when she thought about it too much. When she took stock of the last month, she couldn't believe that in such a short space of time, her mother-in-law had been hospitalised, she'd been half-drowned in the pool, her credit cards vanished and then reappeared, Linda had hounded her, she'd been terrorised by worms and the *pièce de résistance* – she had discovered that her best friend was being abused by her husband.

She had not even thought about her new house. The new start for her and Sam was dissolving right before her eyes. Sophie was adamant they needed to make a fresh start somewhere else. But Flora wanted to make sure they had explored every possible scenario. It would break her heart to have to sell her parents' home. She had already poured her hopes and dreams into it. Plus, Flora could not even envisage a future where she did not work at the centre. Did it make her a bad person not to want to give that up without a fight, when her friend was going through hell?

She shook her head and let out a sigh, rubbing at her throbbing temples. How had her life come to this? She had always told herself that because she had lost her parents and been raised by a psychotic aunt, she had had all of her bad luck in the early years of her life. But it seems life was not done screwing with her. She got up and began to pack her things ready to leave.

Crash.

The sound of breaking glass had her running back into the classroom. The rain was dancing into the classroom from a jagged hole in the large window. Flora raced over and peered through the gap in the glass. Through the rain droplets lashing at her face, she could see a woman with short black hair and a child with dark skin, a boy, pelting down the street as if trying to outrun an avalanche. The woman almost pulled the child's arm out of his socket as she dragged him around the corner and vanished.

Linda.

Before she had thought about what she was doing, Flora had spun around and raced to the door. With her heart beating a drum in her ears, she crossed the busy road and ran as fast as she could after Linda. She hadn't run like this since she did the 100-metre sprint at her school sports day. The wind whipped her hair across her face and she knew she would be soaked to the skin in no time. She made it around the corner where Linda had disappeared and could see they were halfway down the street, still running but Ethan was slowing them down. She could just make out his voice on the wind. Ignoring the stitch in her side, Flora sprinted as fast as she could after them.

Just as she was getting closer, Linda looked back and balked when she saw Flora. Her grip on Ethan's arm tightened and she tried to increase their pace, but Ethan wasn't playing ball.

'Leave me alone!' Linda shouted at Flora, trying desperately to pull Ethan away but Ethan was now holding on to a lamp post, stopping them from moving any further, screaming at his mother, tears pouring down his face. 'You hurt my arm,' he cried.

Flora reached them and had to bend over to try and force air into her lungs. A few seconds later she could speak. 'What have you done, Linda? Why are you doing this to me?'

Linda turned her back on Flora, facing Ethan and trying to pry his fingers away from the lamp post. 'I don't know what you're talking about.'

'I just saw you! You threw a brick through my window.'

'No I didn't.'

Ethan stopped crying for a moment and stared at his mother, bewildered. 'Yes you did, Mum. You said we had to do it.'

'Don't tell lies, Ethan. Now come on. Let's go home and I'll make you spaghetti with the meatballs that you like.'

'I'm not lying, Mum. You said we had to so that woman would give us more money. So you could buy me chalk.'

Linda wrenched Ethan's fingers apart and pulled him away from the lamp post and set off down the street once more.

Flora followed them. 'What woman? Why are you doing this to me, Linda?' she shouted.

But Linda was looking resolutely ahead and would not look back.

'I'm going to have to call the police. You have been terrorising me. You put worms in my bed. Who does that? How did you even get in?'

Linda stopped dead. She turned to look at Flora, her face gaunt and white as a sheet. 'Worms?' she said faintly. 'I haven't got anything to do with any worms. I don't even know where you live.' Linda was about to say more but was interrupted by a notification on her phone. She pulled out an iPhone and unlocked it. Her face went even paler and she wobbled on her feet, as if about to fall. 'I have to go. Come on, Ethan. It's an emergency. You know what that means.'

Ethan nodded his head and turned to move away.

'I'm sorry, Flora. I had no choice. I'm so sorry.'

Before Flora could react, Linda and Ethan turned and marched away. She was about to follow them when her phone went off, distracting her. *Unknown Caller* flashed up on the screen of her phone. She looked up, intending to follow Linda. She needed answers. What woman was Ethan talking about? Cecelia? This could be the evidence she needed to prove to Sam that his mother was terrorising her. But Ethan and Linda had vanished. There were so many routes they could have taken, she would never find them now.

She answered the phone.

'Flora. It's PC Valerie. Where are you?'

'At work.' She turned and began to walk back to the centre, wishing she had thought to put on a coat: her blouse was plastered to her skin, she may as well have gone swimming fully clothed. The noise of cars on the road and the roaring wind made it hard to hear what the policewoman was saying. But it soon made sense when she saw the flashing blue lights outside her centre as she walked around the corner.

Flora ended the call and jogged back to the centre. She opened the door and saw two men boarding up the hole in the glass. Another young PC was clearing up golden leaves that the wind had propelled through the gap, stuffing them into a black bin bag. Puddles had formed near the glass, glistening in the light from the ceiling.

PC Valerie came out of her office and strode towards her. 'Where were you?' she asked curtly.

'I... erm. What are you doing here?' Confused, Flora couldn't remember calling the police. She had chased after Linda within seconds of hearing the crash.

'We've been watching the centre since the incident with the note. Chief Constable's orders. It was just unlucky that this happened during shift change. Now, where were you? Why didn't you call us immediately?'

'I was chasing the person that did it,' snapped Flora, who was not enjoying being treated like a child. She was uncomfortable that her centre had been under surveillance without her knowing. Surely they should have told her that. She might even have felt safer knowing.

'What? That was a very dangerous thing to do, Mrs Cavendish. The Chief is not going to be happy about this. He has known the Cavendish family a while and he stressed the importance of keeping you safe to all of us. We can't very well do that if you go running after a potentially dangerous perpetrator.' She gave Flora a look she couldn't quite interpret but it was not friendly. 'Let's go to your office and I'll take your statement.'

Flora didn't even know how she got home. One minute she had been giving her statement to PC Valerie, the next she was walking through the front door of the house. Her body and mind were weary. She wasn't scared anymore, just fed up. When was she going to catch a break? Linda was intent on ruining her life, possibly egged on by Cecelia. Her best friend in the whole world was suffering. With a groan, she looked at her watch and realised that Sophie would be coming over any minute now. She fingered the necklace. The person who had it made and put in her centre had wasted their time. Now the initial shock was over, the necklace only gave her strength – not fear.

She raced upstairs to change. The bedroom was the only room that she would miss in Sam's house. The guilt at sleeping in an opulent super-king bed had faded now and she loved nothing more than to bury herself in the bed, cuddled by all the cushions and wrapped warm in the duvet. It was a TV bed that meant she could have her own private cinema. It was the only room in the house that did not make her think of Cecelia. It was like her poison stopped at the door to the bedroom – an invisible barrier that she could not penetrate. Sam and Flora had chosen the décor in this room. Hence the massive sixty-five-inch television, hooked up to a PlayStation, a computer, and an Xbox. The rest of the décor had been chosen by Flora and she had painted one wall bright orange just to annoy Cecelia and the rest in an off-white. The orange wall was diluted by the fact Sam had covered it in pictures.

Since she had moved in, Sam had taken to hanging photographs of their lives together. Every so often she would come in the room and there would be a new photograph on the wall. They weren't all photos at occasions like weddings and parties, but silly selfies he had snapped on his phone. From the very first picture they had taken together to the last, it was possible for anyone looking at the wall to see their love had not diminished with time, it had only become stronger.

Could she really give that up without a fight? She looked around the room, trying to contain her misery, realising that unless she could come up with a solution, her days with Sam may be numbered. All she knew was that she needed to find a way that she could save both Sophie and her marriage. How was she supposed to choose between the two people she loved most in the world?

46

'Ah, Sophie. So happy you could join us.' Alistair smiled widely. Only his eyes betrayed the malice behind his words. The pub was a boozer pub, where the floor was sticky, and the air stagnant; not the sort of place Alistair Cavendish would frequent. But the person sitting next to him most certainly would.

Her mother.

The years had not been kind. Lily looked like she had been soaked in alcohol. Her skin was sallow and stretched and had turned slightly yellow. Her hair was mostly grey and greasy. She smiled over at Sophie and revealed a set of yellow and brown teeth with gaps where some had fallen out. Was that a bit of sick staining her blue jacket?

Her eyes hadn't changed, though, they were the same piercing, ocean blue that Sophie remembered as a child. Those eyes had been staring at Sophie whilst accusing her of stealing alcohol and shredding her precious books when she wouldn't reveal where the non-existent alcohol was. Those eyes had burned bright with glee at finding Sophie's stash of money that she had earned cleaning cars in the baking sun. Those eyes had been unfocused and bloodshot after spending that money on three bottles of vodka. Those eyes had almost ruined her life. She thought she had escaped those eyes forever.

'Hello, darling.' Her alcoholic perfume was cloying and it caught in the back of Sophie's throat, trying to choke her. Judging by the way Lily could barely hold herself upright, it seemed she was already half-cut. 'Aren't we all grown up?'

Sophie was surprised her mother recognised her. The last time they had seen each other, Sophie had been fifteen and had managed to use a fake ID to rent her own flat. She had slammed the door on her mother and had never looked back. Until now, she had not even known if Lily was alive as there was every possibility she had drunk herself to death. Without Sophie there to help her when she got so drunk that she vomited while unconscious or tried to light the gas stove, who would save her?

Alistair was looking like the cat that got the cream, and Sophie wished not for the first time that her mother had died. She completely ignored her mother and focused on Alistair. 'What is she doing here?'

'Tsk. Come now, is that any way to speak about your long-lost mother?'

'I said, what is she doing here?'

Alistair smiled broadly. With his Armani suit with the pocket chief, he looked like a champagne glass on a shelf full of chipped, grubby mugs. She was surprised he hadn't been robbed. 'We were just having a very... enlightening... conversation. One of many, I hope.' He turned to Lily, retrieving his wallet from his suit pocket. He withdrew a roll of £20 notes and passed them to Lily, who glanced between him and the money in disbelief.

'Here. Take this and get yourself a drink. Keep the change.' He winked at Sophie. Lily took the money and squealed like a small child on Christmas Day, tripping over in her haste to get to the bar. Alistair chuckled. 'What an interesting woman. I can certainly see the resemblance.'

Sophie bristled, but bit down hard on her tongue. *Do not rise to it*, she chided herself. 'What exactly were you talking about?' she asked, trying to keep the fear out of her voice.

Alistair tapped his nose. 'Never you mind. But safe to say, it was extremely interesting. It has definitely made me look at you in a whole new light.' He stared at her with twinkling eyes.

Her heart pounded and she tried to surreptitiously take some calming breaths. He was bluffing. He had to be.

'Now. Let's get down to business.'

Sophie went cold.

He said, 'I have been feeling very uncomfortable lately. I do not like to feel uncomfortable.'

'My heart bleeds,' said Sophie with more bravado than she actually felt. She was well aware how dangerous Alistair was when crossed.

'Now, now. I'd be very careful how you speak to me, Sophie. Remember, I have the power to destroy your life.' He took her hand and kissed the back of it. 'But I hope it won't come to that, of course.'

Sophie couldn't breathe. He couldn't know. Only two people in the world knew her secret. A secret so powerful that if revealed, could ruin her life. No. There was no way that he knew that. He must be talking about something else. But what?

'I've been having some very disturbing conversations with Greg. I do not like what I am hearing.'

Sophie took a deep breath and composed herself. She had not come to this meeting unprepared. Alistair was trying to intimidate her, insinuate he knew something about her to get her to break and tell her what he wanted to know. Had she not seen him use the same tactic time after time in meetings with entrepreneurs? She may hate the Cavendish family with every fibre of her being, but there was no doubt that she had learnt some useful tricks of the trade. She now always made sure she was one step ahead and never turned up to a meeting without knowing her opponent's vulnerabilities. Luckily for her, Alistair's weakness had fallen into her lap by a happy accident. 'Oh, I'm sorry to hear that. But you can't believe everything that son of yours says.'

'Nice try. But I'm afraid I've known my son long enough that I can tell when he is lying. He's shown me what you have done.'

'I have no idea what you are talking about.'

Alistair leaned forward and hissed at her. 'This is not going to end well for you, Sophie. Just put it back.'

Sophie leaned forward, mirroring his pose. 'Put what back?' she whispered theatrically.

The skin around Alistair's eyes tightened and his eyes were burning with suppressed rage. 'If you want to play games, you will soon realise that I always win.'

'You've lost me. Who's playing games with who? What are you winning?' Sophie put on her best innocent face, eyes wide.

'Let me be clear. Knowledge is power. If you don't return what's mine, then I'm afraid I'll have no choice but to use what I know.'

'But if you do that, then I'll be forced to use what *I* know, Alistair.' She met his eye, unblinking and she could see he was suddenly unsure of himself. The whirring of his brain as he tried to work out what she knew was almost audible. He turned slightly pale and his eyes bored into her, trying to burrow into her mind and work out what she could be talking about. That's the thing about men with power and money. They have so many skeletons in their closets, it was hard to keep track.

'I don't know what you mean.'

'Oh, Alistair. I've watched you long enough now to know

never to reveal my hand. Just like you aren't telling me what you know, I'm not telling you.'

He stared at her, unblinking. She met his gaze, ignoring the sting of protest from her eyes as she refused to blink.

'You're bluffing.' He leaned back in his seat, his composure returned.

Sophie tutted. 'You think that, Alistair? Let's just say, I have evidence of something that if leaked to the press could prove *very* detrimental to the good Cavendish name. What is our tag line again? Trust, honour and integrity. Cavendish is a name you can trust.'

'I don't believe you.'

'Feel free not to believe me. But that would be foolish.' She leant forward. 'I think they call it *mutually assured destruction*.' With that she got up and walked away, resisting the urge to look back at Alistair. Otherwise he might see that her hands were shaking. It took a whole packet of cigarettes before she was calm enough to drive home. Alistair had not left the pub. She hoped he was still reeling from their conversation, that she had done enough to fend him off for now. Things were getting very complicated.

47

Alistair Cavendish exploited the fact his company was supposedly steeped in tradition, having been passed down from generation to generation. He enchanted prospective clients by regaling them with the legend of his family company that had been investing in businesses for hundreds of years.

Which is why Flora was never sure why the company headquarters had moved out of the historic building of its origins into a state-of-the-art skyscraper made by what she thought must have been a drunk architect. Craning her neck back, her eyes soaked up the large glass windows and random juts of metal poking out haphazardly. It was supposed to be modern and edgy but to her it looked like Godzilla had knocked it down and a six-year-old had glued it back together.

At the previous office, large stone pillars loomed at each side of the grand wooden door. The white marble-effect of the stone and the Latin engravings gave a sense of history and credibility. You could not help but feel connected to the past when you were there. Now, Cavendish & Sons were housed in just one of a row of many ugly skyscrapers. She shook her head and followed a crowd of suited men and women into the building. Who was she to judge? Her centre was scraping by month by month and her salary was probably less than they paid the cleaners here. Luckily her insurance was covering the repairs to the window, but it had still meant she had lost money from cancelled sessions.

Flora had only visited Sam a handful of times at his place of work. She always felt intimidated and underdressed in comparison to the sharp suited, perfectly styled women that worked here. Today was no different as she surreptitiously tried to pick off stray hairs from her black jeans whilst she waited. Flora smoothed down her hair, conscious that it had been blown about by the wind outside. A large vase with lilies bloomed in front of her. She felt the urge to move her bag out of the way in response to the irrational fear that she was going to knock it over. The corporate world was not somewhere she would ever be relaxed. In fact, it made her think even more fondly of her centre with the specks of paint engrained into the desks and the stains on the carpet.

Eventually, a large, dark-skinned lady with an unpleasant expression, dressed in a blue security guard uniform ambled over to Flora, dragging her feet. 'Come with me, please.' She sounded exhausted by life.

Flora was searched and her bag was sent through a scanner. The security guard watched the screen that showed an X-ray of the contents of her bag. Flora was captivated, this was a fancy scanner and all the colours were inverted, she couldn't recognise a single item in her bag in the patterns of bright reds, blues and yellows. Before she could ask any questions, the lady turned and shoved a clipboard into her hands. 'Sign here.'

Flora barely had time to finish her signature before the clipboard was snatched from her hands and a visitor's badge replaced it. Flora smiled brightly at the woman and thanked her, but the woman simply turned and trudged back to her seat in the corner.

Flora paused outside Sam's office. The door was slightly ajar, and she could hear voices inside. Taking advantage of this she took several deep breaths, trying to hold her nerve. She felt wretched, knowing she was betraying Sophie's trust. But she had made up her mind: she could not carry on like this anymore. She couldn't sleep. She was cancelling classes. Her whole life was turned upside down.

It was too much to bear and she needed the support of her husband, someone she trusted to help her. Sam was her husband. She had to trust in that. Look at the way he had supported her since the note in her bag. He had come home early as soon as she had told him about the brick through the window. And there was his anger on her behalf and how protective he had been. He'd even told his mother to leave when she'd turned up unannounced to see him. Yes, this was more serious, but she loved him, and she knew that he loved her. It was time to put that love to the test, even if it might ruin her best friend's life. She loved Sam with her whole heart, and she owed it to their marriage to give him the opportunity to be the man she knew he was. Sophie did not know him the way that she did. Her instinct told her that she could trust him and that he would help them.

Flora raised her hand to the door, intending to knock before she talked herself out of it. But stopped when she heard her name. The door was ajar. Turning her head, she moved closer to the gap.

'Flora is my wife. She deserves the truth. How can you expect me to keep this a secret much longer? This has been going on for too long.'

Flora's palms began to sweat. *What was he talking about?*

She was surprised to hear Greg's burly voice answer him.

Sophie had told her Greg was away. 'And I am your brother. Where does your loyalty lie? I'm asking you to keep this a secret.'

'But it's not right. Those bruises.' A banging made her jump. It sounded like Sam had hit the table or thrown something. She had never heard him sound so angry. 'You can't treat people that way and get away with it.'

'Sam, you don't know the whole story. Look, I'm begging you. Don't tell Flora. Please. Just stay quiet and stay out of it.'

'But Flora will never forgive me if she finds out I knew all along. Even worse, that I didn't do anything about it.'

'Please. Just let me handle this my way.'

Sam released a heavy sigh. 'Fine. I'm not condoning anything. But fine.'

Flora turned and ran down the corridor, stopping at a huge terracotta plant pot. She threw up, vomit splattering the roots of the tree and the wall behind it. A bespectacled man in a pin-stripe suit threw her a disgusted look as she wiped her mouth with the back of her hand. She wanted to scream at him. *You'd be sick too if you realised your entire marriage was a sham.*

Sam knows. She ran down the stairs trying to escape the knowledge. *Sam knows.* The words echoed in her mind. Her heart ached. The man she thought she knew had never really existed. He was a figment of her imagination. It was like she had been told he had died. He may as well have. Just minutes ago, she had been reminding herself that at his core, Sam was a decent human being. But she was a fool. Sophie had seen him for what he was. *He'll never choose you, Flora. In the end, his family will always come first.* From what she had heard, Sam had seen Sophie's bruises. How could he see that and stand idly by?

She walked through the foyer in a daze, unable to see the world around her, lost in her grief that the marriage she had been desperate to save was not actually worth saving. She felt a flicker of guilt as she realised that they could have left and escaped by now, but her reluctance to leave Sam, to find a way out that did not ruin her marriage had prolonged Sophie's suffering. She shuddered to think what Greg had been doing to Sophie over the last few days. *How could I have been so selfish?* she wondered. In a way, she was just as bad as Sam. She knew Sophie was being harmed, physically and mentally and she had done nothing about it. Nothing apart from consider how it was going to impact her life and how she could salvage her marriage.

Flora was at her car before she even realised that she had left the building. Her mind was flooded with images of Sophie's bruises interspersed with images of Sam and Greg laughing together, all the Cavendishes together, laughing at Sophie lying broken on the floor. She wiped furiously at the tears streaming down her face. *I need to stop being so weak. Now it's time for action.* Sophie had been her best friend for as long as she could remember. It was time to honour that and do what she should have done when Sophie first told her the truth.

She thought resolutely, *I'm going to save Sophie from the Cavendish scum. I'm going to save her. After all, we've only ever needed each other.*

48

The fury in Flora's eyes took Sophie's breath away. It was the second time she had been in her house that week and it felt strange. Sophie lay back in her bed and watched Flora pace up and down, her hair whipping around each time she turned on her heel and marched ferociously back up the other side of the room. Her brown eyes were alight with rage, her hands waved as she ranted. It was a side to Flora she did not often see, and she loved it. Finally. Finally, it was happening. The rose-tinted spectacles had been ripped off. Flora was finally seeing the Cavendish family for who they were. Including Sam.

Flora had gone to talk to Sam. That was all Sophie knew so far. Flora's anger had so far stopped her from saying anything that made sense.

'They were just in there, talking about it. Bold as brass.'

'You're talking in riddles, Flo.'

But Flora wasn't listening. 'It was disgusting. I can't believe it. I can't believe Sam would do this. How could he? I thought I knew him. But I didn't know anything.' She came to a stop at the foot of the bed, tears glistening in her chestnut eyes. But for once, they were tears of anger. 'You were right all along, Sophie.

We have to leave. This family – Sam, Greg, Alistair, Cecelia – they're evil. We have to get away from them.'

'Are you sure?' Would Flora still feel the same once she had had time to calm down?

'Of course I'm sure.' Flora stared at her, incredulous. 'I just heard Sam admitting that he knew what Greg has been doing to you; and promising to keep quiet.' Flora snatched Sophie's hairbrush off the dressing table and threw it at the wall with all her strength. She turned to Sophie and came to kneel next to the bed, taking her hands. 'I am so sorry for not being a better friend. I should have just listened to you. I should know by now to trust you. That you know what's best.' Flora looked determined. 'You've always looked after me but now it is time for me to look after you, to put you first like I should have done all along.'

Sophie couldn't speak. She was overcome with emotion.

'We need to make a plan. Decide our next move. I can't stay here any longer and neither can you.'

Sophie smiled at Flora. She had been planning their getaway for ages. It was just going to be easier now that Flora was a willing participant. 'Well, I kind of already have a plan. Like I said, it was something that helped me through, you know, everything. We have to be really clever about this, though.' Sophie looked at Flora, trying to convey how serious this was. They could not just up and leave in the night. It would take strategic planning to make it so Greg and Sam didn't come looking for them. 'Can you imagine, both wives disappear in the night. That would make them look so bad. They wouldn't allow it. They'd stop at nothing to bring us back.'

Flora looked sceptical.

'Flora, don't look at me like that. I keep telling you, reputation is everything to these people. They wouldn't be able to look any of their friends and colleagues in the eye if it got out that we had vanished. The rumours could destroy them.'

'All right. So, what do we need to do?'

Sophie stroked Flora's cheek. 'You're not going to like it.'

'What?' She grimaced.

'I know it's going to be hard. But we are going to have to pretend that nothing has happened. Act normal until I get everything ready.'

Flora looked sick. 'I can't. There's no way.'

'You have to, Flora.'

Flora sat back on her heels, horrified. 'Sophie, Sam is going to know in an instant. I am a useless liar. He's going to realise when I can't stand him touching me.' Flora looked repulsed at the thought.

Sophie got off the bed and knelt in front of Flora. 'We don't have a choice, Flora. If Greg or Alistair finds out what we are planning, they would not hesitate to act. You have to realise, they think their money makes them invincible. If they find out, I'm scared what they might do.'

The penny seemed to drop and Flora, pale as a ghost nodded. 'Okay.'

They clung to each other as though they sensed the gravity of the moment. This was the moment their lives would change forever.

49

'Hi, this is Sophie. Sorry I can't take your call right now. Leave a message.' Flora disconnected the call and threw the mobile onto the passenger seat. She'd been to her house; she'd been to Sophie's house and she could not find her anywhere. She'd driven past Sophie's hairdressers and beauty salon but there was no sign of her, and she would not answer her phone. Sophie always answered her phone.

She had woken up with a pit of dread in her stomach that morning. She had not wanted to leave Sophie. Every instinct was telling her to pack their stuff and leave. But Sophie was resolute. After another sleepless night, Flora didn't think she could wait any longer. Flora had stood over Sam as he slept soundly, alternating between crying for the loss of her marriage and wanting to smother him with a pillow, overwhelmed by fury. Her nerves were shot. She couldn't think about anything else.

With difficulty, she had called Charlotte and told her that she was experiencing a family emergency and would not be working for the foreseeable future. She asked Charlotte to run the sessions if she felt comfortable or cancel them. It was up to her. Charlotte didn't say much but that was a blessing: Flora would not have absorbed it if she had. Her entire world was imploding and the only thing on her mind was abandoning it before it cost her everything.

The fear was crippling her. She wanted to talk to Sophie. But couldn't find her anywhere. What if Greg had done something to her? Had Greg found a way to silence Sophie once and for all? Flora's hands were shaking as she took the exit that would lead her back to the Cavendish headquarters. The only place she had left to check was Sophie's office. If she wasn't there then Flora would be left with no choice but to grab the bull by the horns. She would confront Greg if she had to.

The smashed vase lay on the floor, pieces scattered everywhere. Flora watched as droplets of water that used to give life to the flowers in the vase made their way down the magnolia walls. The violence of throwing the vase at the wall had shocked her. It was like all the pent-up emotions she'd had minutes ago had smashed into pieces along with the blue vase. Greg didn't speak either. In fact, he looked pale and sweaty, his eyes darting to the corridor as people gazed in curiously. Meek Flora who always hid behind Sophie had surprised them both.

'Tell me what you've done with her.'

'For the last time, Flora, I don't know what you are talking about.'

'Sophie. You've got her, haven't you?'

'You've lost the plot.'

'I'm not stupid. She told me!'

That stunned Greg. He looked scared and quickly moved over to the door and shut it. Next, he moved to the blinds and twisted the cable, shutting out colleagues who were trying desperately to see what was going on. He turned nervously back to Flora. 'Sit down,' he said quietly.

'Sit down?' she screamed at him. 'Sit down? How am I supposed to sit down when you have been beating my best friend black and blue for god knows how long and now she has vanished off the face of the earth.' Tears coursed down her face and she brushed them away angrily.

Greg walked over to the chair behind his desk and sank into it heavily. He put his head in his hands. Flora stared at him, uncertain what to do next. She had expected anger or sarcasm. Greg looked up at her. She was startled to see tears lining his eyes. She clenched her fists. What did he have to cry about? He had been putting Sophie through hell. Was this his angle, making her feel sorry for him, to try to get her onside? The sounds of ringing of phones and people chatting floated through to them as they stared at each other. She tried to convey that she would not fall for his lies, that he had met his match. Someone had to protect Sophie from him.

'Flora, you don't have a clue what's really going on. You wouldn't believe me, even if I told you the truth.' He put his elbows on the desk and his head back into his hands. If she hadn't seen the damage his anger had done to his best friend's body, she would have believed that he was the broken man he was portraying. His shoulders had sunk and tears dropped down onto the desk, glistening against the mahogany wood. It was very convincing.

'I've seen the truth with my own eyes. Sophie showed me the bruises and told me all about the beatings.' Flora was almost spitting with anger. She moved her hands behind her back, feeling compelled to wrap them around his neck and squeeze with all her strength. She took a step towards him. He looked up and she bent over the desk so they were face to face, eye to eye.

'You think that your money will protect you. Think again. I know what you are. I know that you get your kicks beating up your loving wife when the potatoes aren't cooked to your exact requirements. I know she follows your sadistic commands because she's so terrified that next time you will just kill her. Well, let me tell you, I. Will. Bring. You. Down.'

It was hard to breathe and her whole body was quivering. She felt drunk on adrenaline, but also worried she had just made things a whole lot worse for Sophie. What would Greg do to her now he knew she had told Flora? She took a step back, reminded of how violent he could be, worried about what he would do now that she had stood up to him.

But contrary to her fears, his face was bleached of colour and his eyes wide with shock. His mouth opened and closed like a goldfish, speech failing him. His hands were trembling. He was trying to compose his thoughts, to regain his ability to speak. 'I feel sorry for you, Flora, I really do. You have absolutely no idea who Sophie really is, what she is capable of.' His voice was hoarse and quiet.

'I know exactly who Sophie is. Don't you dare try and blame her. Is that your defence? *Sophie made me do it?*'

'I didn't do anything, Flora. I am not an abusive husband.' Greg's grey eyes bored into her, like he was pleading with her to believe him.

'Don't lie. There is no point. I've seen the bruises, Greg. All over her, up her back, down her legs. She told me everything.'

'She's lying.'

'You're pathetic. Oh. My. mistake! The bruises just magically appeared by themselves. How silly of me not to realise that Sophie had managed to trip and burn the letter G into her side with cigarettes!' The urge to punch him hard rose in her.

Greg looked green in the face. 'She must have done it to

herself.' His gaze was insistent. 'I know it sounds crazy, but she is crazy. You've got to believe me.'

'You're an idiot. Do you honestly expect me to believe that?' Flora began to pace up and down, unable to believe what she was hearing. 'Sophie is one of the most loyal, brave and amazing people I've ever known. Not the sort of person to try and beat herself up. You are going to have to get a better defence than that when it goes to court.'

Greg sank back in his chair 'What's the point? You are never going to believe me. You're too caught up in her spell. You can't see her for what she really is.'

'Stop saying that. How dare you try and drag Sophie's name through the mud when you've been threatening her; stopping her from leaving. You would use all the money at your disposal to bring her back or kill her.'

Greg laughed darkly. 'That's what she told you? That I was using my money as power over her?' He stood up and walked to the window. 'I no longer have any money, Flora.' He began to laugh hysterically, wiping a tear from his eye.

'What are you talking about?' Flora asked, unnerved by his barking laughter.

Greg wiggled the computer mouse on his desk, bringing his computer screen back to life. He tapped a few keys and clicked a few times, then swivelled the screen around so she could see it. He backed away and turned to look back out of the window. On the screen was a list of various accounts and each of them was showing a balance of £0.00. 'Click on the joint account,' he ordered.

With a shaky hand, she moved the mouse and clicked on the joint account. The last four transactions on the account showed four separate withdrawals of fifty million pounds. *Two hundred million pounds?*

'She got into my online banking and transferred all of my

money into the joint and then sent it all to herself. I tried to get it back, but it's an off-shore account that can't be traced. This is our investors' money. Do you understand that?'

Flora was flustered. Her mind was trying to put the pieces together. Why would Sophie hide money at her house when all along she had millions of pounds? Flora looked at the date of the transaction, it was about two weeks ago. All this time, Sophie had taken Greg for all he had. The fight between Sophie and Greg at the barbecue sprang to her mind. Had Greg realised what she'd done then?

'This proves nothing. Maybe she took the money in retaliation for the beatings. She took enough to ensure she could get away from you.' Flora felt like she was swimming underwater in a dirty river. She couldn't see clearly. She didn't understand what she was seeing and hearing. Nothing made sense around her.

'We are rich, Flora. But not rich enough to replace that much money. Everything we have is tied up in assets. Plus, she stole it from the business. We could get done for fraud if someone found out. She has me by the balls. She controls everything. She says if I do what she says she'll put the money back, but I don't think she has any intention of doing that.'

'This makes no sense. Why would she do that to you?'

'Flora, Sophie has been making my life hell for years. It has just ramped up lately. I don't know why. We haven't been happy since–' He stopped abruptly, as if realising what he was saying. 'We haven't been happy in a long time. But recently, it seems taking this money wasn't enough. Now she has been threatening to tell the world that I am abusing her. She even threatened to go to the police. Do you understand the damage that would do to the company? To everything that my family has built? To everything that I have worked for? It would all be torn down and ruined by lies. I swear to you...' Greg came over and knelt in front of Flora. He took her arms in his giant hands and looked up at her beseechingly. 'I swear to you, Flora, I am not an abuser. I admit, I have got angry with her and sometimes had no choice but to retaliate in self-defence when she goes crazy. But I am not a wife-beater. Sophie is lying.'

50

The road was quiet. Sophie sat on the bonnet of her car, pulled over on the side of the road with her hazards on. Any cars that came would have to drive around the crazy woman sitting cross-legged on the bonnet of her car, chain-smoking like it was her last day on earth. But it was the middle of the afternoon and it seemed she had the road to herself. Sophie needed space. She needed breathing space, and this is where she came. This place was special to her. It reminded her of where she had come from and what was important in life.

Sophie was grieving. All of her best laid plans had failed. Nothing had worked. She had tried so hard to fix everything and keep Flora safe, but it wasn't enough. She looked at the phone screen again, unable to believe what she was seeing. What was it they said? *Eavesdroppers hear no good of themselves.*

Whenever she couldn't get hold of Flora, she flicked to her Find My Friend app. Today it had shown she was at Cavendish Head Office. Sophie had navigated off the app and on to her Spy Cam App. No one was more grateful than she for the development of the spy camera. She had actually lost track of the number of cameras she had installed. But the things she had learnt were worth their weight in gold. Flicking through the cameras she had checked Sam's office, but it was empty. Next, she had tried her own office wondering if Flora was trying to find her.

Eventually, Sophie had spotted her friend's chocolate-brown hair flashing into view on the camera she had hidden inside an air freshener in Greg's office.

Sophie held the phone with shaking hands and watched as Flora picked up a vase and threw it at the wall in Greg's office. Her heart sank. It was all over. She had been a finger's breadth away from success. But now she would have to find another way. Flora would understand. She had to understand.

Sophie rested her hands on her head and watched an empty McDonald's bag being blown about in slow circles. Her mind was racing, trying to come up with a Plan B. It would come to her, it always did when she was here. Here, where it all began.

51

Flora's parents were just images in her mind now. Time had erased the nuances she was sure she must have known in their speech and behaviour. There was only one memory she still had where she could remember having an actual conversation with her mother. No longer could she recall her mother's voice, but she remembered her words.

Melissa, the queen bee at school, had told her she could only come to her birthday party at her house with the hot tub if she stopped being friends with Sophie. Sophie was not cool and anyone who was friends with her was not cool either – according to Melissa. Flora remembered sitting at her mother's dressing table while her mother sat behind her brushing her long brown hair. Her mother was appalled at Melissa's behaviour and warned Flora. 'Don't let go of true friends, Flora. They are hard to find and you should not let go, no matter what anyone tells you. Loyalty is important in life. Sophie is a good friend to you. She's worth more than a hot tub, don't you think?'

Her mother had loved Sophie like a daughter. Although they had never talked about it, Flora knew her mother suspected that there was something wrong at home. She was always inviting

Sophie over for dinner and sleepovers. Hearing her mother's words in her mind, she felt ashamed. Sophie had never done anything to make Flora question her. So how dare she be taken in by Greg and his theatrics?

Obviously, it would be easier to believe Greg when he said that he had never hit Sophie because that would mean there would have been no signs for Flora to miss. She would not be the awful, self-centred friend she knew she was. Of course she would rather believe Greg than admit she had been a terrible friend and not seen that Sophie had been suffering. Sophie deserved her loyalty. Plus, hadn't she heard with her own ears Sam and Greg discussing it? They even talked about the bruises. Greg was a good liar. He was so convincing. The look in his eyes when he begged her to believe him... She could not see the slightest hint of a lie; only a desperation to be believed. But Flora felt her mother's presence as she played with the necklace around her neck. There was no doubt in her mind that her mother would want her to stand by Sophie.

Almost back at the car, Flora let out a scream when a hand grabbed her arm. She whirled around to see Sam, face tomato-red and sweaty. He bent over, hands on his knees, gasping for breath, his tie flapping around his neck.

'I've been shouting...' he gasped for breath '...you f-for ages.'

'I'm sorry, I didn't hear you.' Flora felt awkward. She had barely spoken to him since she overheard him in his office. He didn't know that she was avoiding him which made her feel even worse.

'We need to talk.'

'I just can't deal with you right now. I've got to go.' She turned, intending to find her car and leave. She needed to find somewhere quiet she could think about everything. It felt like someone had her head in a vice and with one more twist her head would explode.

'Don't believe everything Sophie tells you, Flora.'

All the muscles in her body stiffened. Her knuckles tightened into fists and the urge to turn and punch Sam in the face gripped her. She breathed hard, trying to steady herself. Slowly, she turned back to face him. 'You'd like that, wouldn't you? Get me to think Sophie is in the wrong here. All to protect your disgusting–' She walked towards him and pushed him with all her might. He didn't move far. '–wife-beating–' She pushed him again, trying harder, wanting to hurt him. '–violent thug of a brother.' Flora was out of breath. Sam, still slightly red from his run down the street, seemed calm in the face of her white-hot rage. It made her want to hurt him all the more.

'Calm down, Flora. There are things you don't understand.'

'Calm down! I've just told you that your brother is a wife-beater and you tell me to *calm down*. Go to hell!' It felt like all the air in the atmosphere had gone. She was suffocating. She turned and ran away from him, clawing for each breath. Sam's voice floated in the air behind her, but she ignored it. Her need to escape was overpowering.

52

Just when Sophie was beginning to think that everything was coming together, her world was once again swept from underneath her. Sophie had watched as Flora fled from Greg's office. She switched the app to show her the camera in Flora's bedroom and waited for Flora to come home. As predicted, Flora had come into view and thrown herself onto the bed. There was no audio but by the shaking of her shoulders Sophie could tell she was sobbing. Her heart had lurched in pain to see Flora cry. Sophie turned off the camera and dialled Flora's number. She had answered on the first ring.

'Where have you been?' Flora had screamed down the phone.

'Hey, what's wrong?'

'Where are you? I've been trying to get hold of you for ages.'

'I'm sorry, my phone died. I was with a client.'

'I... I thought something had happened to you.'

'Hey, don't cry. I'm fine. Please don't be upset. I promise I'm fine. Do you want me to come over?'

'Not right now. Maybe later. I just need to calm down.'

Sophie had watched her for an hour crying on the bed. It

was so frustrating that Flora was alone and upset. Sophie knew if Flora would just let her be there, she could make everything better. Unable to watch anymore, she had turned off the camera and driven home. Taking off her coat and shoes, she went upstairs and lay on her bed, switching between various cameras trying to locate Flora once more. Unable to spot her in the house, Sophie got up and looked out the window. She saw Flora on her patio nursing a glass of wine in the waning sunlight. Her hair the colour of coffee beans shone and even from this distance, she could see strands being blown gently in the breeze. Sophie was overwhelmed by an urge to know what Flora was thinking at that exact moment. Was she thinking about Sophie? Was she still going to keep her promise and leave with her? Or had she been corrupted? Where was Sam? Why wasn't he there? The unanswered questions bugged her.

Sophie wanted to be with her in the garden, to see Flora's face crease into a smile when she was amused, to watch the laughter light up her beautiful earth-brown eyes. She took a deep breath. It was time for Plan B. She couldn't risk Flora's future anymore. She'd tried Plan A. Now it was time for a more ruthless approach. Flora would thank her in the end.

When she had told Flora that people with money could buy anything, she was talking from experience. It took a quick Google search to realise that she needed to get her hands on some ketamine. Cecelia had horses, not to ride but to be able to say that she had horses. They had a family stables and a personal vet. It had not taken long or as many bank notes as she had thought to persuade the vet that she needed some ketamine for back pain. For another few fifty-pound notes he demonstrated how to draw up the dose and explained the best places to inject it for immediate effect.

Sophie pulled out her phone and thought hard about what to put. It needed to be something that would leave Flora no choice but to come and find her. Standing in front of the wardrobe she pulled out her hair dryer. It was not human nature to do something that was going to cause pain. Taking the cable, she let the hairdryer hang, it swung ominously before her. Without letting herself think about what she was going to do, she swung the cable hard and the hairdryer slammed into her back. The pain was incredible. She fell to her knees, breaths coming in rasps. Before she could talk herself out of it, Sophie grabbed the hairdryer and gripped it tightly. She smashed it into her side. Once. Twice. Three times. The pain overwhelmed her, and she dropped the hairdryer and clutched her side. Tears escaped her eyes, running away down her face. She curled up in a ball on her side, still clutching it. Taking deep breaths, she breathed through the pain. When the pain subsided to a manageable level, she inspected her work.

Angry red welts marked her side and the top of her shoulder. She had hit bone instead of flesh, she needed to do better. Taking the hairdryer by the cable, she whipped it around once more so that it struck her between the shoulder blades. Quickly she grabbed it and rammed it higher into her side, aiming for the fleshy part above her hip bone.

Breathing hard, trying to ignore the pain, Sophie placed her hands around her neck. She gripped as hard as she could and began to squeeze. It took all of her mental acuity to not let go. Her instincts were screaming at her to stop, her hands were trying to relinquish their hold, but her mind was stronger. She forced herself to grip harder, ignoring the pain in her throat and her lungs that were screaming for air. In the end, weakness overcame her and she could no longer keep going. She allowed her grateful lungs to suck in air and examined her neck in the mirror. It was slightly red, only visible if someone was really looking.

Steeling her reserve, she placed her hands around her neck.

It was harder to do a second time around. Her brain was still reeling from being unable to breathe. The feeling like her lungs would burst was not something she ever wanted to repeat. But she did not have a choice. It was all for the greater good. She put her shaking hands back around her neck and braced herself for suffocation, digging her fingernails in this time.

The image of Flora floated in her mind, reminding her why she was doing this. It was the only way to save them both. Flora would forgive her in the end. They were best friends.

53

There were some days that Flora believed Sophie had superpowers. Or a tracking system. She was sitting in the garden thinking of her friend when her Fitbit told her Sophie had sent a text. The old Flora would have opened it straight away. But today's Flora was unable to cope with anything else. She didn't want to see anyone or talk to anyone. She'd had enough.

Leaving her key in the front door had stopped Sam from getting in the house. He had knocked so hard the door vibrated. He kept at it until she had screeched at him through the letterbox, begging him to just leave her alone. It had been quiet ever since. Or maybe it hadn't, and the wine had dulled her sense. How much had she drunk now? It didn't matter. She needed to drink herself into an abyss. Her world, her perfect – if you didn't count Cecelia – world had been blown up and everything she held dear was in jagged pieces floating around her feet and she just couldn't put it back together again.

Her brain tried to break it down. Her friend was being beaten up by her husband. Sam knew about it but was pretending that he didn't. Greg denied he had done anything – of course.

Then there was the whole someone putting worms on her and trying to drown her in the pool debacle. She had not thought about that in so long because she had been consumed by Sophie. Now she thought about it, she was relieved nothing had happened to her since the note. She wouldn't have been able to cope with any more.

She fingered the necklace. It had been given to her to scare her, but she found it comforting to wear something so similar to what her mother had worn. It made their connection stronger. It calmed her mind and made her feel less alone. Her marriage was crumbling; the good man she thought she had married was actually an immoral coward. She tried to focus on that as it was much easier to think about leaving Sam when she hated him.

Looking around the garden, she took a big swig of wine. She had always known she would be leaving this house but she had never imagined that she would be leaving Sam as well. *Tonight will be my last night here*, she vowed. *Tomorrow, I will find Sophie and we will leave.*

Another message from Sophie lit up on her Fitbit. Why wouldn't she leave her alone? She needed this night to wallow. To grieve for her marriage. For her centre. For the beautiful children with autism she was teaching who could not cope with change, who would not understand why their teacher, one of the few people who understood them had upped and vanished in the night. A solitary tear ran down her cheek, dropping onto her jeans. She wiped at her eyes. The trail from the tear felt eerily like the slime left behind by the worm on her face. Shivering, Flora tried to quieten her mind. Stroking the necklace again, she finished her glass of wine and poured herself another. It was a Chateau Petrus, 2014. As much as she spurned the wealth Sam came from, she would miss the fine wines she had become accustomed to.

Again, her Fitbit notified her of a message from Sophie. It seemed she would get no respite from the crazy world. She picked up the bottle and her glass and weaved unsteadily back into the house. The wine was working its way around her body, loosening her up deliciously. Her phone was in her bedroom and she made her way slowly up to it. She did not want to see what Sophie had to say. Nothing she heard was good anymore.

As she moved through the house she stopped every now and then to say a mental goodbye. As much as she never felt at home here, it had been the place she had been her happiest. She stopped halfway up the staircase, remembering Sam tackling her to the floor on this very spot. She couldn't even remember why, all she remembered was the laughter that rang off the walls. Her face broke out in a smile despite how morose she felt. They had been so happy. So confident in their future, together forever. But his love of his family had broken everything.

Tipping the bottle, she dripped red wine up and down the steps. She almost wished she could be there when Cecelia saw a £2,000 bottle of wine had been spilt on the carpet she had chosen for her favourite son. She leant closer, fascinated as the red liquid spread across the carpet. It looked like dried blood. Her Fitbit buzzed again and she sighed, taking another gulp out of the bottle, seeking the sweet oblivion only excessive drinking could bring. With each swig she felt the neurons in her brain going to sleep, no longer allowing her to worry about the state her life was in. The alcohol was drowning out her worries and relaxing every muscle in her body. She made her way up to her room, stopping frequently for more sips of wine.

Reaching the bedroom, she tossed the empty bottle on the bed and looked around for her phone. It was charging on the bedside table. She stumbled over to it, the world feeling fuzzy around the edges. Sophie had sent her several messages, but she was struggling to focus on the screen, so she called Sophie instead. 'Well, hello there, Sophie-wophie.'

Silence greeted her words. Flora began to giggle. Why had she never realised before what a great sense of humour she had?

'Flora.' Sophie said her name with such pain and desperation that it instantly sobered her.

'What's wrong, Soph?'

'He tried to kill me.'

Flora's eyes welled up in response to Sophie's gut-wrenching sobs. Her heart hurt and she wanted nothing more than to wrap Sophie in her arms.

'He tried to strangle me to death. The pain. I can barely move. It hurts to breathe.' Sophie began to cry again in earnest this time. Flora didn't know what to do. Her brain was addled from the wine, all she knew was that an unbridled anger burned within her stomach. She threw the wine bottle with all her strength and it smashed against the wall like an explosion of blood, stark against the white wall. Trails of dark red stained the wall as each drip obeyed gravity's pull.

'What was that?' Sophie seemed very jumpy.

'Nothing. Listen, where are you?' Anger was bubbling dangerously inside her, fuelled by the alcohol. It was amazing that she used to be so angry at Sam for his inability to see his mother for who she was, when she had been unable to see what was going on under her very nose. She should have looked harder, listened to that unease she had felt in Greg's presence. Flora had never liked Greg, but she had never thought to wonder why. She had let it go because she thought Sophie was happy. Or was it that she was so wrapped up in this fairy tale of marrying brothers and having her best friend as her sister-in-law that she closed her eyes to the reality. Maybe she should not have been so hard on Sam when she, too, had failed to see.

'I'm in my car. I managed to get him off me and I just ran out and drove off.'

Flora shook her head, trying to clear her mind. The drink-induced haze was making it hard to think clearly. 'I've had too much to drink, I can't think straight. I'm sorry, Sophie. I shouldn't have let myself drink so much.' Flora's anger rose again, this time aimed at herself. She held her head in her hand.

'It's okay,' soothed Sophie. 'Can you come and meet me?'

'Yes. Where are you?'

'If you just walk to the park I'll be there.'

'Okay.' Flora stood too quickly, her stomach lurched, and her vision blurred as her head spun. She slumped back onto the bed, cradling her head in her hands.

'Oh, and Flora...'

'Yeah?'

'Don't tell anyone where you are going. If Greg finds out what I'm planning...'

Flora's mind was instantly filled with images of a broken and beaten Sophie lying on the floor. It didn't matter: she didn't have anyone to tell anymore. Grabbing her coat, she shut the door and locked up with difficulty, struggling to get the key in the lock. She turned around and walked slowly down the drive, unsteady on her feet. She stopped, something was missing. She looked at her house. Looked at Sophie's house. Something wasn't right. Something, that if her brain wasn't addled with drink, that would have rung alarm bells. It was only when she had been walking for five minutes, that it occurred to her what was missing. Greg's car was not on the driveway. Before she could fully understand the relevance of this, she tripped on the kerb and landed face down. Slowly climbing to her feet, she leaned on a nearby lamp post, groaning as she rubbed the gravel from her hands and knees. *Sophie better hurry up*, thought Flora. *I don't know how much longer I can stay awake.*

54

As she got in the car, there was a small part of Sophie that wondered if what she was doing was wrong. Lying to her best friend did not come easily or naturally to her. Lying through omission was a lot easier than lying directly to her face. Shaking her head, she put the car into drive and bolstered her courage. You can justify anything if what you are doing is for the greater good. Soon Flora would see that everything Sophie had done was to save her life. She practised what she was going to say all the way there.

Sophie was a planner. She needed to know exactly where she was going, what she was saying and how she would act in every eventuality. But the rug had well and truly been pulled out from under her and she was acting on instinct and trying to plan what she could in the brief time that she had.

Flora had ruined it all. By denying the natural order of things in the Cavendish world, she had put herself at risk. Only Sophie could see what Flora couldn't or wouldn't see. Cecelia and Alistair would not allow their son to move out of the family fold. He had to be exactly where they wanted them. How else would they ensure they had the ultimate control of him? Sophie had tried everything to help Flora save herself voluntarily, but nothing had worked. She now had no choice.

Slowing down as she reached the park, she saw Flora at the corner holding onto a lamp post like a lifeline.

This is going to be easier than I realised. As Sophie slowed down she glanced at her driver side compartment. The needle was still there, primed and ready to go.

55

Now she was sitting in the passenger seat, Flora turned to appraise Sophie. She seemed to be struggling for breath and hunched over in her seat, eyes creased in pain.

'What happened?'

'Same old.' Sophie chuckled heartlessly. She would not look at Flora. She never looked at her when she talked about Greg. Just stared off into the distance as she described the fight that had happened when she had not ordered the right takeaway. 'He just lost it. It was worse this time. Usually, he hits me once and then walks off. But tonight, once was not enough. His hands were around my throat. I thought it was the end.' Sophie stroked her neck, her voice choked with tears, and then she winced and clutched her side.

Flora flicked on the car light and moved Sophie's hand. Gently, she lifted her shirt and could just make out a large patch of red, swollen skin on Sophie's side. Flora blenched. It spread around her hip bone, angry and large. It was going to be a very bad bruise. Sophie pulled her top back down. Flora gasped in horror as she saw nail marks gouged into the skin around Sophie's neck.

'I don't think he broke anything this time. It was just the violence on his face.' She looked at Flora with terror and tears in her eyes. 'I was scared for my life.'

Flora tried her best to hold Sophie. But with the gear stick between them she couldn't get a proper hold. Sophie let out a cry as Flora's arm went around her shoulders. Flora pulled back, devastated to have caused more pain. 'I'm sorry.'

'It's okay. He just whacked me with something as I went to run away. I don't even know what with. I just got up and ran out the house.'

'We have to go to the police, Sophie. You've got evidence. Look at the state of you.'

Sophie shook her head emphatically. 'We've been through this, Flora. It's no use. Look what he did to me because I got his dinner wrong. What do you think he'll do when he finds out I've reported him? I don't want to take that risk. Do you?'

Flora punched the dashboard in frustration. She was just so damn angry and frustrated. 'We'll just have to leave tonight.'

Sophie was leaning down, reaching for something in a compartment in the door. Her head swivelled to look at Flora, her face ashen and shocked. 'Tonight? But I told you I needed time.'

'Look at you, Sophie. By tomorrow you are going to be black and blue. What sort of person would let their friend go back into a house where they are being beaten up? I can't stand it.' She punched the dashboard again. The alcohol stopped her feeling pain so it felt good to let out some of the anger beating a drum in her head. If she opened her mouth wide enough a jet of lava would spew from her. She was ready to erupt with the hatred that was burning within her.

'You really want to leave. Now?' Sophie did not look convinced. Flora stared into her eyes, trying to let them confirm the sincerity of her words.

'Yes. Now.'

Sophie moved her hand away from the syringe, she wouldn't be needing that anymore.

56

Sophie squeezed Flora's hand and switched on the car. They would need another car. She knew just where to get one. The plan she had loosely outlined before she had given up hope that Flora would leave with her resurfaced. The neurons in her mind were firing on all cylinders as she tried to rapidly adapt her plans and enhance them. She had to be very careful with her next moves. She thought about discussing it with Flora. But that would just slow her down. No, this was where Sophie's strengths lay, she was going to outmanoeuvre the Cavendish family this time.

'Okay, let's go.'

She drove the car towards Flora's house on Trelawney Close. The streets were relatively quiet, and she passed few cars. The car was dark except for the intermittent spotlight of a street light. Sophie glanced over at Flora and saw her mouth open, head back, lolling with the gentle turns of the car. The alcohol on Flora's breath had filled the car when she had first got in, but Sophie hadn't said anything. It seemed like she had finally fallen into a deep sleep. Judging by the drool on her face, she wouldn't be awake for a while. Tonight was going better than Sophie could have ever planned. She drove with a smile on her face. For the first time in a long time she no longer had a knot in her chest. Her whole body was relaxed, and she even began to hum gently to herself. Everything was going to work out.

With bated breath, Sophie turned off the car and looked over at Flora. Her head was leaning against the window, each breath fogging up the glass. Her hair covered her face making it impossible to tell if she was awake. After a few minutes, Sophie quietly opened the car door, she had switched off the interior lights so they would not come on when the door opened. Again, she stopped but Flora's breathing was still even and she did not stir. She leaned over and reached into Flora's coat pocket, she gently coaxed out her keys, her eyes on Flora the whole time.

Opening the front door, she looked back at the car and could just make out Flora's slumped body in the passenger's seat. As soon as she shut the door she was assaulted by the smell of fresh paint. The change in the house was astounding and she marvelled at what a fresh coat of paint could achieve. The house was no longer neglected and depressing. It was vibrant and welcoming. It gave her a momentary pang of sadness. Flora would have been so happy here. It made her anger at the Cavendish family explode. She strode through the house with a sense of purpose, locating the money exactly where they had left it. Hauling it from the hiding place, she turned to leave when she stopped suddenly.

If they were leaving forever, then Flora would get nothing. She would lose her centre and this house would stand empty. Sam might even lay claim to it. Her mind raced with the possibilities of what could happen to this house. Eventually, she looked around and nodded. There was only one thing to do. She pulled out her lighter and looked around her. Now, how to do this... It could not look like Flora had done it, it had to look like arson or an accident. Her mind raced with the possibilities. She needed to think quickly. Who knows when Flora would wake up?

The house was an empty shell due to the renovations. The only thing that had been finished so far was the kitchen. A pile of unopened mail lay on one of the worktops. It was such a pokey kitchen. The paint job had done wonders but there was no getting away from the fact the house was so small. She fingered the cooker and wondered if that was the answer. Pulling out her phone, a quick Google search told her what she needed to do. She pulled out her pack of Marlboros and lit one. It was the same cigarette brand she used to steal from her mother's purse when she was younger. It was the only link to her past that she had permitted herself.

Inhaling deeply, she felt the smoke unfurling in her body and revelled in the seductive numbing effect as it smothered all her stress and anxiety. Slowly, she put the unfinished cigarette on the side and moved towards the gas hob. The last time she'd used a cooker like this was when she lived with Flora in their student flat. She supposed they would have to get used to cooking their own food again.

Turning the hob, she listened to it clicking before the gas ignited, a small roar and then a ring of blue fire burst forth and lit up the room. She had an irrational urge to touch it, to feel the burn of the blazing fire on her skin. Switching off the hob, she twisted the knob until she could hear the hissing of the gas. Positioning the cigarette on top of the junk mail that had been left serendipitously on the side, she quickly left the room, shutting the door firmly behind her. When only moments before she been disparaging the small room, now she was grateful for it. According to Google, the smaller the room the faster it would fill up with gas. She rushed to the front door, heaving the bag of money with her, she needed to be well away before the house went up in flames.

Opening the door, she realised that the gas was more potent than she realised. The air that raced towards her was bracing and clean. She took a deep breath and her lungs gratefully drank the pure air. As she raced back to the car, the only sound was the hoot of a nearby bird, the rustle of leaves tossed around by the autumnal wind and her heels clip-clopping on the tarmac. She knew she had done the right thing. The house would be destroyed and from its ashes, they would rise, leaving behind the past and starting afresh.

57

I t was the ache in Flora's head that pulled her from sleep. She felt like someone was pounding her head with their fists. Once again, she chided herself for drinking red wine: it always punished her viciously. Her temples throbbed and she almost cried out in pain. Cradling her head in her hands, she waited for it to become more bearable. After a few minutes, the sharp pain dulled, and she could open her eyes. It was almost pitch-black except for the faint glow from a distant street light. She was in a car... Sophie's car.

Where was Sophie? Why was she in her car? Flora groped through the murky recesses of her mind, trying to work out what her last memory was. Red wine, running down a wall. Sophie on the phone crying. Agreeing to leave. That was it. They were leaving, that's why they were in the car.

She struggled to work out where she was. The light was so faint and coming from behind the car so she could not see anything out of the front window. Just all-consuming blackness, like she'd be swallowed up. The door opened and Sophie leapt into the driver's seat, she lugged a heavy bag onto the back seat. Then, before Flora could say anything, the car was reversing, the wheels squealed in protest as she launched them backwards, turning hard. A faint, indistinct smell accompanied her, Flora tried to work out what it was but was distracted as the headlights lit up the outside and she realised where they were. She turned and had only a fleeting glimpse of her house before they passed the street sign for Trelawney Close and she was flung back into her seat by the speed of Sophie's acceleration.

'What's going on?' Fear and confusion were only increasing the pounding in Flora's skull. It felt like a battering ram was being launched at her head at frequent intervals.

'Nothing, nothing. It's all part of the plan.' Sophie drove furiously, swerving around a silver Vauxhall on a blind bend.

Flora swallowed the bitter bile that had risen in her throat and closed her eyes. As they lurched around a corner, she was forced to open them again: having them closed made it worse. 'Sophie, slow down. I'm going to be sick.'

Sophie did not slow down and she did not respond. Her eyes were manic and fixed on the road. Strands of her long blonde hair were falling out of her bun. She would be horrified if she could see herself.

Flora braced herself as best she could. 'Sophie, what is the plan?'

'The plan to leave. Tonight. Remember?'

'Yes. But what are we doing now?'

Sophie did not answer straight away. 'Can't you just trust me?' she asked. 'I need to focus. I really don't have the time to explain it to you and answer all of your questions. Just know that I have spent a lot of time plotting my escape, planning for each scenario. Like I said, it was all that got me through the beatings.' Sophie's grip on the steering wheel tightened, her knuckles going white. The electronics in the car gave off a gentle blue light, enough for Flora to get another glimpse of the dark marks lining Sophie's throat.

Flora felt the gut-punch of shame at all her friend had endured alone. It strengthened her conviction that they were doing the right thing. Her resolve had been ebbing away without the synthetic courage the wine had given her. She had felt scared of the unknown, of leaving the life she had known behind. She took Sophie's hand and squeezed it because she was unable to find the words to say how sorry she was for letting her down and for not seeing that she had been suffering all this time.

'Okay, I'm sorry. I trust you,' said Flora.

Sophie didn't answer, just gave Flora a small smile and continued to drive aggressively, as if she was running from something. She supposed they were running from their old lives. Flora just wished she knew where they were running to. All the plans for her future had been smashed to smithereens by the violence of one man and the overwhelming power of a wealthy family.

58

Her mother's house looked even worse to the adult eye. Sophie had always known that she had lived in a run-down council estate but the decaying flat in front of her looked more like a building that had been abandoned after a raid. Bin bags littered the pathways and graffiti decorated every inch of wall. Had it always smelt like a urinal? She didn't remember that. Was that why no one wanted to be her friend at school? Because she smelt like a boy's bathroom? She couldn't imagine there was enough soap in the world to erase the potent smell of urine currently damaging her nose lining, making her want to gag.

Flora was reluctantly waiting in the car. Sophie had seen her guilt written all over her face and was shamelessly using it to ensure that Flora did as she was told. It was the only way the plan would succeed. Flora was too emotional. Until they were away from Manchester, she couldn't take any chances.

The spare key lay under the pot of a long-dead plant, shrivelled and black, surrounded by cigarette butts. It took several attempts to open the door as it was blocked by piles of junk mail that her mother was too lazy to put in the bin. The flat smelled like a run-down pub, a foul mixture of cigarette smoke, alcohol and a hint of vomit. Putting her sleeve over her nose, she tried to focus on the smell of her Chanel perfume. The carpet was covered by months and months of takeaway cartons and empty beer bottles.

It was hard to walk without making a noise, but she need not have worried. A herd of elephants would not wake Lily. She was lying prostrate on the floor, her yellow-stained dress bunched up around her armpits exposing her body. Sophie could just see a white thong peeking out between her mother's buttocks. She still clutched a can of Stella in her hand. Sophie kicked at her mother's bare foot, confirming what she already knew: her mother was passed out drunk. Letting fireworks off next to her head would not wake her.

Seeing her mother in this state, Sophie felt nothing but pity. There used to be ball of rage in the pit of her stomach that flared to life every time she laid eyes on her mother. But now, with the benefit of age, Sophie knew that Lily had a sickness, albeit one she appeared to have no desire to fight, instead choosing to relish in it. Almost all of her memories were tainted by Lily and her alcoholism. But staring down at her mother now, looking vulnerable and almost childlike in her slumber, she began to recall that there were some good times.

When Lily used to wake up from her binges, she would either be like an angry bull or full of remorse. Sophie had lived for those brief episodes of guilt, when Lily seemed to remember that she was a mother and that she had responsibilities. She would grab blankets from their rooms, and they would spend hours snuggling together on the sofa. On the rare occasion that Lily had any money left, she would pop to the off-licence and then come back and make them both a fry-up.

She didn't know if Lily was technically still drunk during these times, but it was the only glimpse she ever got of what she thought was her real mother, the mother she could have been without the alcohol. It was the only time Lily would wrap her arms around her, and Sophie would feel that mother–daughter bond everyone talked about. For a few precious moments, she would feel loved and not the burden that her mother would remind her she was when drunk.

For a couple of hours, she would enjoy the loving and affectionate relationship with her mother that the children at her school took for granted. But these moments were so scarce among the episodes of neglect and drunken rage that she had begun to think she had imagined them. She thought of them now as she gently moved her mother into the recovery position and then laid a blanket over her, tucking it around her to keep out the frost of the night. If tradition was anything to go by, the heating was not on as her mother preferred to use alcohol to keep her warm.

As she rose, she spotted the car keys on the floor, partly covered by a McDonald's takeaway bag. She would have been here all night trying to find them, but fate once again had shined on her and her act of kindness meant she had found the keys. It had been a slight gamble. There was always the risk that Lily would have been out in the car or sold it for more cash. But she knew Lily enjoyed being one of the few in the block that could afford a car, even if she barely spent money on fuel for it. She preferred to put her money to better use lining the pockets of the George and Dragon down the road.

But Sophie was grateful: it was the only way to get a different car. She needed a car that would not attract attention. Something the Cavendish family would not know to track. She needed to be long gone and nowhere near her BMW. Her only worry was that she should really be disposing of her car, burning it as she had Flora's house. Or hoped she had: she'd relied on Google to help her set the fire. That was an impulsive decision; maybe she should have waited to see if it actually worked. Too late now.

She stared at her phone for a long time before she finally sent the message to Alistair. This was it, the final stage of the plan.

I'm ready to make a deal. Meet me at the Basilwood Estate.

With any luck, this would be the last time she would ever see his wrinkly old manipulative face again and she and Flora would finally be safe.

59

The buzz of the alcohol had well and truly worn off. All the benefits of drinking had evaporated, leaving Flora with a raging headache and increasing sense of trepidation. Was this really happening? Was she really about to leave her husband and the life she had built for herself and run off into the unknown? Her heart ached when a small voice reminded her about the centre.

Sophie seemed to have it all planned out, but she wasn't sure where or when they would be able to settle.

On the run. Flora smiled at the ridiculous thought. This sort of thing just didn't happen in real life. Surely Greg would get over it. He wouldn't really spend the rest of his life chasing them, trying to get Sophie back. Would he? But then what did she know? She hadn't seen that he was capable of strangling his wife. Sophie had told her time and time again the ruthless way they worked at Cavendish & Sons, but she had never really taken it in. Flora had no interest in what they did. It was corporate greed and she did not want to hear it.

Leaning her tender head back against the head rest, she thought back to some of the stories she had only half listened to.

Sophie had been so full of enthusiasm when she had first joined the business. When she regaled Flora with stories of her day she would almost be bouncing up and down with the excitement of it all. But in the montage playing in her mind, she realised that gradually and almost imperceptibly the passion began to dull. Now she thought about it, Sophie seemed to almost drag herself to work and she spent more time with Flora than at the office. Again, she felt so overcome with shame that it took something like this for her to actually focus on her friend long enough to realise the shift in Sophie's behaviour. She was really lucky to have Sophie in her life. Sophie loved her unconditionally. *Despite the fact I've been a shitty, shitty friend.*

Her phone screen lit up the car and she winced in pain. Sam was calling. She already had seventeen missed calls and three voicemails. Her stomach rolled but this time it wasn't the effects of the alcohol. It was the knowledge that she had no home and would likely never see her husband again. Even though she despised his actions, she still loved him. It was impossible to turn off that level of emotion as much as she was trying. Before she knew what she was doing she answered the phone. A longing to hear his voice one last time had swept through her and taken over her subconscious.

'Flora. Thank god.'

'Sam.' She didn't know what else to say.

'Where are you?' His voice was laced with concern.

'I love you, Sam.'

He paused. She could hear rustling in the background. She thought she could just make out Greg's voice. He sounded angry. *Oh god.*

'Flora, tell me where you are.' Sam sounded scared.

Flora could see the dark figure of Sophie making her way back to the car.

'Goodbye, Sam.' And she meant it.

'Flora, no. You have to listen to me. Sophie is–' Flora cut the call and put her phone between her legs.

Sophie opened the back door and Flora could see she was shoving something into a black rucksack. Heaving it onto her back, Sophie came around to her side. 'Come on. We are changing cars.' She led Flora to a battered Ford Mondeo that had so many scratches and dents it looked like it had taken on a car crusher and won. Flora didn't bother asking any questions. Sophie's face was set with determination and Flora was too ill from all the wine to string more than a few words together. She wanted to ask what was in the black rucksack on Sophie's shoulder. It was a far cry from the Prada handbag she usually had with her. But instead she focused on breathing and keeping down the bile that kept rising up inside her.

'Get in,' ordered Sophie. She was twitchy and nervous, looking around them as if expecting the police to show up at any moment.

Flora's laugher rose unbidden. It was like they were acting out parts in an 80s crime television show. It just was not real. This could not be her life. Swallowing her laughter, she got in the car. The perfume of rotten food hit her hard and she opened the door she had just shut and vomited across the tarmac.

'Shit!' cried Sophie. She flung open her door and ran around the car to Flora's side. She held Flora's hair as she retched.

Finished, Flora wiped her mouth gingerly. Sophie's cool fingers stroked her face and smoothed her hair. Flora moved back into the car and Sophie let go and went back around to the driver's side. The smell was overpowering, and Flora looked in the back and saw several half-eaten cheeseburgers that were now a shade of green. The rest of the car was decorated with an array of beer bottles. A pattern of suspicious dark stains across the back seat stopped her inspection and she looked straight out of the window, trying to breathe only through her mouth.

Sophie wound down her window and then lent over Flora to wind down hers for her. The scent of Sophie's perfume was a welcome relief in comparison to the vile bouquet of mouldy food and stale beer. She put her face in Sophie's neck trying to block out the invading stench and Sophie let out a giggle. She pulled Flora into an awkward hug and they stayed like that for a few minutes.

Sophie was the first to pull away and she put the key in the ignition and twisted it. The car made a pitiful whirring noise but did not start.

'Damn it!' Sophie hit the steering wheel hard. She tried over and over, her language becoming fouler with every failed attempt. 'Come on, you bastard.' Sophie looked like a wild animal, close to spitting with rage.

'Do you want–'

Sophie turned to look at Flora with fury in her eyes. Her voice so loud it reverberated around the car. 'No, Flora. I don't want you to do anything. Just fucking sit there and shut up!'

Flora was stunned into silence. She looked away, out of the window so that Sophie would not see the tears welling in her eyes. But Sophie would not have noticed. She was beating the steering wheel, her hair unruly. Almost all of it had now escaped the confines of her hair tie. It was such a contrast from her usual chic appearance, she seemed almost deranged. Sophie hit the steering wheel with a strength that belied her thin frame. One more time she twisted the key in the ignition and seemed to sag with relief when it finally caught and the engine whirred into life. But Flora didn't really care. Sophie had never spoken to her with such venom before. The way she had looked at her... It was as if she hated her. Wiping at the tears, Flora tried to reconcile this maniacal woman with the best friend she loved.

Sophie is just stressed, she reasoned. She had lived with a violent bully for so long and it was obvious she was terrified of him. It was understandable then that she was anxious that their escape did not go wrong. After all, Sophie was making all the decisions, she was the one taking all the steps. It was all on her shoulders. The pressure must be immense. Flora thought back to Sophie's face when she was telling her about her other failed escape attempts and the things that Greg had done. Now she had involved Flora, that would probably incite even worse repercussions. No wonder she was lashing out. If it was left to Flora, she would have over-analysed everything so much so that she'd still be in her back garden deciding on a name for Plan A, whereas Sophie had Plans A, B and C, probably all the way through to Plan Z.

Thankfully, when Sophie put her foot down on the accelerator, the car was too old to respond as quickly as the BMW, so Flora was not treated to another nauseating rollercoaster ride. When they hit the A-roads, Flora reached for Sophie's hand which was resting on her lap. She squeezed it gently and felt a rush of happiness when Sophie squeezed it back. Everything was okay again. Flora didn't ask where they were going or what was next. She knew that Sophie had everything under control. Her job was just to be there to support her. She trusted Sophie with her life after all.

When she would look back on this moment, she would despair at how naïve she had been.

60

Ever since their confrontation in the pub, Alistair had kept a very close eye on Sophie. He had attended all of her meetings, he sent her constant emails asking questions about decisions that she had made, he'd even turned up at their house, telling Greg he fancied a drink with his son, but spent the whole time staring at Sophie. Everywhere she turned he was there. He was trying to intimidate her, but it wouldn't work.

Fate had given her a weapon against this man. She knew he was not all powerful and infallible and she had to use that to her advantage. Stealing the money was not enough to keep them under control. She could see that now. Luckily, in the rucksack behind her seat she had the tools to overpower Alistair, to ensure that he not only let them go, but that he would ensure the whole family would toe the line. Sophie had tried to explain it to Flora. Alistair's whole world was built on reputation. You could have all the money in the world but if people didn't trust you, if they knew who you really were, that money may as well be Monopoly money. No one would want an investment from Cavendish & Sons if there was a whiff of a scandal. The investors would take their money and run, and the building blocks would fall until the entire company collapsed.

Sophie had the power to do that. It had fallen into her hands at Alistair's birthday party and she could not believe her luck. She just had to work out the best way to use it. If she used what she had to bring down Cavendish & Sons, she would make a dangerous enemy. Although Alistair would lose money, he would not be penniless and there was no doubt he would spend his remaining days trying to track her down and exact some form of heinous revenge. No, it seemed far safer to hand over what she had in return for their freedom.

Pulling up at the estate, it was so dark she could barely see her hand in front of her face. She pulled out her phone and turned on the torch and Flora did the same. Flora was quiet and Sophie was surprised she had not asked any more questions. It seemed Flora had realised that Sophie knew best and that she needed to trust her. All Sophie had done since she had met Flora was make sure she was safe and happy and she wasn't about to stop now.

Sophie groped blindly in the back seat, wincing as her fingers brushed the contents of a takeout container. She was glad she couldn't see what it was. She pulled her hand back and wiped whatever it was on her jeans. Reaching back in she managed to find the rucksack and pulled it out gingerly, not wanting to jostle the contents too much.

The estate was the first investment she had made, the impossible challenge that Alistair had set for her on her first day at the company. The client was finally building the first estate of flat-pack, affordable homes. Only one had been built so far, a show home for buyers. She had helped him secure this beautiful plot of land. It had a campsite feeling as it was surrounded by a man-made forest of Douglas fir trees. They passed by the domineering trees, which were dancing and swaying in the bracing wind. Street lights had been erected but were yet to be turned on, given that no one was actually living here. Wooden boards made a crude path up to the show home. It was here she led Flora, the beam of their phone torches lighting up the way. The silence was eerie. In another situation she may have felt a little nervous, but she was too focused on the task ahead. Her whole body was tense, like an elastic band being pulled so taut it was in danger of snapping.

This was the final part of her plan. A journey that started when Flora announced that she and Sam were moving. Everything she had done since that day had led to this moment. She could not screw it up. Her torch eventually lit up a forest-green front door that belonged to a wood-clad home. It was deceptively small on the outside but could easily house a family of four inside. She heard Flora swear next to her and the world got darker. 'Shit, my phone has died.'

'It's fine. We are here now. Hold this up so I can unlock the door.'

Sophie unzipped the small pocket at the front of the rucksack and reached in for the keys. Unlocking the door, she took back her phone and used it to locate the light switch. The house had that new-build smell, a blend of wood chippings and fresh paint. The furniture would be arriving the following week, but it was just an empty space at the moment. It was the perfect place for the final chapter of her war with the Cavendish family.

61

Flora was finding it harder not to ask questions. Sophie had taken them to a remote forest, half a mile from the main road. Giant, imposing fir trees formed a tight circle around them. The only break in their guardianship was the small road that they had driven down. They were nature's version of prison fences, whether they were there to keep the world out or to stop people from leaving she was not sure.

The dark was oppressive and the whispering of the wind between the trees chilled her. She felt vulnerable being this far away from civilisation. Were they going to stay here? Was this part of Sophie's plan, to hide here for a while and lay low? But she had seen building equipment and piles of sand near the boards they had walked on. The builders would be coming back, surely.

Flora was starting to wish she was back at home. She thought of Sam, being tucked up in bed with him, safe in his arms. What was she doing? People didn't do this. She and Sophie needed to stop this and go to the police.

Sophie believed that Greg was above the law and his friendship with Doyle would be enough to prevent the police from helping her. But surely if they shouted loud enough and told enough people, they would start to listen? Wasn't that better than giving up everything they had built to disappear into the wilderness. But then, could she really expect Sophie to watch her and Sam play happy families, knowing that his brother was always going to be in the picture. Sam could no sooner cut out his family than he could cut off his own arm. No, she had to leave with Sophie. It was the only way. Anyway, at least she would make Cecelia happy. There would be no more worms in her bed or people trying to drown her in the pool.

Flora sincerely hoped they weren't staying here. She followed Sophie into the little cabin and was pleasantly surprised by the space inside. Although there was electricity, there was no heating. They were sheltered from the wind, but the temperature was no less biting. She pulled her coat around her, wishing she had brought something warmer. This wasn't going to keep her warm tonight when the temperatures dropped further.

'What are we doing here, Soph?'

'Meeting someone.' Sophie put down her rucksack and opened it. She pulled out a book and laid it on the floor. Reaching further into the bag she pulled out a gun.

A gun?

Flora's heart stopped beating. She was rooted to the floor and tempted to pinch herself. Surely she was in a dream. This was getting ridiculous now. Swapping cars was crazy enough but a gun? Sophie didn't know how to use a gun. Where would she have even got one from? Flora watched in stunned amazement as Sophie held the gun in one hand and pulled out the bottom of it. Bronze bullets glinted in the light as Sophie reloaded with the confidence of someone who knew what they were doing.

'What the hell are you doing with that?' Flora's voice rose and sounded almost hysterical.

Sophie stood up straight nonchalantly and tucked the gun in the back of her jeans. 'Calm down. It's just for protection.'

'Protection from what? Sophie, I don't like this.'

Sophie wrapped Flora in her arms. She made soothing noises and stroked her hair. Normally this worked – but Flora was wired. Sophie had a gun. A real-life killing machine. *What else does Sophie have that I don't know about?* Flora couldn't process this. She pushed Sophie away, more forcefully than she intended and she saw a hurt expression flash across her friend's face as she stumbled backwards.

'You have to tell me what is going on. This is crazy.' Flora gestured to the outside. 'I mean, where the hell are we? Why do you need a gun? Who are we meeting?' The questions rushed out of her like she was a popped inflatable.

A loud knock at the door echoed around the empty room. Sophie jumped around, breathing hard. Her shoulders went back and she went to the bag, picking up the book and gripping it tightly.

Flora's heartbeat increased, the tempo pulsating in her ears. The hairs on the back of her neck rose as Sophie reached out a shaking hand to the door. They were two women on their own in the middle of nowhere. What could go wrong?

Alistair Cavendish was the last person she expected to see at the door. His white hair normally combed back had been tousled by the wind, but this was the only thing that marred his appearance. His pristine black overcoat flapped in the wind, revealing a black suit underneath. It was one of those obviously expensive suits that was impervious to creasing. He smiled widely at Sophie as he waited to be let in. It was not a friendly smile. It was the smile of a predator. He was like the wolf at the door, trying to get the little pigs to let him in.

Flora let out a whimper as Sophie stood back to admit their father-in-law.

Oh no. Is Cecelia on the way? Did the Cavendishes know they were going to leave and were intending to stop them? Maybe he was here to negotiate. He wouldn't want the world to know that his son was a violent thug who beat up his wife.

'Sophie, Flora. How delightful.' He sounded like a kindly old man, but his eyes betrayed him, a wicked glint spoke of his true feelings.

Sophie shut the door and quickly moved so that she was stood in front of Flora, blocking his access to Flora but also Flora's view of Alistair. Shifting slightly, she moved so that she could see around Sophie.

'Alistair. Thanks for coming.'

Flora was reeling. Why the hell had Sophie invited the very person she had been warning her about?

'I wouldn't have missed this for the world. I was very intrigued when I got your message, I must say. So, what deal do you have for me?' He rubbed his hands together, looking expectant.

Sophie held up the hardback book, its jacket was shining in the light. 'This. In exchange for mine and Flora's freedom. We can leave. No one follows us.'

'And why might this book *What to Expect When You're Expecting* be of any interest to me, dear girl?' He sniggered derisively.

'Don't you recognise it? You found me in Cecelia's office, and I said I was borrowing it.'

Alistair bowed his head in acknowledgement.

'Well, it turns out it isn't a book about babies.' Sophie pulled off the book jacket and dropped it to the floor, revealing a mahogany Moleskin notebook. 'This is, in fact, Cecelia's diary.'

Flora saw the colour drain from Alistair's face. He moved towards her, but Sophie was quicker, she pulled out the gun from her waistband and pointed it at Alistair. He backed off straight away, hands in the air.

'Now, now, Alistair. Where is your sense of decorum? That's no way to act in a business meeting.' Flora could hear the smile in Sophie's voice. She sounded confident and powerful. She was now the wolf in the room and there was no doubt in Flora's mind she would blow this house down, with Alistair in it.

'Really, Sophie. A gun? I would never hurt you.'

Flora did not believe him. The fury on his face as he had dived for the book was undeniable.

'Look, let's quit messing around. I've made a copy of every page of this book. It's quite heart-wrenching, really. Almost made me feel sorry for the old bat. No wonder she was such a bitch to me and Flora when she has to put up with all the things you did to her.'

Alistair's knuckles clenched and Flora knew without a doubt that if there was not a gun trained on him, he would have lashed out at Sophie. Flora gathered that Sophie was talking about Cecelia. But what did she mean, she felt sorry for her? Why had Sophie not told her any of this? Flora was beginning to realise that there were a lot of things Sophie had kept from her. Dread flooded her.

Alistair was holding himself back and almost shaking with the effort.

Flora was captivated by the whole scene in front of her. It was like she had been living in a separate universe for the last five years. She thought of Alistair as an aloof and ruthless businessman, but it seemed there was much more to him than that. The scene before her was like something out of a wildlife documentary, like two male gorillas fighting for dominance. Only instead of a violent, bloody fight, it was a battle of wills.

'I see. Can I look, to verify that it really is Cecelia's diary?'

Sophie turned to Flora. She passed her the book and then

nodded towards Alistair. Flora grabbed the book with shaking hands. She moved slowly towards Alistair, scared to make any sudden movements.

'Don't let him touch it, just open it and show him some pages.' Sophie's voice instructed her from behind and Flora could feel the stare of the gun that was pointed at her and Alistair. She opened the book almost halfway in. She had a glimpse of handwriting and a few words leapt out at her – 'blood' and 'fists' – before she turned it around so that Alistair could see the pages. His eyes roved hungrily over the words and his face seemed to be turning grey.

Sophie taunted him. 'Doesn't make for very pleasant reading, does it?'

Flora shut the book and moved back behind Sophie, pleased to be out of range of the gun.

'Do we have a deal?'

Alistair wasn't looking at Sophie. His eyes were darting here and there as if trying to work out a complex maths problem. Sophie continued when he didn't respond. 'I don't care about you or your stupid business. All I want is to be free of you all. For me and Flora to escape this viper's nest and start afresh somewhere new.'

It seemed the shock of Sophie's revelation about the book had worn off, the colour seemed to be coming back to his mind and his eyes began to twinkle menacingly as his composure returned. 'Viper's nest?' He began to chuckle. 'I wonder if dear Flora knows that she will be leaving one viper's nest for another. Probably the most deadly and poisonous of them all.'

The dread in Flora's stomach worsened.

'Oh, Alistair, you're so pathetic.' Sophie turned her face slightly, so her voice was directed at Flora. 'Flora, don't listen to anything he says, he's just trying to drive a wedge between us. It's his classic business strategy. Divide and conquer.' Sophie turned to look back at Alistair. 'But he doesn't know that we cannot be divided. Nothing he can say can tear us apart.'

'Oh really?' Alistair looked like all his Christmases had come at once. He stepped forward and stared straight at Flora. 'Not even the knowledge that Sophie's mother was the drunk driver that killed your parents? That Sophie was there when your mother and father died. She watched their car explode and did nothing to save them. That she has known all along that her mother is the reason that you have no parents. Not even that could destroy your friendship?' His smile was as wide as that of the Cheshire cat.

62

'It was Sophie's mother who killed your parents. It was her mother's car that ran them off the road.' The secret she had kept from Flora for so long was finally voiced. It was both a relief but also terrifying. Memories rose unbidden of Flora's mother's screams as the flames licked her body and burnt her alive. This wasn't how it should have come out. Flora wouldn't understand unless she explained it to her.

Sophie lowered the gun and turned to face Flora, terrified by what she was going to see on her best friend's face. Her mother had betrayed her once more. She was foolish to think the threat of prison would stop Lily from spilling her darkest secrets for the promise of alcohol. She should have known better. All this time she had had plenty of opportunity to silence her, but she had been foolish.

Flora's eyes were wide, and her skin was ashen. It looked like her spine had been removed and she was going to collapse any minute. She stared at Sophie, waiting for her friend to deny it.

But the fight had left Sophie. This secret had taken up a whole shelf in her mind and there was no going back. She would have to explain everything. They had been best friends for so long. She knew if she could just get Flora to understand then it would be fine. 'You've got to understand, Flora. It wasn't my fault. I couldn't save them.'

Alistair's smile lit up his face. Having thrown the grenade, he was now watching the devastation with fascination and enjoying every splinter of pain that he had caused.

'Flora, I'm so sorry. You have to let me explain everything. You'll understand everything if you just let me explain.'

Flora wiped her mouth with the back of her hand and looked at Sophie with fury and pain in her eyes. 'You knew.' Flora's voice was eerily calm. 'All this time, you knew it was your mother.' Her face contorted in pain. 'You comforted me, helped me grieve, knowing all along it was your mother's fault I had no parents.' Flora spat the words at her. The look of revulsion on her face was like a physical wound to Sophie's heart.

'How could you be my friend all these years? Knowing what you knew? How could you not tell me something like that?' Disgust flushed across Flora's face and she looked like she was about to launch at Sophie and attack her.

'I was doing what your mother asked me to do.'

The words rang out, silencing the room.

'Everything I've ever done, I did it because your mother asked me to.'

63

Flora felt like she was looking through a kaleidoscope, seeing both Alistair and Sophie but also a montage of her parents dying in a car with Sophie and Lily watching from above. Bile rose in her throat, but her stomach was already empty. She could not wrap her mind around this. Her mother. Sophie.

The front door banged open. Sam strode into the room, closely followed by Greg. Sam's eyes were on Flora. He strode over to her, covering the distance in seconds and wrapped her in his arms. Before she could appreciate his warmth, he pulled away, taking her face in his hands. 'Thank god you are okay. Are you all right? Has she hurt you?'

Tears poured down Flora's face in response. Her whole world was disintegrating before her. Nothing made sense anymore.

'What have you done to her?' he spat at Sophie. He didn't appear to notice the gun in Sophie's hand. She was leaning against the wall, seeming to need it for support. Alistair had moved so he was sitting on the windowsill, a spectator at the cinema. He just needed snacks.

'I haven't done anything. All I've ever done is look after her and try to make her happy. You have to let me explain, Flora.'

'Explain what? How you let my parents die?'

'I was still a child, fourteen. I tried to get them out.' Tears coursed down Sophie's anguished face. 'She was begging me to help her, but the door wouldn't open. The car was upside down and on fire. Then my mother dragged me away. She forced me into the car and made me leave with her. I loved your mother. I would never have let her die. You have to believe me. There was nothing I could do.'

Flora had tried to block out images of her parents' final moments. It was bad enough they were gone. When she was younger, she would torment herself with wondering what the last thing they saw was. Wondering what the last thing they thought before they died. Were they thinking about her? Flora felt faint. Sam's arm came around her, holding her up. Greg looked sick, still staring at the gun in Sophie's hand.

'She was talking to me through the window. She told me to leave her and make sure I looked after you. The last thing...' Sophie choked on her tears, then wiped her face and tried to compose herself. 'The last thing she said to me was that I had to take care of you.'

Flora did not know how to feel. Her mother was thinking of her before she died. But Sophie, the woman she loved most in the world, had kept the most devastating secret from her; had spent most of their lives lying to her and protecting her drunk mother instead of telling Flora the truth.

'From that moment on, all I've done is try to keep you safe. Keep you happy, the way your mother would have wanted.' Sophie reached out a hand to Flora. 'Your happiness has been the only thing I've cared about for most of my life.'

Flora recoiled from her touch. 'You're a liar!' she yelled.

'Flora, please!' Sophie looked stricken. 'You don't

understand, I've sacrificed my whole life to make you happy. This is the only thing I've ever lied to you about. I spent my life making amends for what my mother did. There was no point telling you. All it would do would drive us apart when you needed me the most. So, I made a decision. I could ensure your happiness in the future. Look at you, how does knowing this make you happy? I would never do anything to hurt you intentionally.'

Sam stirred next to Flora. 'But that's not true is it, Sophie? This is not the only thing you've lied about, is it?'

Sophie looked at Sam, as if only just remembering he was there. 'What are you talking about?' she asked.

'You are the one that has been doing all these things to Flora. Hiding her cards, putting worms in the house... having her attacked in the pool, it was all you.' Sam looked down at Flora. 'I've not been away in Cardiff, helping to start a vegan business. I've been looking for Linda. I've been staking out the centre, trying everything I can to find her.'

Sophie jerked as if she'd been slapped.

Sam ignored her. 'It was hard, but I found her. She told me that when Sophie met with her to tell her Flora couldn't have Ethan at the centre, she offered her money to terrorise you. A lot of money. Sophie organised for her to meet the journalist, made her drown you in the pool and even got her to throw that brick through the window. But Linda got cold feet after her run-in with you and so Sophie ran her out of town. That's why she was so hard to find. I'm presuming the other things, the rat and the worms were Sophie herself.'

Flora's legs didn't just weaken, they lost all feeling. She crumpled and it was only Sam that kept her from falling. He took all her weight and held her close to him. Flora suddenly recalled Charlotte, trying to tell her something about Sam. She must have spotted him watching the centre and wanted to warn her. If only someone could have warned her about Sophie.

'What is he talking about, Sophie?' she whispered.

Sophie paced up and down. She gesticulated with the gun as she talked, apparently forgetting that she held it. 'No. No. No. He's twisting everything.' She pointed the gun at Sam. 'He's not explaining it right. You don't understand.' She was talking quickly, almost manically. She scratched her head with the hand holding the gun and stared at Flora, eyes begging to be understood. 'Listen, I had to make you want to leave.'

Flora shook her head. 'You aren't making any sense. Why the hell would you torture me like that? You are supposed to be my best friend.' Flora felt bereft, as if Sophie had died and she was staring at her ghost. The Sophie she thought she knew had disintegrated right in front of her. Her whole world no longer made sense. She had no one she could trust anymore.

Sophie screeched at her, seeming to lose all her composure. 'This is all your fault! You are making me out to be the bad guy when you started all of this. If you had just stayed where you were instead of trying to move away none of this would have happened.'

'You're crazy,' whispered Flora.

'I had to keep you safe. How was I supposed to do that when you wanted to move away from me?' She gestured to Sam and Alistair with the gun. 'I made a mistake, Flora. These people are poisonous. I thought at first that I had found the perfect home for us. I did everything in my power to engineer a relationship between you and Sam and when we both got married, I thought, *This is it. The perfect family we both deserve.* But then I got to know them.' Sophie walked over to Alistair, pointed the gun at his head. 'Now him. He is a power-hungry sadistic cretin. He takes pleasure in controlling other people's lives and then destroying them without another glance. The things I've seen him do in the name of entertainment.' She spat in Alistair's face.

Unperturbed, Alistair pulled the pocket square out of his suit pocket, wiped his face and smiled at Sophie like she was the most entertaining creature he'd ever met.

She moved over to Sam, prowling towards him. 'He's the most dangerous of them all, Flora. When you said you wanted to move away from me to be with him, I just knew I had to save you from yourself. He's a coward, Flora. Stitched to his mother's apron strings, he would never keep you safe. If it ever came to a "them or you situation", he would always choose his family. I had to get you away from him. It was different when I was next door, when I could pop by in an instant and keep making sure you were safe.'

Sophie was now in front of her, but Flora was seeing a stranger. This wasn't the Sophie she knew. She felt empty. The desperation to be understood was leeching from her, but all Flora saw was Sophie stood over her bed, tipping worms into it whilst she slept.

'I had to make you scared enough that you would leave with me. It was for your own good. Surely you can see that?' She looked at Flora imploringly.

Flora could only stare back. Her mind reeling.

'Only I can keep you safe. I promised your mother. She charged me with your protection. No one else can do it. Especially not this weak, pathetic mother's boy.' She spat the words, looking at Sam with utter disgust. 'He thought you were crazy, you know. Didn't believe you when you told him all the things that were happening to you. Stood back and let you be tormented. He's not worthy to even lick your shoes.' She prodded Sam with the barrel of the gun.

'That's not true. I am the one that worked out it was you.'

Flora said, 'Why didn't you tell me this? If you suspected it was Sophie, why wouldn't you tell me? You let me think you didn't believe me.'

Sam looked down and gently stroked her face. 'If I told you that I thought your best friend in the whole world, someone you loved possibly more than me was tormenting you, would you honestly have believed me? I know how you feel about Sophie. You are like me when it comes to my mother.' He gave her a gentle smile.

Flora bowed her head. He was right. She had not once considered it was Sophie. Which is crazy considering she had suspected her husband but not Sophie. Flora felt ashamed. But mostly she felt pain. Sophie's betrayal was cutting her apart inside, tearing her heart to pieces. Destroying the happiest memories of her life with each revelation. The depth of her betrayal was crushing her, physically and emotionally. A thought occurred to her. She looked at Sophie and then at Greg. Before she could voice it, Sam addressed Sophie once more and what he said next almost made her faint.

'I also know what you've been doing to Greg.'

Sophie flinched. Greg shifted from foot to foot and looked down, unwilling to meet anyone's eye.

Flora had forgotten about Greg. The whole reason they were here was because Sophie was being abused by Greg. 'Greg?' Flora questioned, her voice croaky and weak. She didn't know how much more she could take.

Sophie stamped her foot, frustrated. 'I didn't do anything to him that he didn't deserve.' She looked around at Alistair. 'It was actually you that gave me the idea in the first place. I read all the things that you had done to Cecelia over the years. Flora still wouldn't leave, even after everything I'd done to scare her. I needed something stronger, something that would give her no choice but to leave.' Again, Sophie tried to pin Flora with her gaze. 'You don't understand. I had to make you leave. The worms and the drowning weren't doing it, so I had to do whatever it took. I didn't enjoy lying to you. Making up these things. But doesn't it just show how desperate I was to help you? To keep you safe. I was willing to burn myself, to turn a weapon on myself, to take all of that pain, just in the name of your safety.'

Flora was aghast. 'How could you do that? How could you burn yourself with cigarettes? You made me think Greg was hurting you. It was all lies.'

'Flora. Please try and understand. He deserved it. He killed my baby!'

Flora stopped breathing. Greg's head shot up and Sam looked at Greg, nervously.

'He did what?' asked Flora.

'That is not true, Sophie,' said Greg forcefully.

Sophie swung around to him, pointing the gun in his face. 'Yes it is!' she shrieked at him. 'You *forced* me to get an abortion.'

Flora looked at Greg in horror. This wasn't making sense. If Greg wasn't a violent bully, why would he do something that atrocious?

Sophie turned to look at her, snot and tears were dribbling down her face. She wiped at them angrily. 'Do you remember, Flora, when you got engaged and I fell ill? It was complications from the termination that *he* made me have.'

Sam looked over at Greg, startled by this revelation.

'I am now infertile thanks to him. He killed my baby!' screamed Sophie. She was screaming into Greg's face.

Greg stepped closer to Sophie. 'I'm sorry that happened to you, but you have to stop blaming me. We both agreed to that abortion. Neither of us could have predicted that it was going to go wrong. Ever since that day, you've made my life hell. Stealing money, ruining business deals, starting fights. It's not fair.'

'Not fair! Not fair?' Sophie was spitting with rage. Her usual mask had been demolished and all composure had fled the building. 'I can't have children because you said that you would leave me if I didn't get an abortion. That's not *fair*.'

Greg looked shamefaced. 'I know I said that. But you always knew that I didn't want a baby. I made that very clear. But that didn't mean you couldn't have had it yourself if you really wanted it.'

'Of course I wanted it. I just couldn't do it alone. Who would have looked after Flora if I went off and raised a baby?' Sophie said this as if it was a matter of fact and she was unable to see the lunacy of her words. Flora felt faint when it dawned on her that Sophie had terminated her pregnancy in order to stay close to her. To 'look after her'. The true extent of Sophie's madness was disturbing. She let out a gasp and it drew Sophie's attention back to her.

'You see it now, Flora. Don't you? You see it was his fault. You understand that I couldn't leave him as it meant leaving you. He gave me no choice. I promised your mother I'd always protect you.'

Sophie didn't wait for an answer. Apparently convinced that Flora now understood, Sophie took a deep steadying breath. She put her hand out to Flora and kept the gun pointed at Greg. 'Come on, Flora. It's time to leave.'

Sam stepped in front of her. 'She's not going anywhere with you.'

'Get out of the way! You don't deserve her. You can't keep her safe. She needs to be with me,' Sophie yelled, brandishing the gun, eyes blazing with determination. Flora wanted to push Sam out of the way, concerned by the crazed look in Sophie's eyes, they now knew what Sophie would resort to in order to keep Flora 'safe'. She remembered the blood of the guy in Prague and couldn't bear the same thing to happen to Sam, especially as this time Sophie had a gun.

64

The gun was heavy and Sophie's hands were so slick with sweat that she was worried she was going to drop it. She adjusted her grip and held it with two hands. It would stop anyone noticing how much she was shaking. Sophie couldn't believe it had come to this. She had brought the gun as a last resort. *We should have been gone by now*, she thought.

But Flora was looking at her in a way that chilled her to the bone. Everything was going wrong. Flora did not seem to comprehend that Sophie was the one that loved her. That Sophie had given her entire life to look after Flora.

How could she not see that they were all evil? That Sophie was the only one really interested in her happiness. They needed each other. *Once we escape, I can make her understand*, Sophie told herself. *It's just a lot to process. Poor Flora, she hasn't had time to take it all in.*

'Get out of the way, Sam,' Sophie repeated.

Alistair chuckled from behind, moving so that he was stood next to Sam. Greg moved to stand on Sam's other side.

'We both know you aren't going to use that,' said Alistair.

Movement caught her eye, she saw Sam trying to edge slowly around her, taking Flora with him.

'No!' cried Sophie. 'Stop!'

'Just let Flora go, Sophie.' Sam stepped forward.

She tried to look around him, to see Flora behind him. She just hadn't explained it properly. They just needed to sit down and talk this through. The thought of Flora leaving without her, going with Sam made her feel hysterical. She could not lose her. Not until she had made her see sense. 'We are leaving together, Sam. Me and Flora. Haven't you heard everything I've said? Don't you understand?' Anger flared and the urge to press the trigger overwhelmed her.

Sam seemed to sense she was losing control as he twisted and almost threw Flora towards the door.

It was an involuntary reflex. She hadn't known she was going to do it. Her finger just responded to the possibility that Sam was going to run away with Flora. She had to keep Flora safe. Even if that meant saving her from herself. The bang echoed, the emptiness of the room amplifying the noise.

She had time to register the smell of gunpowder and feel the kickback of the gun twinge her wrist, before she turned to Alistair, who was standing still, open-mouthed, shock written across the deep lines in his face. He began to speak, but she didn't give him the chance. She pressed the trigger again, ready for the kickback this time.

Alistair's body fell backwards and hit the wall. He did not move again. Blood began to pool steadily around his neck, glistening red in the glow of the solitary lightbulb.

Greg darted towards the front door. He opened the door just as she fired at him, but the bullet missed him, lodging itself into the wall a hair's breadth away. Greg ran into the pitch-black night. The door slammed behind him.

The sound of the gunshots had died out, leaving a deafening silence in the room.

Flora stood where Sam had crumpled to the floor, hand to her mouth, staring down at him in abject terror. Flora took off her jacket and bent down next to him, putting his head in her lap, she clumsily bunched up the jacket and pressed it to the patch of red that had spread angrily across his white shirt.

What have I done? Realisation hit Sophie like a steam train. She collapsed backwards against the wall.

65

'Wake up, Sam!' Flora shook him roughly. His face was deathly pale. His eyes fluttered open, but he did not seem able to focus. She cradled his head, stroking him and leaving bloody streaks down his face. Her tears fell on to his face, the pain that she might lose him was visceral. If he died, she would lie down next to him for as long as it took to die too. She couldn't imagine a world without him in it. Flora took gulping breaths of air between her sobs. Rocking Sam gently in her arms she prayed that he would survive.

'Talk to me, Sam. Stay with me,' she whispered into his hair. She kissed him all over his face but he stayed silent. All she could hear was rasping breaths.

Sophie was still slumped against the wall, the black gun at her feet.

'He needs help! Call an ambulance, Sophie!' screamed Flora.

But Sophie did not move. She looked entranced.

Gently setting Sam down on the concrete floor, making sure not to move the makeshift bandage she'd tied around him using her jacket and his jumper. Flora ran over to Sophie, clutching at her jacket, looking for a phone. Sophie just looked at her with vacant eyes. It appeared she had shocked herself as much as Flora when she had shot Sam and Alistair. Flora found Sophie's phone in the pocket of her jeans and wrestled it out.

At this, Sophie seemed to return to herself as before Flora could press '9' for the second time she snatched it from her. 'No. You can't do that.'

Flora tried to wrestle the phone back, but Sophie was stronger than she looked. They grappled. Flora was crouched down and Sophie used this to her advantage and kicked her feet from underneath her. She fell backwards, hitting her head on the floor. Sitting up, she felt dazed and slightly sick. Holding her hand to her head she screamed at Sophie. 'Sophie! Sophie, what are you doing? Sam needs help.' Flora began to cry in earnest. Tears burning in her throat and eyes, tracking down her face, into her mouth. She was going to lose control.

'I can't. I've just shot two people. They'll put me in prison. God. This wasn't supposed to happen.' Sophie began to pace. 'I don't know what to do. This wasn't supposed to happen.'

Flora crawled back over to Sam. Sitting behind him, she pulled him as hard as she could, so his upper body was lying in her lap. He was a dead weight and her muscles strained and popped. She buried her head in his sunflower hair, drinking in the subtle smell of coconut, his favourite shower gel. She pulled her arms around him and pressed down on the place where he had been shot. He made a small moan of pain but did not move or talk. His body was trembling, but she saw beads of sweat on his forehead.

Her mind whirled in confusion. In a few hours she had gone from drinking wine in her back garden to seeing her best friend shoot her husband. She held Sam tighter as she sobbed. She loved this man so much it felt like her heart would burst. The thought of not seeing him every day, not being held in his strong arms, not seeing him in her pink dressing gown in the mornings, it made her want to die.

A week ago, Sam and Sophie were the most important people in her life, the concrete foundations of her whole life. One of them had turned into a psychopath and the other might not live to see tomorrow. The world would no longer have any meaning. She would be alone. She cried into Sam's hair, pressing as hard on his wound as she could.

Sophie walked over to Alistair. He had hit the wall behind him when she shot him and a trail of blood, like a gruesome arrow guided the eye to his body. She seemed to be trying to check his pulse. But then Flora realised she was checking his pockets and pulling out a wallet and a phone. She stood up and began looking through both of them.

'We are just going to have to make a run for it, Flora. It's the only thing we can do.'

There was no way on this earth that Flora was leaving Sam. Sophie would just have to shoot her as well. She opened her mouth to say as much when the door opened again.

The weather had worsened and a rain-soaked figure with a black umbrella entered the house. The face was hidden behind the umbrella, but Flora could have sung for joy when it snapped shut, and there stood Cecelia.

66

Cecelia was the only person that could walk through howling rain and still look pristine. She closed the umbrella and neatly stowed it up against the door, on the mat so it wouldn't drip onto the floor. Greg followed closely behind her, his hair flattened to his head, rain dripping down his face.

Sophie was pleased to see that Cecelia's bravado faltered when she saw her son lying on the floor, bleeding into Flora's hands. *Wait, this might actually be a blessing.* If she could convince Flora that Cecelia would make sure Sam was okay, then she would be able to get her to leave. It was just making sure that Cecelia did not come after them. If Sam died, there was no doubt that she would want revenge. She needed to get out of here and quick. Everything was unravelling.

'What are you doing here, Cecelia?'

'What have you done to my son?' asked Cecelia at the same time.

'It was an accident. I didn't mean to hurt him. He'll be fine.' Sophie raised the gun and pointed it at Greg and Cecelia. 'Everything will be fine.'

Cecelia looked pale and she could not take her eyes off Sam.

Unsurprisingly, she did not seem to give Alistair more than a cursory glance. When choosing extracts of Cecelia's diary to leave for Flora to find, it was hard to narrow it down to which was the more harrowing. The years of abuse this woman had withstood was inconceivable. If Sophie hadn't shot Sam, she wondered if Cecelia would be thanking her for shooting Alistair.

Greg whispered in his mother's ear. It made Sophie nervous. How *had* Cecelia got here so quickly?

'What do I have to do for you to let me take my son to the hospital?' asked Cecelia.

'It's just not as simple as that, Cecelia. I know that as soon as you take him you are going to tell the police and Flora and I will have to spend our lives in hiding.'

Cecelia paused, she seemed to be thinking hard. 'What if I was to incriminate myself as much as you? That way, if I told the police about this, they would find evidence that makes me just as guilty as you?'

Sophie didn't know what to think. It sounded too good to be true. 'I don't understand. What could you do that was worse than this? You're trying to trick me.' Sophie felt sick. She held on to the gun with both hands and moved it between Greg and Cecelia, worried that one of them was going to rush her. She couldn't think straight, nothing had gone right, and she couldn't think of a new plan. All she kept thinking of was the feel of the gun when she shot Sam; the shock and pain in his eyes as he looked at her, utter disbelief etched into his face; his lips forming a perfect O before he crumpled to the floor. She looked back at Cecelia trying to work out her angle. What was she planning?

Before she had time to react, Cecelia pulled out a small silver handgun from her pocket. She walked over to Alistair and shot him five times in the head. His body jerked grotesquely with each shot. Putting the gun on the floor next to his head. She raised her hands in the air and slowly walked back over to Greg.

'There, now I'm more guilty than you. It was my gun that made the final killing blow. If anyone were to investigate, they would find bullets registered to my gun. You only shot him once, that is easily self-defence. But five times? Complete overkill.'

Sophie stared at Cecelia in awe. 'It's no secret, I've wanted the both of you out of my sons' lives for a long time.' Cecelia looked at her diary lying haphazardly on the floor where Flora had dropped it. 'Now I'm going to get my wish, with the added bonus of no longer being subjected to the malevolent torment of my husband.'

Sophie could see no downside. Cecelia had wanted them gone for so long. If she let Sam go, then she would have everything she wanted. The company name would be intact, there would be no scandal. It was win–win.

'Okay. You let me and Flora go first and then we've got a deal. I've still got your diary. I made copies, so I could use that against you... you know that, right?'

Cecelia bowed her head in acknowledgement. 'I do not want a fight. I just want to save my son and go on with our lives. Without either of you in it.'

Sophie motioned to Flora. 'Come on, Flora. You heard her. Let's go.'

67

'No.'

Flora's voice rang out in the silence and all three heads turned to look down at her. It was like they'd forgotten she was there.

'Flora, come on. We haven't got time for this.' Sophie looked at her, confused.

'I'm not going anywhere with you!' she screamed at Sophie. If she hadn't been holding on to Sam with all her strength, she could have happily scratched her eyes out. But Sam was getting ice cold and heavier in her arms.

'Don't be so ridiculous, girl.' Cecelia moved over to her and Sophie's gun tracked her movements. Cecelia knelt down next to Sam and took his hand in hers. Her eyes went wide with fear when she too felt the iciness of his skin. Cecelia looked at Flora until she met her eye. It looked like she was trying to communicate something silently, but Flora didn't know what.

'Go. Sam will be okay. Just go,' said Cecelia. She motioned to Greg to help her. He walked over and stood behind Flora, he bent down and grabbed her roughly under her arms. She tried to fight but he was too strong. Cecelia moved so that Sam was now on her lap instead. She stroked his hair softly and whispered into his ear. But Sam made no sound. Greg held Flora with one arm around her chest, with the other, he rammed something hard and cold into her back, sliding it into the waist of her jeans. He whispered, 'Be careful,' before pushing her towards Sophie so hard she stumbled.

Sophie took the advantage and grabbed Flora's arm.

'No. I'm not leaving with you. I'm staying with Sam.' Flora tried to wrestle free from Sophie's grip.

Cecelia looked up. 'Get out of here. Can't you see you've done enough already? It's because he fell in love with you that he's lying here in the first place. I never want to see either of you again.'

Before Flora could reply, Sophie had grabbed her by the throat and dragged her to the front door. Flora was clutching at Sophie's arm that was wrapped around her neck, cutting off her air supply. She was too focused on stopping her windpipe from being crushed to try and escape.

Outside Sophie continued to wrestle Flora towards the car. They stumbled without the light of the torches. Suddenly, the world spun upside down and Flora was flung to the floor: Sophie had tripped over something in the dark. The landing forced all the breath from her body and she lay there winded. Something hard and cold was digging painfully into her back. She rolled to the side and reached behind her and pulled out a gun similar to the one Cecelia had used to shoot Alistair. Why would Greg give her a gun? She didn't even know how to use one.

She could hear Sophie's heavy breathing somewhere close by but could not see her. Her eyes were struggling to become accustomed to the obsidian night sky. Not even the stars wanted to shine on this scene. She clambered to her feet and held the gun in front of her, hoping that if she did run into Sophie it would deter her from dragging her into the car. Flora would not be leaving with her. There was no doubt in her mind about that.

Flora turned in slow circles, trying to get her bearings. She was just able to make out the light from the cabin. Slowly, she moved delicately in that direction, stopping every time a twig snapped under her foot. She couldn't hear Sophie anymore. Flora stumbled as her foot hit something hard. With relief, she realised it was the boardwalk. She started to run and focused her attention only on the light that was getting bigger with each stride.

Something hard rammed into her from the side, sending her sprawling onto her back once more. The gun flew from her hand, landing a few metres away from her, partly obscured by a patch of nettles.

Before she had time to move Sophie had jumped onto her, straddling her. 'Flora! Stop running away. Didn't you hear her? We aren't wanted there. We need to go.'

'I'm not going anywhere with you,' snarled Flora. She was fed up of Sophie and her insanity. Hurt swept over Sophie's face but Flora didn't care. She wriggled and fought to get free, but Sophie had the height advantage. She pinned down Flora, arm by arm, her legs gripping tightly, keeping her under control. Flora thrashed uselessly, refusing to give up.

'Don't be silly. You just haven't fully understood everything I've said. How could you with all this drama going on? You'll soon see why I've done what I've done and be grateful.'

'YOUR MOTHER KILLED MY PARENTS!' roared Flora.

Sophie flinched at the ferocity in Flora's voice. 'Well, I can explain all that too. Please. Let's just go and we can sit down and talk all of this through. I love you, Flora.' Tears sprang into her eyes but it just infuriated Flora further.

'I'm not going with you. I don't want to see you ever again. I love Sam. I am going to be with him. Let me go, I want to see Sam.' She fought against Sophie's weight, but it was futile.

'You don't love Sam.' Sophie smiled down at her, talking to her in a voice normally used with children. Patient and understanding. 'You think you do but that's just because I pushed you into a relationship with him. I am so sorry, Flora. I shouldn't have done that. That part is my fault and I'm trying to put it right.' Sophie was panting now with the exertion of holding Flora down and resisting her escape attempts. 'Will you stop fighting me! I don't want to hurt you, Flora, but you are giving me no choice.'

'I love Sam. I HATE YOU!' Flora shrieked. Unable to wound Sophie with her body she tried with her words. 'You disgust me. You will never keep me away from Sam.'

'Oh, Flora.' Sophie gave her a pitying look. 'You'll thank me eventually. I know you will.' She forcibly moved Flora's hands together above her head, holding them tightly in place with one hand. Satisfied that Flora could not move, she reached around her back and pulled out her gun. She held it by the barrel this time. Flora realised what she was going to do with growing dread. Sophie raised the gun high above her head.

'I wouldn't do that if I were you.' A clicking noise came from behind Sophie's head and Cecelia stepped into view, behind Sophie.

Sophie twisted around and aimed her gun at Cecelia. Her other hand still holding Flora's arms captive. 'Stay back!' ordered Sophie, her voice uncertain.

'But why would we do that, Sophie?' Greg appeared on her other side. Flora felt Sophie's panic. Sophie twisted the gun between Greg and Cecelia, unsure who was more dangerous. She lessened the weight holding down Flora's hands and Flora took the advantage. Twisting her body quickly, she pushed up on the ground to buffet Sophie to the floor. The gun fell from Sophie's hand and arced towards the undergrowth.

Standing, she raced towards Greg's outstretched arm. He grabbed her and pushed her behind him as Cecelia strode towards Sophie, kicking her gun further into the weeds and out of reach as she stalked towards her prey like a lion about to make the killing blow. Raising the gun, she held it a hair's breadth away from Sophie's forehead. She pressed something on the gun, and it clicked.

Sophie flinched at the sound.

Realising what Cecelia was about to do, Flora cried out, 'No!'

Cecelia looked up, surprised but still as polished as ever. 'This girl's mother killed your parents. She has lied to you most of your life. She tried to kill Sam. Why on earth are you saying no?'

Flora stepped forward from behind Greg, though he kept a precautionary hand on her arm. 'Killing her is too easy. I don't want her to get the easy way out.'

'You just want to let her go?' Cecelia looked gobsmacked.

'No. She would be too dangerous. We all know what she is capable of. Can't we... you know, pay to have her committed somewhere?' She felt uncomfortable insinuating that not only were they all in this together but that she had any say in what happened next. But she hoped that if they could pay someone to take care of Alistair's body – which she presumed they would – then they could accomplish this. 'If we have her committed, she'll have to spend the rest of her days knowing I'm out there with Sam and she is never going to see me again. She told me that the whole reason she did all of this was for me. She's got some crazy obsession with me.'

Cecelia looked at Sophie. An evil smile breaking out on her face. 'That would kill you, wouldn't it? Take away your precious Flora.'

Sophie looked at Flora, open-mouthed, agony in her eyes. She was looking at Flora as if to say, *how could you betray me like this?*

Flora stared back, unwavering.

Sophie let out a cry of pain. She pulled Cecelia's gun to her forehead, clutching at it. 'Shoot me. Just shoot me. Sam could still die. It would all be my fault. Just shoot!'

But Cecelia lowered her gun, forcing Sophie to let go. Sophie fell to her knees howling, her sobs wracking her whole body. She looked up at Flora. 'How could you do this to me? I love you. Everything I've ever done was to keep you happy. Your mother wanted me to be with you.'

Flora had no words left. All she wanted was to go and be with Sam. She turned and looked up at Greg, who was holding her arm with such tenderness that belied his muscled strength. He was every bit the gentle giant that Sam was. 'Can we go to Sam? I can't stand the sight of her.'

Something pulled at her legs and she turned to see Sophie clutching her. 'Please, Flora. Please. I can't be away from you. You need me.' She looked so pathetic, scrabbling on her hands and knees.

Greg reached down and ripped Sophie's arms off Flora's legs, he threw her backwards so that Cecelia had to dodge out of the way as Sophie landed hard, sprawled out on the grass.

'It's over, Sophie,' said Flora quietly.

'It will never be over. Not as long as I'm alive. You'll never be free of me. We belong together.' She smiled manically up at Flora.

Greg pulled her gently away. Cecelia pulled out her phone and ordered a 'clean-up' crew. When she was done, she knelt down close to Sophie. 'Don't worry, Sophie. I'll look after Flora now. It's the least I can do.'

68

To the world, Sophie Cavendish is dead. This was one of the last things Cecelia told me. But I'm not. I am rotting away in this godforsaken place. I don't even know where I am. I can just make out the sea from my window, through the bars. No one will tell me. I see no one. My meals are delivered through a letterbox. I have a toilet and a bed and my memories. My memories are all that sustain me.

Each day I choose a new memory to devour, to help me escape the confines of my cell. Today I conjure up the day that Flora's parents had died. It was regretful but I had always known that it was for a reason. I didn't mean to run them off the road. That part really was an accident. It was down to fate. I'd always believed in fate ever since I was a child.

Until that day, I thought fate had forsaken me. She had always shown me the path, but Flora moving away, my only friend in the entire world, was unbearable. She was the only person who didn't judge me for my alcoholic mother. It was Flora who had helped me clear up the sick and hide my mother's neglect from social services. The one who let me into her home and made it so I was a part of a different family. A better family. She was my entire world. She was the reason I got up in the morning and practically ran to school. My life was only bearable because she was in it. But then it seemed she was going to be taken away. Her dad had been offered a new job and they were going to relocate. I cursed fate. I yelled and I screamed. I was going to be abandoned. Left to deal with my disgusting mother on my own. Who was I if didn't have Flora? I would have no reason to live. No reason to smile. Nothing.

But fate was there to step in and help. The memory overtakes me. I had learnt to drive by the age of twelve at my mother's insistence for those times when she'd had too much to drink. It was her fault I was driving that day.

It is supposed to be a shopping trip, not a drinking trip but like a moth to a flame, Mother finds her way to the vodka and begins to drink before we have paid. We are asked to leave and as my mother stumbles her way back to the car like a baby deer walking for the first time, I have no choice but to drive us home.

She is trying to look in the back for more drink, convinced there is something she has missed, stupid woman. I turn away to see what she is doing. I only glance at her for a few seconds but when I look back, I am on the wrong side of the road driving at a red car. I yank the wheel hard.

In my peripheral vision I see my mother flung into the back seat, I hear a clunk as her head hits something. I slam on the brakes and pump the clutch. I just manage to stop the car teetering over the edge into the ditch that runs either side of the road. In my rear-view mirror, I can see the red car has not been so lucky.

I undo my seat belt, rubbing at my neck where it has almost strangled me. I clamber down the ditch towards the red car. It is upside down. I can hear screaming from inside. I kneel down and to my horror I see Flora's mum, Mrs Harper. I have run my best friend's parents off the road. Mr Harper is on the other side.

He isn't moving and there is blood all over his face, making him barely recognisable.

I reach for the handle and try to open the car door, but it won't budge. Flora's mum is screaming for help. She can't get her seat belt off and is frantically pulling and pushing at it. Then, she realises I am there and looks at me. Recognition lighting up her face.

'Oh, Sophie. Thank God it's you. Help me. Please, I can't wake up John and I can't get my seat belt off.' Tears are mixing with the blood on her face. A small cut across her temple is still bleeding. The blood drops to the ceiling.

'I can't get the door open,' I say.

'Smash the window,' she says.

I turn to find a rock and a thought occurs to me. Flora is leaving with them. They are taking Flora away from me. Then it dawns on me. Everything happens for a reason. I can't open the door for a reason. I am not meant to save them. I stand stock-still and examine the thought further. If I saved them then Flora would move away. Fate does not want that to happen. Why else would it be her parents' car that I run off the road?

'I'm sorry. I can't help you,' I say to Flora's mum. I take a step back. She looks confused. Yanking at the door handle, she thrusts her body weight at the door, but it is stuck fast. Her hand moves out of sight, but I can see she is winding something. The window in the door begins to move but then it jams. She can get only her fingertips through it. She lets out a howl of anguish.

'Sophie, please,' she begs. 'Flora needs me.'

'No, she doesn't,' I cry. Tears running down my face. 'She needs me.' I'm about to walk away when there is a whooshing noise.

Flames spring up and engulf the back of the car. Panic consumes Mrs Harper and she yanks and yells, trying to escape the car. She hits Flora's dad, trying in vain to wake him up.

'Don't let me die, Sophie,' she pleads, tears coursing down her face.

'I'm sorry. I can't help you.'

I feel awful but I am resolute in my certainty that this is what should happen. That Flora needs to stay with me. That fate has engineered this situation to keep us together.

Realisation dawns. She knows that she is going to die. I can see it in her face. She is calm now. No longer panicking. Reaching around her neck she unhooks a necklace and pushes it through the gap. I walk forward and reach down to it. It is the necklace I have seen her wear since the first day I met her.

'Give that to Flora,' she sobs. Through the tears she fixes me with a piercing stare. 'Promise me you will look after her. That you will keep her safe and always protect her.'

'It's what I am doing now. I will always look after her. You don't have to worry, Mrs Harper. Flora is safe with me.'

I walk away to her screams of pain. When I glance back the entire car is burning. The screaming stops abruptly.

I grapple with my unconscious mother until she is out of the car and then I slap her hard. It is *very* satisfying. She drinks in my lies about her driving and running someone off the road. It sobers her up immediately. Who knew that was what it would take? She drives us home and tries to live with what she has done, whilst I focus on keeping my promise and always thanking fate for not taking away the only good thing in my life.

The memory dissipates and the bars on the windows come back into view.

You were safe with me. Until we got caught in the spider's web of the Cavendish family. That was my fault, Flora. I will fix it, though. Cecelia will not look after you. She doesn't care about you. I am the only one that loves you. Truly loves you. I've loved you since I met you when I was four years old. No prison in the world can break that bond. Someone will make a mistake.

Someone will slip up and when they do, I'll be free. I've already managed to increase the time the man who delivers my food spends at my door. It won't be long until he feels compelled to help me. Then I'll find you, Flora. I've spent my whole life loving you, keeping you safe. We will be together again.

THE END

ACKNOWLEDGEMENTS

There was a point where I honestly didn't think this book would ever get written. But thanks to the support of some incredible people, it has.

This book is very much about the power of friendship. I've moved around a lot since I was a child and although it taught me how to make friends easily, I've struggled to keep hold of them. But thankfully I have managed to ensnare some unlucky people and persuaded them to stick around, and I want to thank them from the bottom of my heart.

As ever, I need to thank my best friend Elle. Without you in my life, I wouldn't have got to this stage. I'd also like to thank Meggie, Nathan, Antony, Mike, Mark, and Jen for showing me what true, long-lasting friendship is so I could write about it and for all your kindness and support whilst I've been writing this book.

To Rachel, we met trying and failing to set-up a book club in Worcester, but I think we'd both agree we got a friendship out of it that more than makes up for it. Rachel, thanks for being my sounding board and for all those discussions on how to write about worms authentically. Jen Lucas – I know you don't like hugs, so this is the next best way to demonstrate how indebted I am to you. Your support with this book has been amazing, thank you for listening to me ramble, for giving me constructive feedback, for going with me on a writing retreat and boosting my confidence when I needed it as well as some straight-talking when that was also needed. I'm looking forward to our next writing retreat, somewhere with fewer distractions next time! I'm very lucky to have you as a friend.

A huge thank you to Sara, the first person I had the courage to send the completed book to before publication. Your words gave me a confidence I cannot explain. I also want to say thanks to Joanne Beacham – also known as Alexa – you gave me the help and support to leave my job and go freelance. Without that, I would never have written this book, of that I am sure.

I'm also grateful to Kerry and Leann for your encouragement and support, you are two of the nicest people in the world and I feel lucky to have you as my family. Especially Kerry – who taught me how to cheat at board games.

It was through blogging about books that I started my journey to writing. I have had the privilege of meeting some wonderful book bloggers that love books just as much as me. I am lucky enough to call some of these people friends. I'd like to thank all book bloggers – your passion and support are underrated – and all my friends in the book world. But I'd also like to give a special mention to Sandie Bishop, Nicola Southall, Teresa Nikolic, Joanne Robertson, Alexina Golding, Sumaira Wilson and Heather Fitt.

Special thanks to Jane Flaherty and Linda Tyler for taking the time to help me with legal advice for this book. Another thank you to Linda Tugwell for entering my competition to have her name included in the book.

I would like to thank all of the team at Bloodhound Books for everything they have done to get this book to publication, my editor Clare, Tara, the whole team are amazing. I'm especially grateful to Betsy for saying just the right thing to get me out of my head and persuading me to finally submit the book. Betsy was the first person to read this book and her reaction gave me a boost in confidence I desperately needed.

Family is so important and I'm very lucky that I've had my

mum and sister supporting me my whole life. It's always been just the three of us and always will be. My mother raised us single-handedly, and it's only because of her strength that I am strong enough to put myself out there and try to follow my dreams. As I know that she will always be there to catch me if I fall.

And last but by no means least, my long-suffering husband. I am not an easy person to live with and I don't know how you cope. But I'm so grateful that you are mine. Thank you for being my best friend in the world and for protecting me from flying cows and meteors.

A NOTE FROM THE PUBLISHER

Thank you for reading this book. If you enjoyed it please do consider leaving a review on Amazon to help others find it too.

We hate typos. All of our books have been rigorously edited and proofread, but sometimes mistakes do slip through. If you have spotted a typo, please do let us know and we can get it amended.

info@bloodhoundbooks.com